ZAVEN

JED CULLEN

Publishers:
Inspiring Publishers
P.O. Box 159 Calwell ACT 2905, Australia.
Email: inspiringpublishers@gmail.com

National Library of Australia Cataloguing-in-Publication entry

Author: Jed Cullen

Title: **ZAVEN**

ISBN: 978-1-922792-06-8 (Hardcover)
ISBN: 978-1-922792-04-4 (Paperback)
ISBN: 978-1-922792-05-1 (eBook)

Chapter 1:
Four Friends

Hi, I am Tyler Graham. When this all began, I was your average five-foot eleven, sixteen-year-old male. I was not overly muscular nor was I entirely skinny. I was a fresh-faced teenager with a mat of curly brown hair, large brown eyes and a prominent nose. Anyway, now that you understand that I'm nothing special, this is my story.

After an extremely boring and non-productive summer, it was back to school. "Take care, darling!" my mother said, smiling warmly.

I know she was just showing affection, but that is the last sentence you want to hear when you're waiting for the bus with Rufus beside you.

Rufus Smith and I have been close friends for many years. Unlike his adoptive parents who were unnerving and irate, Rufus was a cheerful, scrawny fellow. His identity was defined by his wiry blonde hair, buck teeth and bog eyes. He was literally as stupid as he looked. I disliked my mom's loving words, as Rufus had a habit of being a clown. However, today was different... he was not mocking me at all...

I was sitting on the bus next to him when I asked, "Dude, is everything okay?"

He glumly stared out the window. "Yeah..." He sighed. "I have just been thinking about that new drug spreading throughout Russia, like it's all over the news, with army soldiers getting deployed and stuff... What would happen if it were to reach us down here in Florida?"

"Is that what you are worried about?" I laughed. "Our military would clean it up so fast, that it wouldn't even make the news!"

Rufus turned to me and grinned.

I regretted putting his mind at ease, as for the rest of the trip, I was getting pinched, pulled and joked about. The amount of enjoyment I got when the bus finally came to a halt at our school was heaven.

I was hopping off when I felt a nudge in my back. It wasn't much, but I still hit the ground with a loud thud.

I laid face down in the dirt. "Rufus, you cheeky bastard!" I cried.

To my embarrassment, some freshmen stepped out from behind me and ran away.

Rufus stopped sniggering and extended his arm. "I wonder where they are heading off to."

I gripped his hand and lifted myself up. "Let's go find out."

Now as seniors, we strolled through the school like superiors. The commotion was easy to find as every kid seemed to be running in the same direction. We followed until we came across a crowd gathered in a circle. From previous experience, a crowd like this only meant one thing. A Punch-up. Rufus and I pushed over the freshmen and squeezed our way to the front. I stopped chanting "fight" when I noticed who it was between. In the center was my buddy Jake getting held high up in the air by some unknown massive student.

I leant over to Rufus. "Want to do anything?" I whispered in his ear.

"No ha-ha," he replied, shoving me backwards. "Look who's coming..."

Almost as soon as he said it, Eli came charging through with his arm elevated and fist clenched.

Thwack! The new student dropped to the ground like a brick. It had to be one of the best thumps I had ever seen.

"Thanks..." Jake trembled, fixing his shirt.

"No worries." Eli laughed. "Who knew some dick would try and pick on you the first day back from summer. Hey, Tyler! Rufus!" He pointed to us. "Why didn't you guys help? Were you too busy fiddling with your little peckers?"

Rufus gave a cheeky grin. "Maybe?"

The entire crowd cracked up laughing. Some people looked as if they had just heard the funniest joke in the world. I had already experienced my fair share of Rufus's jokes for one day, so I just found the situation bemusing. Still, everyone else knew that when the toughest kid in school made a joke, that joining in was the safest option.

Eli Cooper was not only tough, he was also a boxing champion. He had won multiple international under-sixteen heavyweight titles. In junior high, he was the skinniest of all my friends. It was only until senior high when puberty struck that he became as muscular as he was tall. Standing at six-foot four, Eli was a white-skinned individual with a patch of short black hair sitting on top of his oversized head. He had small, pursed lips and a perky nose, which resembled that of a woman's. However, with his thick black eyebrows over-shadowing his beady, hazel eyes, he was far too intimidating for anyone to mock.

When at school, Eli would dress in a pair of white Nike skate shoes, white jeans and a red jacket over a pure white shirt. His appearance, complimented with his hygiene made him one of the most handsome students in the year. I was always astounded to see how a little wimpy kid could transform into an intimidating adult in just under thirteen months. He was scary to most, including the teachers, but to me and my friends, he was the same old Eli.

The laughter was disturbed by Jake. "Hey, guys! Let's get to class before Mr Vander finds out."

We all knew why Jake wanted to get to class. Jake may have been short and pudgy, but he happened to be the smartest kid in the year. His large turquoise eyes always showed a sense of understanding in everything... except sport. At first sight, with his mop of brown greasy hair and unnaturally tan skin, Jake resembled that of an overweight surfer. However, his lack of fashion degraded him to one of the most undesirable students in the school. Wearing a combination of red wife-beater shorts and a faded indigo Batman shirt, Jake would appear to most as a purebred red-neck. Nevertheless, with appearance out of the way, Jake was renowned as a nerd. And due to his surname being Newton, classmates often referred to him as Isaac Newton.

The unknown massive student rose from the ground and jogged out of sight, tears running down his cheeks.

The bell rang and the crowd slowly dispersed. I met up with Jake and started walking towards B block. Our first class of the day was mathematics.

It was two minutes in and our teacher was already asking really complex questions. "And what is the answer when the quadratic formula is used in this hypothesis?"

Jake swiftly shot up out of his seat. "Seven hundred and thirty!" He squealed.

Every student in the class could have sworn Jake had a bad case of Asperger's. "Correct!" exclaimed Mr Vander. "Great work, Jake!"

Jake turned to me to see if I was impressed. To be honest, I couldn't have cared less about mathematics. I was not good at it and in fact, the only subjects that I did enjoy were technology classes that allowed me to work on metal and wood. So, propping him the middle finger seemed like a suitable response.

"Tyler Graham!" Mr Vander shouted, glaring at me in anger. "We do not use those vulgar gestures in class!"

I tried to reply but it came out as if I had just been shot with a taser. "But...but... I was..."

"No buts!" He screamed. "See you in detention this afternoon!"

"Damn it!" I shrieked.

Just my luck, first day back and I happened to be the only one in detention. The rest of the lesson was also unenjoyable. Jake kept giving me the middle finger and giggling like a little kid. At one point, I swear Mr Vander witnessed it. It didn't matter, though, as he would never harm his class pet. The only option I had left was to ignore Jake the only way I saw fit... by actually calculating questions.

Mathematics was awfully slow and painful. Just before the bell rang, I leant over to Jake. "Yo," I whispered. "Tell the rest of the guys that we should catch up after school."

Jake gave me a concerned look. "Dude, you have detention... You don't want to get in any more trouble, do you?"

"She'll be right," I shrugged. "It's not the end of the world."

School dragged past and by the end of the day, I was keen on catching up with the gang. I was walking out the back exit of school when Jake, Rufus and Eli dashed past.

"Last one across the creek is a rotten egg!" Eli yelled.

I sprinted after them, ecstatic that they could all make it.

Rufus was leaping across stepping-stones when he accidentally slipped on some moss. *Smack!* He slammed his head hard against a rock and splashed into freezing cold water. Our laughter arose like fireworks. Rufus tried scrambling to his feet, attempting to not be last. It was a waste of his effort.

"Rufus, the Wet Rotten Egg," Jake joked, stepping out of the creek.

"You could say hard-boiled egg!" Eli cackled.

The rest of us, including Rufus who was still perched in the middle of the creek, glumly shook our heads in shame. Eli was usually gifted at saying jokes. However, this one in particular was a disgrace.

Eli noticed our expressions and stopped laughing at his own joke.

After a few minutes' walk-through woodlands, we arrived at our destination. All of us knew this treehouse from our childhood. We built it years ago as a gathering spot. Every few months we would return to it as a group. It was constructed high in the air with a retractable ladder leading up to it. We may have been teenagers, but this place was a nostalgic paradise. None of us could resist the temptation of revisiting it.

We were standing at the entrance of the treehouse. Knowing Rufus was leading, Eli took a step back and gestured me to go forward.

"Tyler." He smiled. "You are in front of me."

Rufus poked his bum out and ascended the ladder. "Yeah, I didn't wipe today." He chuckled.

Eli drastically pulled me in front of him.

I gripped onto the first rail. "Good to know..." I sighed.

One after the other, we climbed up the ladder and stepped inside the treehouse. All of us were shocked to see what we found. Looking around, it was as if we had been in a time machine for a couple of centuries. The treehouse we originally knew was almost completely unrecognizable. The walls were charred black and cracked. Panels were missing and in fact the only thing we did recognize was the old two-way radio. It was a bit melted and damaged, but still in working condition. Years ago, Rufus stole it from his adoptive father. We mainly used it to prank call people and listen to music broadcasts. It was a valuable source of entertainment.

Jake pounced on it and switched it on. All four of us instinctively started dancing as it played our favorite song, 'Paradise.' "What luck?" I shrieked.

"Yeah." Jake agreed. "Look at Eli's new dance moves! They are going off!"

We all turned and to our astonishment saw Eli breakdancing. I always thought dancing was kind of lame, yet Eli somehow made it look cool.

"Guys, watch this!" yelled Rufus.

Everyone turned and gawked at the awful sight.

Rufus whirled around on his ass, attempting to copy Eli.

"Ouch!" He squealed, lying back, with tears filling his eyes. "I got a splinter in my glute."

I began fist-pumping towards him. "I thought my mom told 'me' to take care," I said cheekily.

Rufus slowly rotated around with a serious expression on his face. "Oh, Tyler..." he replied. "She did, darling..."

All of us burst into hysterics. I wasn't quite sure how Eli and Jake got the joke, but I didn't care. This was the best time I had had in months. How did I make it through a whole summer without any of them? Jake abruptly stopped. "Hold on... shush guys..." he whispered.

The laughter died to silence. We all stared at the radio. The music had stopped and was now playing a high-pitched alarm...

CHAPTER 2:
First Encounter

We crept up to it as if it was an alien. Each of us fiddled with the antenna and dial. After a brief moment, a monotone trebled, utterance became clear: "Breach, we have a breach in the Psyriviox drug. Everyone stay inside. Lock all doors and windows. Keep calm and loved ones close. Repeat, there has been a breach." The siren gradually became vibrant again.

We all looked at each other with troubled gazes. All was quiet. I cupped my hands over my ears to ignore the alarm, leaned against the wall, and thought about what Rufus had said to me earlier on the bus. To my utter disbelief, he was correct... Eli broke the stillness. "Don't worry, guys," he said. "I have got my mobile with me. All I need to do is call my parents."

It was a great idea. "Yeah, go for it!" we all agreed.

Eli whipped out his flash new mobile and proceeded to dial his home number.

The phone rang about three times before a voice answered: "I'm sorry, your call cannot be connected, please check the number and try again."

"Try mine," I said.

"Okay," Eli replied.

Eli continued to go through each of our home phone numbers. All of them returned with the same wretched response.

Jake then asked Eli to call the emergency number in order to confirm whether the problem was with the mobile or the area.

"It's worth a try..." Eli said, dialing 911.

We all huddled around him, anxiously hoping for an answer.

To our amazement, someone picked up. "...Lock all doors and windows. Keep calm and..."

I slammed my fist against the floor. "Dude!" I shrieked. "That is repeating the same advice that was on the radio. How useless can some people get? I mean... they could at least tell us what to actually do if we are not at home..."

Everyone sat down and attempted to evaluate the situation.

We listened to the siren for a while before Eli probed the question that no one else would. "Soooo... do you think we should go home?"

Jake restlessly played with his fingers. "No, didn't you hear them?" he replied. "They said it is unsafe to be outside."

"Technically, aren't we already outside?" Rufus said, smirking.

Rufus's remark instigated an argument between Eli and Jake and whether we should go home. The argument became so heated that they ended up screaming at the top of their lungs.

It was both annoying and deafening. After a short while, I couldn't stand any more of it. "All right!" I burst out, infuriated. "We don't know whether we are outside or inside! Let's just have a vote whether we should go home or remain here. Put your hand up if you agree, keep your hand down to disagree."

I knew it was going to be a very biased vote, but I couldn't tolerate the bickering.

"Okay, who wants to go home?"

Eli and I shot our hands up high in the air. Rufus took a moment before also raising his hand. "Staying at one of your houses sounds a lot better than hanging around here," he said.

Jake stared at me, gritting his teeth. "All right," he growled. "Let's just walk home then…"

Eli pinched Jake's cheek. "I'll protect you, baby," he teased.

Jake overlooked Eli's ridicule and proceeded to climb down the ladder. We followed single file until we were safely on the ground.

As we ventured towards the creek, the echo of the radio eventually disappeared. However, as one faded another began to manifest. Yet, this siren was different to that of the radio's… We had heard this siren plenty of times before, mainly around Rufus's house. It was a police siren…

I got excited at the noise. I knew that an officer would be able to help us out.

We hurriedly tripped through bushes onto the creek bed. As we were about to hobble across, we noticed something on the other side. Where the alarm was coming from…

Straight across the creek was a bunch of mixed colors: blue, red, brown, black and white. It was a police car that had crashed into a tree. Its lights were still flashing and its motor was still running.

We were all busily gawking at it when Rufus laughed. "Ha-ha look at the tomato sauce on the front windscreen."

The rest of us seized up in shock. We knew that police did not have lunch at five o'clock.

It was blood... and a lot of it.

It took a while, but Rufus eventually realized why the rest of us were exchanging nervous glances. This was the first time any of us had ever seen a crash in reality. What were we supposed to do? Call for help? The emergency line was of no use. What happens if someone died and we could have saved them? None of us could live with that burden. "Sh...should we go check it out?" I stuttered.

"No," Jake replied. "It could be dangerous. Let's travel a bit further up the creek and find another crossing."

All of us agreed and started walking parallel to the creek. We'd only travelled thirty meters before coming to another halt.

Eli grabbed my shoulder. "Dude... is that Mr Vander?" he whispered.

"Yeah, right!" I laughed. "You are not fooling me today!"

Eli aggressively spun me, facing towards the school.

To my shock, he wasn't joking... On the other side of the creek, my math teacher was aimlessly strolling around.

"Mr Vander!" Jake yelled. "Mr..." I placed my hand over Jake's mouth as I did not want him to know I had skipped detention. However, it was too late. Mr Vander crookedly twisted and began walking towards us.

"I'm sorry, sir!" I pleaded. "I forgot about detention!"

My pleas did not seem to affect him. It almost seemed like he was accelerating towards us... *Thump!* Mr Vander fell forward.

"Ooooo!" Rufus sniggered. "He must be really angry with you, Tyler."

We were completely oblivious to what Rufus had said, as we were all horrified at what was happening in front of us. Our math teacher was up and running towards us, now with a thick branch poking out of his guts, intestines swaying with each step.

"Guys..." I whimpered. "I do not think that's Mr Vander...." I looked around but everyone had disappeared.

"Pace it, Tyler!" a voice echoed from behind.

I quickly turned and sprinted after them. Even though they had a huge head start, it only took four seconds before I was beside Jake.

We were lunging past trees when I glimpsed at the whereabouts of Mr Vander. To my terror, he was rushing across the creek, a wake of dark red blood trailing behind.

Completely forgetting about how my friends had ditched me, I decided to hang back and reassure Jake to keep moving.

"Come on!" I heaved. "We are nearly there!"

We all had the same idea of where to run. The nearest house was a few miles away. The closest shelter was where we had come from: the treehouse.

As we made it to the ladder, knowing Jake was the least athletic, I allowed him to climb first.

"Let's move! Let's move!" I encouraged.

Jake slowly climbed up and tumbled into the tree house. I was just about to climb in when something gripped my leg.

"Holy hell!" I shrieked. "Get it off! Get it off!"

Mr Vander had one hand on the ladder and the other on my ankle. The ladder was awkwardly swaying back and forth.

"Guys, help!" I squealed. "He is trying to bite me!"

Rufus immediately grabbed hold of the ladder and pulled it towards the tree. I proceeded to violently kick my free leg like a maniac.

Whack! Thud! Crack! Blood sprayed everywhere. My boot connected with my teacher's face, his grip loosening with each blow. I wound up my leg and threw a final kick. *Crunch!* Mr Vander let go and stumbled back. I clutched hold of the rails and shot up the ladder. I was in a midway dive into the treehouse when I screeched, "Pull it up!"

Bang! The ladder shot up as quickly as a bullet. Eli grasped it while Rufus retracted it. Jake and I perched our heads over the edge to look at the pulverized mess I had made.

Mr Vander had no nose. It was impounded so far into his face that one of his eyes was bulging out. There was a mix of blood and intestine shredded along the ground. He had been ripping his exposed organs further into the extruding branch while trying to capture me.

"Far out!" I exclaimed.

Rufus finished retracting the ladder and popped his head out to look at the teacher. "Wow, Tyler, you made a mess!" He chuckled.

Eli looked at me confused. "I have seen some brutal knockouts in boxing, Tyler, but what you have done there to the math teacher... it should... it should have killed him." He staggered.

"How is he still moving?" I questioned. "He looks totally unaffected..."

Rufus sophisticatedly placed his thumb on his chin. "Well... a logical explanation would be that he has contracted the Psyriv... whatever it is, and turned into a zombie..."

Jake gave him a dumb look. "No... that's the most irrational theory ever...!"

"Well, explain to us why he isn't dead?" Eli requested.

Jake opened his mouth to respond but Rufus interjected "...Guys we have seen plenty of zombie movies and we know what they are like. I'm afraid to say Mr Vander appears to be a prime example."

Jake shot out in a dispute straight away. "Don't be ridiculous, you dumb ass."

Rufus began naming movies: "Dawn of the Dead. Land of the Dead. World War Z..."

It went on for quite a while before I yet again had to interrupt.

"All right!" I shouted. "I have a proposal... Without any medical attention, by morning Mr Vander should most definitely be dead, right?"

"Correct..." Jake agreed.

"Well... it's simple, then... We will wait for Mr Vander to seek help. If he doesn't, we will remain up here until the morning. If by then he is missing or received therapeutical care, we will agree with Jake. If he is still aimlessly stumbling around like an idiot, we will all agree with Rufus."

Everyone dazedly nodded in approval. It was obvious that arguing when out of breath required a lot of effort. It was the most adrenaline any of us had ever experienced.

Hours passed before we felt calm again. The sun receded behind the horizon and we were left in the glowing midst of a full moon.

Jake's eyes were beaming under the stars. "It's beautiful, isn't it?" he offered in solace.

The rest of us were getting content with Jake's remark, when Rufus cried, "What's for dinner? I'm soooo hungry!"

Rufus had been complaining for the last three hours. Eli stood over him. "This tree is your dinner, you stupid beaver!" he screamed. "One more peep from you Rufus and I will throw you down with Mr Vander for you to endure another math lesson!"

Rufus instantly shut up. We all knew that Eli was joking. But just the amount of aggression he could portray through an irritated look was enough to scare anyone. I was quite thankful that he did it.

Rufus uncomfortably rested down on the hard-wood floor and nodded off to sleep. I tried to follow, but the constant moaning from Mr Vander was keeping me alert.

Another hour passed, Eli and Jake had drifted off to sleep. I was left by myself staring at the stars. Jake was right you know. Tonight, the stars were stunning. However, the sparkle in my eyes was not reflected by the stars. No.

I was thinking, planning, and preparing for the path ahead. None of us could survive another day of Rufus's sulking, which in turn only left us with one option. Tomorrow, we would be escaping this prison. Tomorrow, we would discover the truth.

Chapter 3:
Logic versus Reality

Slap! My right cheek began to burn, painfully. "What... the... hell..." I murmured.

I opened my eyes to see Eli leaning over me, lining up his next hit. "No!" I screamed. "I'm awake, I'm awake!"

Eli laughed and withdrew his hand. As my eyes regained focus, I revolved around to see Jake and Rufus kneeling by the entrance.

I let out a deep yawn and stretched to my feet. "What's up?" I sighed. "Look!" Rufus screeched.

"Huh? Look at what?" I replied.

Jake lowered his head in shame. "Rufus was right..." he muttered.

I had no idea what he was talking about. It was only until I peered outside did I succumb to the severity of our situation. It was as if staring into another dimension.

The sky was concealed behind thick, gray smoke. Glittering ashes hailed down in the distant flickering lights.

I was concentrating on a red-hot cinder blissfully falling to the ground when I suddenly shuddered in horror. From behind the glow I noticed not one, but two objects pointlessly stirring around. Without their uniforms, they both would have been indistinguishable.

Mr Vander now had a clear hole straight through his gut, his innards were stretched around the foliage like colorful streamers. A police officer was stumbling beside him. He appeared to have a splintered bone bulging out of his blood-ridden neck. Both were tinged green and, judging by the strong smell of vinegar, they seemed to be decaying.

A sudden gust of wind bellowed through the tree house, amplifying the putrid stench. It quickly overwhelmed us all. The other three began to cough and gag while I unfortunately commenced to vomit.

I held my head over the edge. "One thing's for sure," I spluttered. "They are definitely zombies."

"Yeah, they sure do reek," Eli teased. "But you need to harden up, princess!"

I attempted to reply, but incidentally choked on my regurgitation. Jake swiftly leapt forward and slapped me on the back.

The sudden thump made me profusely barf everywhere. Rufus and Jake blocked their noses as I uncontrollably saturated the zombies below.

The officer, completely startled by my expulsion, took a quick step forward and tripped over Mr Vander's intestines.

"Now that's a sight to see on your second day of school!" Rufus laughed.

It was a disgusting but lucky set of events. As if I didn't witness this blunder underneath, a very articulate idea would have never crossed my mind.

I rotated around and wiped spew off my chin. "We are escaping!" I cheered.

Jake sat down and rubbed his forehead "Huh? We are getting out of here?"

"Of course, we are!" I shrieked. "Don't you guys want a cheeseburger and Coke?"

Rufus licked his lips "Yeah... that would be nice." He sighed.

"Absolutely, anything to stop Rufus's whining," Eli agreed.

"Fine..." Jake accepted. "What's your brilliant idea, Tyler?"

I raised my eyebrows. "Ok... Here's the plan."

After half an hour of explaining, I stood up and waited for a response. "All right, let's do it!" Jake yelled.

"Yeah, should be fun!" Eli smiled.

Rufus gave me a confused look "What was the plan again?"

I slumped my head in agony. "All right, new proposal. Rufus, you stay up here and keep on the lookout. Eli and I will give you the 'okay' when it is safe to come down."

Rufus bowed heroically. "I will do my best!"

After ten minutes of warming up and stretching, we were ready. "Let's do this!" I roared.

Eli began ripping off a loose plank while Jake unfolded the ladder. After both objectives were complete, it was my time to shine.

"Go! Go! Go!" Rufus yelled.

I jumped out and slid down the ladder like a fireman. By the time I hit the ground, Mr Vander and the officer were charging towards me. Even with their horrible injuries, they were still quite fast. All I needed to do was outpace them. I took a deep breath and initiated a full sprint around the tree. I completed three revolutions before shouting out the signal: "Coooooeeeeee!"

Eli vaulted down with his plank raised. I quickly ducked as he swung at a zombie behind me. *Crack!* The officer fell lifeless on his back.

"One down!" Rufus screeched.

I completed another loop before coming to a dead stop. To my relief, my plan had worked. Mr Vander was standing two meters in front of me, his mouth wide open, arms outstretched.

"It's okay to come down!" I heaved.

Rufus and Jake hastily advanced down the ladder. In a flash we were all surrounding and scrutinizing what used to be our math teacher.

Mr Vander was unable to move. His intestines were tangled so far around the tree that they immobilized him. It was the equivalent of a dog on a chain.

Rufus was busily prodding him with a stick when we were disturbed by a feminine high-pitched squeal.

"Eeeeeeee!"

To my disbelief, Eli had accidentally trodden on some intestines. A yellow liquid oozed over his shoe.

It was karma at its finest. I promptly marched over and slapped him on the back. "Who is the princess now?" I laughed.

Rufus and Jake joined in, calling him names.

Eli grew as red as a tomato. He was so embarrassed that he couldn't even respond. We were able to torment him for five minutes before the hilarity finally dissipated.

I observed Mr Vander. "What should we do with him?" I asked.

"Let's double check that he is 'actually' a zombie," suggested Jake. "I still have my doubts..."

"How are we going to...?"

"Easy!" Rufus screamed, jabbing his sharp stick into Mr Vander's chest.

"Oh, shit!" I screamed.

The prodding stick seemed to have broken the intestinal chain, because as soon as it sliced in, Mr Vander got loose.

We were all stumbling backwards and falling over when... *Thwack!*

In the blink of an eye, Eli managed to crunch what was left of Mr Vander's face through the other side of his skull. The teacher dropped to the ground with a loud thud. "What were you guys saying to me before?" Eli questioned, abruptly.

Each of us looked away in humiliation.

"Errrrm nothing..." I croaked.

"Like how cool you are and stuff..." whispered Jake.

"Yeah... yeah... like... what the other two said..." dribbled Rufus.

Eli hurled the plank at the tree. "That's what I thought!" he shouted.

We were venturing back towards the city when Jake asked a very important question. "Where are we actually going?"

"To McDonalds, of course!" Rufus said, rubbing his tummy. "Jake, were you even listening to Tyler?"

I gave a hesitant look. "Yeah...." I muttered. "About that.... That was just for inspiration, Rufus, I was not actually planning on fast food..."

Rufus slumped his head in defeat, "Well, where then?"

Eli moodily spun around. "I know where I'm heading... I'm heading home."

"No, you can't!" Jake blurted.

"Why not?" Eli questioned.

"Well... We concluded that they were zombies, right?"
"Correct." Eli agreed.

"I don't know about you, then," Jake said. "But I have seen plenty of zombie movies as well and I will tell you what... we need more than just weapons.

"What is that, genius?" I mocked.

"Armor," Jake replied.

It was the simple ideas that Jake always had that made the rest of us feel stupid. I mean, here we are walking towards a probable zombie-plagued city, without any weapons or protection. "Screw that," Eli said, picking up a stick. "I have got all the protection I need."

"Don't be stubborn," Jake replied. "It is unsafe and illogical to split up. We must stick together even if it hinders us from seeing our families for a few days."

Rufus slapped Eli on the back. "Yeah ..." He sniggered. "They are probably all dead, anyways."

The rest of us stopped in shock. We had been so worried about ourselves, that this was the first time any of us had thought about our parents. It was horrible to think about the actuality of our parents dying. And it was even worse that it could be expressed as a joke.

I suddenly became immobile as all the memories of my mother flooded into my mind. It was as if a train had rammed into my chest. I felt quite nauseated as I pictured my last confrontation with Mom. I began to question myself: What if she is dead? Would I have been able to help her?

We must have been thinking of the same thing, as at the same time, Jake, Eli and I collectively burst into tears. In fact, the only person who wasn't crying was Rufus. He did not have a single expression on his face.

I glared at Rufus with running eyes. "Why aren't you upset?"

Rufus sat down. "You don't know my parents," he muttered.

"Neither do you!" I blubbered, crying. "You have adoptive parents."

Rufus forcefully slammed his fist into the ground. "Who else do you think I am talking about?" He screamed. "My biological parents? They ditched me the first chance they got!"

All of us stopped sulking and turned our attention to Rufus.

"Every afternoon I dread going home!" he wailed. "My apparent 'adoptive parents' are nothing but a bunch of useless slobs. They would not even bat an eye if I died, let alone go to my funeral. Why do you think I am always at your house, Tyler?" Rufus began to mope.

It was the most unexpected event I had ever witnessed. Rufus's adoptive parents were regarded as odd, but how were we to know the extent of their incompetence? Rufus had always been the happiest person any of us knew. We were completely clueless to what he was masking behind his cheerful appearance.

After hearing his story, I wiped tears off my face, walked over to him and gently patted him on the back. I empathized with him as I, for one, had affection for my parents. Rufus, on the other hand, had never even met his biological parents.

"You guys are the closest family I have..." he sobbed.

Eli and Jake advanced to cheer him up. We talked about all the fun he had brought into each of our lives and how we could not live without him. After about twenty minutes, Rufus managed to force a smile. "All right, where to?" He struggled.

Jake enthusiastically stood up. "We need to go somewhere with lots of equipment and gadgets," he replied. "It needs to provide food, water and shelter. It also has to be close and a place that we all know."

All of us rose to a stand, exchanging the same cheerful looks. We all knew where Jake was leading us. It was a colossal structure that met all the requirements. We had all been there plenty of times. It was a place I always hated, but a location that Jake valued. I didn't want to serve my detention, but yes, we were heading back to school.

Chapter 4:
Diverse Strengths

We journeyed through the forest and were scaling across the creek when a faint, depressing noise was heard. "Urgghhhh."

"Zombies!" I screamed, throwing myself face-down in the water.

I was under for close to ten seconds before something grasped the back of my shirt.

To my humiliation, Eli hoisted me to my feet. As it turned out, the noise I heard was not actually zombies but Jake's exhausted moaning.

Dripping wet, I gazed around in total embarrassment. "You have got to be kidding me," I muttered.

Rufus crossed his eyes. "Urghhhh, my name is Tyler and I am as dumb as a zombie."

"Shut up," I snapped. "Yesterday, you were in the same position as me."

"Yeah," Eli teased. "But Rufus had an actual reason. He was making a dam."

"Ha-Ha-Ha..." Rufus laughed sarcastically. "Well, at least I don't have to 'live' in the water like big Elephant Seal Jake over here."

For once, Rufus's joke was quite clever. Jake's overweight body combined with his exhausted moaning, directly resembled an elephant seal in mating season. I didn't want to acknowledge it and laugh, but Jake splashing in the water forced me to.

"Hahahaha!" I cackled.

"Yeah... yeah..." Jake puffed, angrily. "Let's just hurry up and get to school."

It was quite remarkable. Half an hour ago we were the saddest bunch on earth. It was like our depressive conversation never even happened.

After a little more jogging and joking, we eventually made it to the back entrance of school. Rufus eagerly approached the door and looked through a small glass panel. To our relief, he turned around and gave us the thumbs up. All clear.

Rufus gripped the handle and shook it. The door wouldn't budge. "It's locked!" he shrieked. A low rumble echoed back. "Urghhhh..."

Eli whirled around. "Come on now, Jake... Joke's over."

"That wasn't me," Jake replied.

My heart began to race. "Where are they?" I whispered. The moaning got increasingly louder and muffled.

Rufus fidgeted with the door handle. "They must be attracted to noise," he said, quieting. "Keep your voice down while I picklock the door."

"Okay," I whispered. "I'll go check how close they are."

I don't really know why I wanted to see the uproar. I think my curiosity had got the better of me. I dashed up the side of C block, the noise becoming louder every few meters.

As I got to the end of C block the noise was unbearable. I peeped around the corner and stumbled back in shock. "Find another entrance!" I screamed.

"I've nearly got this!" Rufus replied.

I initiated a full sprint towards him. "No, you don't!"

A horde of thirty uniformed students tumbled around the corner chasing me, with bones puncturing through their flesh and blood dripping from their mouths. I was only able to distinguish one student. Her name was Lucy. She had huge watermelon-sized boobs. They were out of her bra and freely bouncing around. It would have been nice if I had got to see them while she was alive. As now that they were blue, saggy and maggot infested, they didn't have the same appeal...

Eli, Rufus and Jake gaped in horror and staggered back into a full gallop.

I ran after them. Once again, I caught up to Jake with ease. He was so slow and worn out from our previous trek that Eli had to hang back and shove him along. Rufus was the opposite. He was so speedy he was nowhere to be seen.

We were running down D block when I swiftly looked behind me. To my horror, our classmates were gaining on us. "Faster!" I shrieked. "Faster!" I ran over to Eli and helped push Jake ahead. Our acceleration was not great, but it was enough to maintain our distance from the zombies.

Jake was about to collapse from exhaustion when we were saved by a familiar voice. "Up here! Up here!"

We wildly looked around to see Rufus's two skinny arms poking out of a school window.

Eli picked up Jake and launched him through the window. Rufus caught him and fell backwards. Eli then dove through the window, followed by me. I was halfway through when a deadly grip seized my ankle.

"Slam it!" I wailed.

Eli grabbed the window and smashed it shut. I tumbled and slid along the ground; a convulsing arm still attached to my leg. Rufus dashed over and repeatedly smacked it with a chair until it lost its grip.

Eli locked the window and turned to me. "Holy moly!" he cackled. "They sure do love your ankles, Tyler."

I was breathing so heavy that I could barely speak. I drowsily looked at him and noticed he wasn't the slightest bit dazed. "Are you superhuman?" I heaved. "You don't look tired at all..."

Eli gave me a wink. "Fitness, bro."

I attempted to sit up, but an overwhelming sensation forced me back down. There was a high-pitched ringing in my ears before everything died black. The last sight I recall was zombies clawing at windows.

I awoke with a dry mouth and aching back. I stretched to a stand and looked around. The room in which I had fainted was now silent and dark. The only body I could decipher was Jake. He was asleep on a nearby table. I walked over and kicked him in the side. "Wake up!"

Jake opened his eyes. "Huh? What's happening?" he groaned.

"Where are Rufus and Eli?"

Jake shrugged and stood up. "Why is it so dark?" he murmured.

I realized that Jake was as confused as I. "Let's just go find the others." I sighed.

Jake stood up and inspected the windows. He approved of their safety and we walked out of the room.

Standing out in the corridor, I noticed a subtle light flickering from within the cafeteria. I grabbed Jake. "Do you see it?" I whispered.

Jake responded with a fearful nod.

Both of us tiptoed up the corridor, trying to make as little noise as possible. We had no idea what was in the cafeteria and we didn't want to alert it. As we closed in on the cafeteria, I halted Jake to a stop. From inside, pots and pans could be heard falling over.

"There is definitely something in there..." I mumbled. Jake glanced at me, worried.

I reached down and picked up a nearby trash can. "All right, on the count to three..."

"One..."

"Two..."

"Three!"

I burst open the door with a loud *bang!* when... "Wait! Wait! Wait!"

"What the fuck?" I screamed, launching the trash can.

The trash can connected with a bewildered figure, sending them flying onto their back.

Jake heard the commotion and came rushing in with his hands over his head. "What happened?" He squealed.

To my relief, Eli strolled out of the kitchen holding a can of baked beans. "Yeah, what are you doing, Tyler?"

To be perfectly honest, in the position I was in, I had no idea what I was doing. I was so caught up in the moment that I couldn't even respond. The best I could do was quiver my lips.

Rufus broke the stillness. "Nice shot..." he joked, rubbing the top of his head. I looked at the bin beside him and realized what I had done. "Sorry..." I sighed.

Rufus gave me a humble smile and picked up a packet of mac 'n' cheese. "It's all right," he replied. "My knock yesterday at the creek was worse."

Eli sniggered at the thought.

"Soooo... enough joking... What's going on?" Jake asked.

Eli ate a spoon-full of beans. "Don't worry," he said. "While you guys were asleep, Rufus and I reconfigured the school to a safer environment."

"How?" Jake questioned.

"Well, for starters," Eli answered. "We locked all the windows and doors to the mainframe of the school. We also butchered the cafeteria lady. So far, she has been the only zombie we have seen inside."

Eli dropped his baked beans and ecstatically pulled a woman's body out the doorway. Her head was smashed into a pulp. Jake and I stared down at it in disgust. It was weird. Even though it was horrific, Eli had done the right thing.

"Well... Nice work..." I replied.

Rufus shoveled mac 'n' cheese into his mouth. "You guys want some food?" he spluttered.

Jake didn't waste any time. He immediately dove on some assorted packets of chips. I wasn't hungry though. I was thirsty. I raced over to the sink and turned on the tap. The water passed through my parched lips, quenching my thirst.

I was wiping my chin when Eli gleefully threw a can of asparagus. "Dig in!" he cheered. I hated asparagus. Instead of catching it, I pounced on Eli's stray can of baked beans.

Eli smiled and opened up another can. "There is plenty to go around!" he cheered.

Ten packets of chips, four cans of baked beans and four packets of mac 'n' cheese later, we were all finally full.

I looked around at the rubbish, thoroughly impressed by the mess. "Wow!" I exclaimed. "We eat a lot!"

Eli kicked an empty can. "We are definitely not cleaning this up." He laughed. "So, what do we do now?"

Jake rubbed his tummy. "Well..." he replied. "Where in the school are there tools and material to construct armor and weapons?"

"Stop giving me riddles," Eli replied. "You know I am not good at them."

Rufus's eyes lit up. He looked as if he had just seen an angel. We all knew what he'd done, though. He'd solved the riddle. "The industrial room!" he answered excitedly.

Hearing those words, a wide smile spread across my face. In my industrial class, I had always wondered what it would be like to have total freedom within the room. Now that there were no teachers to boss me around, I had no boundaries. "Awesome!" I rejoiced.

Each of us grabbed a handful of snacks and headed towards the industrial rooms. Walking through the school was a lot different at night. The lockers and tiled floors glimmered like silver in the dim light. Along the sides of every corridor the classroom doorways were now frighteningly obscure.

The industrial room was located at the opposite end of the school. After a five-minute walk, we were standing in the last corridor to the industrial room.

I stared down the dark tunnel, thankful that Eli and Rufus had boarded up the school's windows. The pitch-black doorways were already eerie enough knowing that there weren't zombies inside. "Wow, you guys have done well to secure this part of the school," I beamed.

Rufus turned away from me. "Yeah... about that..." He mumbled.

I knew this was going to be bad news. "What?" I groaned.

Eli punched Rufus in the arm. "This big hungry beaver over here stopped us from locking the classrooms down this hallway... Apparently, Rufus can't work on an empty stomach."

I shook my head in dismay. "So, what do we do now?" I replied. "For all we know, zombies could be climbing through the windows at this very moment."

Jake rested against the wall, tired. "Tyler's right," he said. "I think our safest bet would be to sleep in the industrial room tonight and finish securing the windows in the morning."

We approved of Jake's idea and crept down the corridor. By now, we had learnt that zombies were attracted to noise and as such, to keep safe, we tried to make as little noise as possible. We were halfway down the corridor when Rufus sprinted ahead of us. "Last one to the end is a rotten egg!" He shouted.

"Rufus, you fricking idiot!" Jake screamed.

Jake's voice echoed up and down the hallway. Rufus got startled by the noise and fell over with a deafening slap.

"Ooooo!" we said, cringing.

Rufus was never intentionally trying to kill us. But some of his mistakes appeared remarkably planned. A red light faded in and out above us, followed by a piercing screech which sounded off throughout the school.

"Oh... fuck," Eli muttered. "He fell over the fire alarm..."

"Turn it off!" I shrieked.

Rufus sprung to his feet. "I don't know how?" he squealed.

All of us sprinted over to the alarm and tried to turn it off. The light and noise disappeared as I flicked the switch upwards.

"Thank god..." Rufus exhaled. "That was close..."

Jake dashed ahead of us. "Not close enough!"

Dozens of silhouettes poured out of every open door. "Quickly!" I shrieked.

We ran for our lives. The zombies rushed towards us, groaning hysterically. We ducked and weaved around each of them as if we were playing professional basketball, inadvertently dropping our snacks while doing so. As we neared the industrial room, Jake was already standing at the entrance. He impatiently signaled us forward. The fear in his eyes made me worry that he'd shut the door on us. Thankfully, he didn't.

Eli, Rufus, and I collectively plummeted through the door. Jake slammed it shut and locked it behind us. A loud thumping sounded from the other side. The excited zombies pummeled against the door like a battering ram. Jake walked over and flicked a switch. The industrial room's large, fluorescent lights flickered on to a constant.

From watching the Russian pandemic on the news, just like every zombie movie we had ever watched, we knew that the zombie contagion was able to spread through biting. As we had just escaped a tight situation, we needed to ensure that we hadn't been infected. All of us sat at a table and examined our bodies. After a thorough and scary inspection, we confirmed that none of us had been bitten.

"Yeah! Baby!" I cheered. "Damn, we are good at surviving!"

My remark was unnoticed for everyone's attention was on Rufus. He was wiping metal shavings off the table and placing food out in front of us. Remarkably, he had managed to recover all the snacks that the rest of us had lost. He divided the food evenly between us.

Eli pushed his share aside and walked over to the door. A small glass window within the door allowed a full view of the zombies outside. They were crowding around it like vultures. Eli observed the zombies and sat back down at the table.

I pulled my share towards me and turned to Eli with inquisitive eyes. "How many zombies are out there?" I questioned.

"I don't know for sure," Eli replied. "But from my little assessment, I counted around twenty-eight."

It was a significant amount, but I didn't care. I was happy that we had made it into the industrial room in one piece. I turned to Jake. "Hmmm..." I said. "Well, as we have supplies... I think we should work on some weapons and armor before we leave the rooms."

"If we ever leave..." Jake muttered. "But yes... that is the best chance we have." Jake observed the room and its materials. "Tyler, as you are the master craftsman, we will leave the construction to you. As of right now, though, we need to figure out what items would suit us best."

Having been friends with all of them for many years, I had a good idea of what everyone needed. "Well, Eli's strengths are endurance and power," I responded, confidently. "Plus, he is the only one out of us to have successfully killed a zombie. I think it seems reasonable that we allow him to do it more efficiently."

Eli raised and tensed each arm in approval.

"As we will be on the move a lot, we are going to need an individual who can carry our supplies. Rufus being the quickest, he should be that person."

"Sounds kind of lame," Rufus sneered. "What is your part in this, Tyler?"

"I already have an idea up my sleeve," I answered, winking.

"And what about me..." Jake stammered. "I am a burden to you all..."

"Oh, Jake..." I said, preciously. "You are the brains of the bunch. The brain needs heavy protection. Thick armor should do you just fine."

Jake forced a smile.

"So, are we at an agreement?"

"Yes, sir!" Eli cheered.

"I guess so..." Rufus muttered.

"Plan B?" Jake questioned.

I stood up and smiled. "Fellas, let's get to work!"

Chapter 5:
New Instruments

Bang! Clangour! Hssss!
The noise we were producing sounded like a heavily packed death metal concert. It was six o'clock the following morning and all of us were still hard at work. We had been creating the equipment for Jake throughout the night. Due to the low rations of food, Jake instructed that we work as quickly as possible.

Each person had tools dedicated to them. Eli the hacksaw, Rufus the drill press, Jake a ruler, pen and paper, and due to me being in my zone, I was the welder and overall instructor.

By midday, I was hosing down Jake's cindering plate armor. Steam was filling the room and it felt as if we were in a sauna.

"All finished, Jake!" I yelled. "Let's see you in it."

It took us a combined two minutes to equip Jake with it. After connecting the last latch, we all took a step back and admired his armor.

Jake was sweating profusely. "How do I look?" he puffed.

"Awesome!" Rufus cheered.

"Show us if you can move in it," I said, observing him.

"It's quite hot and heavy in here, but here I go," he said, acquiring a slow jog. His heavy metal shoes clunked with each step.

"Nice!" Rufus applauded.

"Yeah, good work!" Eli cheered.

Jake managed to gallop ten meters before coming to a standstill. "I can't go much faster than that," he puffed. "I know that it is zombie-proof and all, but it seems wrong for you guys to risk your lives for me. I can't really help us out in this suit. It pretty much makes me a big slow liability."

I jogged over to a table. "Don't worry," I replied. "Let's just have some lunch."

"Hey! A little help over here!" Jake shouted.

I ran back and removed Jake's suit. "Sorry, Ironman," I teased. "I don't want any trouble."

With Jake out of his armor, all of us sat down at the table and ate lunch. As we were eating, I realized that one of my packets of food was missing.

I glared at Rufus, automatically assuming it was him. "Who stole my food?" I snarled.

Rufus immediately dropped his mac 'n' cheese on the table and pushed it towards me. "Sorry, Tyler," he mumbled, worriedly. "I had breakfast this morning when you guys were asleep... I didn't know it was from your pile."

"Come on, man," I said, shaking my head. "Jake has already established that with the low amount of supplies, we can only spend another two days in here. Breakfast not included."

"My bad..." Rufus sighed.

After finishing our meals, it was back to work. I walked past the entrance door to see the zombies still standing outside. They did not look any different from yesterday. Their rotted bodies seemed to have stopped decaying.

"Look at that," I said, laying out my sketches for Eli. "They haven't changed a bit."

Jake was the only one to look up. "Weird..." he replied. "I have got no logical explanation on why they aren't decomposing. Guys, maybe we should check..."

"Cool!" Eli burst out. He excitedly stared at my sketches. "You know me all too well, Tyler."

Everyone crowded around and observed the sketches. "This will be in combination with some light armor," I announced. "It will have less protection than Jake's suit but will not weigh you down."

Eli patted me on the back. "Sound's good!" he replied. "I can't wait to test out these killer gauntlets."

We exchanged smiles and went back to work.

Eli's items were lighter and easier to shape than Jake's. However, it still took us until midnight before we'd finished. And even though it was chilly, all of us were still dripping with sweat.

Rufus rested on the ground. "I'm exhausted," he groaned. "Try them out, Eli, before we go to sleep."

Eli impatiently suited up. He wrapped cloth around his knuckles to reduce the impact of his rigid gauntlets.

"Are they comfortable?" Jake asked, yawning.

Eli began punching a table. Each blow formed a deep indent in the hardwood "Yeah, great!" he replied. "Though, it would be nice if they had a little more impact."

I rested beside Rufus and closed my eyes. "Just get to sleep," I mumbled. "Rufus's items have to be made in the morning."

Listening to the thumping of metal against timber, I drifted off to sleep.

When I awoke, Rufus was busily sketching away. I got up and rubbed my eyes. "Are you keen, Rufus?" I said, dozily.

Rufus looked at me and grinned. "Tyler, wake the others," he cheered. "We have got some work to do."

I walked over and kicked Eli and Jake. "Come on, everyone! Up and at it!" I shouted. Both of them drowsily sat up.

Eli groggily looked at me with bloodshot eyes. "Whose turn is it now?" he asked.

I pointed at Rufus who was already sitting at the drill press. "By the way, Tyler..." he said. "I made an adjustment on my gear."

I walked over and examined his sketch. From my point of view, it looked as if some little kid had drawn lines all over his weapon.

"What is it?" I questioned.

"Nails!" he replied, excitedly.

I twisted my face up in confusion, trying to comprehend how a person could not possess the ability to draw a nail. I shook my head in disbelief. "Easy done, Rufus," I said, smirking, trying not to laugh. "Everybody, back to the same positions as yesterday."

All of us went back to construction. This time it was easy, though. Rufus's lightweight materials allowed for easy construction. In the end, we managed to complete his items in a little under four hours.

I helped Rufus equip his newly constructed items. "All right, Rufus," I said, fiddling around with his armor. "Just tuck that in there... Push that out and... *Bam!* You are our master scavenger." I took a step back and examined him. Rufus was fitted with armor made from old aprons and a canister on his back made from sheet steel. A long metal baton, riddled with nails, was clenched tightly in his hand. Although his armor wasn't as robust as Eli's and Jake's, he still looked very threatening.

Rufus stared at himself in the window's reflection. "This storage canister on the back looks a bit dumb," he muttered.

"Don't worry, it suits your personality!" Eli teased.

Rufus raised his baton. "Eli, when I shove this up your arse it will suit 'your' personality, you cocky moron."

"Rufus, that weapon is meant for zombies," I retorted. "For all we know it could go all the way in out of Eli's ass and still come out clean!"

Jake and Rufus burst out laughing. Eli opened a can of food. "Good call, Tyler." He smirked.

I ran over to Eli. "Early lunch!" I rejoiced.

Rufus wildly swung his baton around. "Wait for me!" he squealed.

Jake untied the apron armor fastened to Rufus and we all sat down for lunch.

"We have got ample time now to complete my gear," I said, swallowing some food. "I have already found a weapon of choice. It's only my armor that we have to create now."

"True," Jake replied. "So does that mean tomorrow we are leaving?"

I looked around at the empty food wrappers spread over the table. All but three of our food supplies had been consumed. "Yep," I answered. "Tomorrow we leave."

All of us devoured our meals and went back to work.

Due to the armor being constructed for myself, I wanted something a little extra. Jake, once again, started off with a lot of measuring, most of it being around my waist.

"You don't need to measure my groin that much," I joked.

"Well, Tyler..." Jake said, slapping me on the testicles. "If you have nuts, we wouldn't want them getting sliced open by some dead people's teeth, would we now?"

I attempted to ignore the pain as well as what he had just stated as I knew that to some degree, it was quite possible. "Okay, Jake, get on with it," I moaned.

After a thorough examination, Eli began cutting thin strips of metal. Once he had finished, I was able to get started.

I crisscrossed and welded the thin metal strips together. The armor that I was constructing for myself was somewhat like a chain mail.

By the time I had finished, everyone else was already asleep. It was ten o'clock and I was testing my armor. Looking at my reflection, it wasn't the flashiest-looking bit of gear. But I didn't care, it was comfortable.

I excitedly climbed out of my suit. *What now?* I asked myself. I placed my armor on the ground and stared at everyone else's equipment. Hmmm. They all wanted something changed... What did they ask for? Words appeared in my head one at a time: *puncture, untie, hot, aprons, liability, impact...* I matched up the problem with the person and thought of suitable solutions. Knowing that the solutions were time consuming, I began the modifications right away.

It was one of the hardest working experiences I had ever had, almost torture. However, I still managed to finish. I swung a hammer one last time and collapsed on the ground.

I was asleep for two hours when: "Wake up, Tyler! Wake up!"

"Huh?" I groaned, getting to my feet.

Eli raised his gauntlets to my face. "Tyler, it seems to me that you are our secret Santa."

I understood why they had awoken me. They were thrilled with their equipment's modifications. "Yeah," I yawned. "Hope you like the alterations."

Rufus was wearing his armor. "Do we ever, Tyler!" he replied. "I can't believe you managed to make my armor into a one-piece set!"

Eli was admiring his gauntlets. "Yeah, these spikes on my gauntlets should come in 'handy'." He smirked, waving his hand.

"Nice pun," I muttered. "I got that idea from Rufus's baton."

Jake stomped over to me in his heavy metal suit. "And what does mine do, Tyler?" he questioned. "Apart from providing a little ventilation, I don't understand why you went to the effort to cover my armor with angled holes ..."

I trotted over to a cupboard. "Don't worry," I answered. "You will know what they are for when we experiment with it."

"What are you doing?" Rufus questioned.

I reached into the cupboard and pulled out an industrial tool. "Getting my weapon, of course!"

"What?" Jake screamed, staring jealously at the tool in my hand. "You get a nail gun... It seems dangerous, don't you think?"

I shuffled nails into Rufus's canister. "Don't worry," I replied. "I will be a master marksman."

"That's a joke!" Eli teased. "Let's just hope you kill more zombies than you do your friends."

I rubbed my eyes. "Ha-Ha-Ha..." I laughed sarcastically. "There are three packets of chips left. As I get the best toy, I think it's only fair that you guys have the rest while I prepare."

The three of them joyfully sprinted over to the table and began scoffing down the food.

I was equipping my chain mail when the actuality of what we were about to do crossed my mind. We had to be ready for this; it was almost thirty undead against four teenagers who had seen way too many zombie movies. We were in way over our heads.

I fastened up my shoelaces, shot a nail into the wall and joined the others. The food was quickly diminished and before long all of us were stretching and double-checking our armor. After confirming that our armor was fitted and safe, we strutted over to the exit.

As we approached the infested door, I grabbed a welding mask off a rack and placed it over my head. I flicked the shady frame up and looked at our oncoming mission: the zombies were staring at us, chattering their teeth.

Rufus skipped up and down on the spot. "Zombie killing time!" he said, encouragingly.

I flicked the lock and slowly turned the handle. The zombies got increasingly louder with each passing second.

Jake trembled with fear. "Are you sure I'm safe?" he stuttered.

I abruptly swung open the door. "Let's find out!" I shouted, pushing him headfirst into the horde.

CHAPTER 6:
Dire Decisions

The putrid smell of decay shot up our nostrils. It was so powerful that it made my whole body cringe. Without having several exposures to it over the past few days, there would have been no way I could have withstood its intensity without vomiting.

"Help me..." Jake cried. His body disappeared into the mass of zombies and his cries for help faded to a low gag.

We stood in silence. Thick blood flowed out from the horde like a river of lava. As I stared at the blood, a slight smirk spread across my face.

"Oh, my God!" Rufus howled. "You killed him."

Eli looked at me in disgrace. "How could you let him...?"

"I'm not dead!" snapped Jake.

I raised my nail gun and fired into the mass of flesh. *Shif! Shif!*

Eli gaped in astonishment. "Are you hurt?" he stammered.

"Just shut up and help me!" Jake shrieked.

With that, Eli trampled forward. His huge steel boots crushed any zombie that was unlucky enough to cross his path. To avoid shooting him with the nail gun, I stopped firing at the zombies that were enclosed around Jake and started targeting the stray ones that were peeling off to the side.

Rufus, not equipped to be in the middle of the fight, followed my lead. He dashed to the side and smashed his bat down on a fallen zombie. "Yeah!" he screamed.

Eli reached the cluster of zombies and swung powerful haymakers. Each blow caved in a zombie's head like a wrecking ball. His gauntlets were heavy, but he swung without rest.

The fight became a massacre, chunks of flesh flew around like a hurricane and before we knew it, only one zombie remained. With its mouth stuck to Jake's armor like a parasite, Eli plunged his fist directly into the back of its head and jerked upwards. Brain and blood splattered all over him.

Rufus looked around in awe. "Wow!" he exclaimed. The entire hallway was painted red. I could barely make out Eli's eyes under the dripping liquid.

Jake pulled himself up off the ground. A loud rattle sounded from within his armor.

Eli shook his body like a drenched dog. "What is that noise in your armor?" he asked Jake.

I walked over and unclipped the back of Jake's armor. Hundreds of teeth toppled out over my shoes, little stringy bits of flesh peppered throughout.

Rufus took a step back in disgust. "Well... on the bright side, at least we know what those holes in Jake's armor do..."

Jake angrily turned to me. "I don't care about the defanging improvement!" he shouted "You may have altered my armor into a teeth grater. But how you just tossed me into the zombies... you did wrong, Tyler!"

I was not going to argue. He was right. Pushing him headfirst into a horde of zombies was actually very dangerous. The excitement had clearly got the better of me. "Err...

yeah... sorry about pushing you ..." I replied. "I thought it would be best if you got their attention while we killed them... You aren't hurt... are you...?"

Jake hated the idea of being used as bait. "Not that I know of!" he shrieked.

Eli stepped in-between us and pushed Jake backwards. "Whoa! Don't blame Tyler..." he said. "Jake, he actually made you helpful for once."

Although he shouldn't have, Rufus felt as though he should have some input. "Yeah, you should just be thankful that Tyler knew that zombie blood wasn't toxic."

Jake shook a few more teeth out of his armor. "Is that right, Tyler...?" he said, inquisitively. "Please explain to me how you know that 'zombie blood is not a carrier of the contagion'."

To be perfectly honest, apart from biting, I had no idea how the contagion was spread. I could have just told him that, however I felt as though I could redeem myself with a clever lie. "Well..." I croaked. "I umm... the other day by the tree... I like... figured it out from Mr Vander..."

Jake squinted at me. "Go on," he said.

Under pressure, with no airflow under my mask, I was becoming very hot. To cool myself off, I pulled my mask up over my head. It was not a good idea, as with Jake examining my face while trying to lie, I only felt more nervous. "Well... I, umm... looked at Mr Vander's blood and I could just tell...." I murmured.

I thought it was a decent lie. However, the look on Jake's face proved otherwise. "See?! I told you Tyler knew!" Rufus cheered, ecstatically.

Eli shook his head at Rufus's stupidity.

Jake unbuckled his helmet and threw it on the floor. "Un-fucking-believable!" he screamed at me. "You push me into a horde and now you lie straight to my face!"

I looked at the ground in an attempt to avoid eye contact.

Jake gripped my chin and lifted my head up so that our eyes locked. "You are lucky that I forgive you!" he shouted, spattering slobber in my eye.

I wiped my face. *Huh?* I thought. *Did I just hear what I thought I heard?*

"I have to..." he said. "We have come this far together. And as I've previously stated, it's far too dangerous for us to split up."

Eli mockingly applauded us. "Okay, so Tyler's forgiven," he said. "That's great and all, but we need to progress onwards."

Jake gave Eli a dirty look, furious at the fact that he didn't care about the argument.

Rufus winched blood out of his apron. "Yeah!" he agreed with Eli. "We can gather food from the cafeteria and wash ourselves at the creek."

The abrupt enthusiasm was a nice change from the argument. "And after that, then what?" I eagerly questioned.

"Simple," Eli answered. "We check our homes. I know that all of us have parents. But since I am the only one who owns a pet, we should visit mine first. I could never forgive myself if something were to happen to Bruce."

Jake moodily shrugged. He was trying to treat Eli the same way in which Eli treated him. It wasn't working, though, as instead of uncaring, he came off looking like a child throwing a tantrum.

Aside from Jake's amusing tantrum, in actuality, Eli did have a valid point. His dog was old, and if zombies ate animals, Bruce was certainly in more danger than a person. "Sounds good to me," I said. "First things first, though. We are washing ourselves before breakfast."

Rufus frowned at my comment, knowing that he was going to have a late breakfast.

After a short trek to the creek, we were splashing in the water, washing the blood and gore off our armor.

The creek seemed to lighten the mood. Jake, for one, was no longer grumpy. He was enjoying himself. He pulled off his shirt and shook his flab around for us all to see.

Disgusted by the sight, Eli shouted, "Tsunami!" And jumped into the shallows.

Unfortunately for Eli, the splash he created was the equivalent of that of someone stepping in a puddle. As he resurfaced, I belly-flopped on top of him. After a few seconds of holding him under, he shot up out of the water, breathing heavily. I patted him on the back. "Sorry." I laughed. "I forgot how bad you are in the water..."

"Yeah, yeah..." He coughed. "I probably deserve that for splashing you."

I chuckled and rinsed the remaining blood off my armor. It dribbled off and faded into the water as if it were completely fresh. "Dead people are not meant to bleed, are they...?" I asked Jake.

"Correct," Jake replied. "Blood clots when dead."

I curiously gazed at the murky water. "If that's true, then why does zombie blood remain liquid?"

Jake shrugged. "Their biology is beyond me," he replied. "Anyways, don't worry about it now. We have more important things to do."

Rufus sprinted out of the creek towards the school. "Yeah.... We have to eat breakfast!" he shrieked.

Jake had previously stated that *it was unsafe for us to split up*. Since I had finished cleaning my armor and was also hungry, I felt as though I should be the one to join Rufus. I climbed out of the creek, picked up my nail gun and started jogging after Rufus. "You guys can catch up," I yelled back to the others.

"Yeah, no worries!" Eli replied.

Rufus accelerated ahead and I quickly lost him. By the time I got to the cafeteria he was already demolishing his second can of baked beans.

"Where are Eli and Jake?" he choked.

I sat down and ripped open a packet of chips. "They will be up here soon," I replied. "They have a bit more to wash than me and you."

He snapped open his third can of baked beans. "Okay," he said. "But they better be quick if they want some food."

Ten minutes passed by and we'd almost finished our meals. I shoveled the last of the chips into my mouth. "How long are they going to be?" I asked.

Rufus burped and rested back on the ground. "Who knows?" he replied. "They are probably frolicking about, comparing their 'armor'... if you know what I mean..."

I wiped my chin and rested beside him. "Yeah ha-ha, they probably are." I grinned.

Another ten minutes passed and they still hadn't returned. It was at this point that I started to worry. "Do you think we should go search for them?" I asked.

Rufus got up and stuffed his container full of food. "Okay, just after I fill this," he answered.

After Rufus had finished packing his container, we trekked towards the creek. As we stepped outside, my concern for Jake's and Eli's well-being was immensely increased. The creek was clear and no one was in sight. Both of us anxiously moved up in search for clues.

I was glaring at the water when something caught my eye. "What's that?" I stuttered.

Rufus walked over and picked up a round, metal object. "Huh? That's weird," he said. "I wouldn't expect Jake to leave his helmet in the water."

The lonesome piece of armor made me feel very eerie as I knew that Jake would have never parted with his armor unless he was forced to.

I sat down at the side of the creek. "Where do you think they went?" I questioned.

Rufus looked around. "Well, you did recently push Jake headfirst into a horde..." he answered. "He seemed pretty pissed off about it. Do you think they just ditched us to go do their own thing?"

"Maybe..." I said. "That, or they were chased away by zombies."

"Hmmm..." Rufus pondered. "Well, if so... I think either way, Eli would have swayed Jake to go back to his house. I mean he really does love that dog..."

I thought about how eager Eli was to see Bruce. It made perfect sense. "Yeah, you are right," I said. "But there is just one problem... how do we get there before dark?"

Eli's house was a massive white mansion located in the far northern sector of the city. Only the prestigious and wealthy families lived in his district. If we were to ever walk to his house, it would take a very long time even without zombies running rampant in the streets.

Rufus squinted at the crashed police car down the road. "That plan is already set." He smirked.

After a hundred-meter walk, we were sitting in the police car. Myself in the driver seat, Rufus in the passenger.

"Do you know how to drive this thing?" Rufus chuckled. "I'm pretty sure it's got a driving stick."

I clipped in my seatbelt. "Yeah, I have driven my mom's automatic a lot. An extra stick shouldn't be too difficult..."

I turned the ignition and pressed my foot hard against the accelerator.

The noise and power in gear one was as if I was firing up a jet engine. In fact, it was so brilliant, it took me a few seconds to realize that instead of reversing out of the tree, we were climbing further up it.

By the time I'd taken my foot off the accelerator, the car was stationed upright against the tree with its wheels violently rotating in mid-air.

Rufus was dangling in his seat. "Even I know how to put it in reverse!" he screamed.

All of a sudden, a branch came crashing through the front windscreen, narrowly missing my head.

I wiped sweat off my forehead. "Phew," I sighed in relief. "That was close."

Rufus unbuckled his seatbelt. "Well... at least it can't get any worse..." he muttered.

I knew he shouldn't have said it, because as soon as he did the car alarm triggered, erupting an ear-piercing screech.

After our previous experience with the school's fire alarm, we were absolutely certain that zombies were attracted to noise. Stuck in a vehicle out in the open, we were sitting ducks. "Let's get out," I squealed.

Rufus climbed out his side door. I had a bit of trouble unbuckling my seatbelt, but after a couple pulls and twists it eventually came undone. With no time to spare, I opened up my side door and plummeted to the ground.

As I stood up, I looked around to see zombies rushing towards the vehicle from all directions. Like insects attracted to light, they were uncontrollably piling towards the siren.

I had to think fast. I gazed up and down the road looking for another vehicle. In the distance, I noticed a pickup truck parked in the middle of the road. "That pickup!" I shrieked.

Both of us started sprinting towards it, as always, Rufus left me trailing in his dust. The zombies' attention span on the alarm was a lot like mine in mathematics. It was extremely short, and soon all that were previously concentrating on the siren were now chasing us.

By the time Rufus had reached the pickup, the zombies had enclosed me into a tight tunnel. With my final few strides, the passenger door swung open and I dove inside.

My face landed directly on Rufus's lap. Just before the zombies could grab my ankles, Rufus reached over and slammed the door shut behind me. Filled with a mix of disgust and respect, I pushed myself off his lap and rubbed my tainted face.

Rufus started the engine. "Sorry, Tyler!" he sniggered. "I thought only Mrs Graham placed her face down there?"

After a near-death experience, his joke was actually quite suitable. I smiled and shook my head. "On the bright side..." I replied. "Landing face-first on your lap was still better than another ankle lock..."

Rufus laughed and pushed his foot down on the pedal. "I will show you how it's done!" he shouted.

The smell of burning rubber filled the air. A heavy smoke screen surrounded us. He slammed down the handbrake. "Hold on tight!" he screamed.

The pickup took off flying forward. *Thud! Crack! Bang!* Oncoming zombies splattered into the bumper bar like roadkill. As the smoke dispersed, I peeked into the rear-view mirror to see the horde slowly fade out of sight.

The path we followed to Eli's house was very time consuming. Although we happened to be the only vehicle on the road, the blockades, crashes, fires, oil spills, and occasional horde accounted for a very strenuous drive. As we approached the entrance to Eli's street, we noticed a few lost zombies moping about.

"All right..." I assured. "Rufus, you move slowly. This is a drive-by shooting."

Rufus lightly revved the engine. "Why don't I just ram them?" he asked.

I signaled him to stop revving. "If Eli and Jake are in the house, we don't want any attention drawn to us," I replied. "You saw how that horde reacted to noise. Let's just play it safe."

Rufus cooperated and proceeded to drive very slowly down the street. Once I was in range for a clear shot, I wound down my window and started firing at the nearby zombies.

At the speed at which we were travelling, it was difficult to miss. The quiet nails hit the zombies perfectly in the forehead. One by one they fell over, stiffly. By the time we'd reached Eli's driveway, only two remained, a male and a female. The male stumbling across the road was the easiest target.

I lined up his head and fired. The nail splintered through his skull and he collapsed on the ground.

Only one more to go, I told myself. The female zombie was hobbling towards the car, dragging one leg behind it. I aimed the nail gun and fired. Rufus nudged my arm at the last second, making me miss. *Ting! Smack! Bang!* The nail ricocheted off a bin and struck an overturned car.

I angrily turned to Rufus. "Dude, what the hell was that?!" I yelled.

He pointed at the female zombie. "Check out that face," he said. "Doesn't that look familiar?"

I assessed the zombie's face and opened my mouth in shock. "That... that is Mrs Cooper!" I shrieked.

Before I could even comprehend the severity of what I was witnessing, the airbags of the overturned car burst, triggering yet another car alarm.

An immediate rush of adrenaline pulsed through my body. I leapt out of the car and sprinted towards the house. "Jake, Eli we have to go!" I screamed.

I smashed through the side gate and sprinted into the backyard. As I darted around looking for Jake and Eli, I was stopped by something that made my heart drop.... Next to the pool, in the far right-hand corner of the backyard a hunk of fur lay chained up to a peg in the ground. Eli's German shepherd Bruce was dead, and by the looks of it, it died from dehydration. From a playful puppy to a tail-wagging guard dog, I always remembered Bruce as being Eli's closest companion. I walked over to him and gently stroked his spiritless head. Maggots toppled out of his empty eye sockets and fell squirming to the ground. It was truly upsetting to see him lifeless and decomposing, however, with the hurry that I was in, I knew that I had no time to mourn and that I had to keep moving...

I sprinted through the house's backdoor and into the kitchen. To my surprise, in comparison to the yard, the inside of the house was relatively clean. Only after spotting a streak of blood across the kitchen sink and fingernails burrowed into a wall beside it, did I realize that something dreadful must have happened inside. I gazed around in bewilderment. *What the hell happened here?* I asked myself.

The uproar of zombies snapped me back to consciousness. With all that was happening around me, I'd discerned that it was unlikely that Eli and Jake were in the house. However, on the slight chance that they were, I dashed upstairs in search for them. Running through the upstairs hallway, yelling at the top of my lungs and inspecting every room, eventually I made it to Eli's bedroom.

It was a large, clean white room with a king-sized bed in the center. Around the sides of the room were numerous tall, hardwood cabinets filled with photos and trophies of Eli's boxing achievements.

I was staring at a photo of Eli with one of his familiar-looking friends when I heard a clatter from inside the cupboard. Curious about what could have made the noise, I walked over and opened up the cupboard door.

To my horror, a hulking creature, wearing a blood-soaked lab coat was hunched over inside the closet, furiously glaring at me.

Drizzling down its neck like a waterfall, blood was uncontrollably escaping from a gaping hole where its jaw was meant to be. I don't know how it had happened, but Eli's father was a zombie... his jaw completely torn off his face...

He let out a blood-gurgling groan and stumbled towards me. "Holy shit!" I screamed.

I tried to sidestep him and make a break for the exit. However, his massive frame made it impossible to get past him. Unable to escape, I staggered backwards and reared my nail gun at his head. Although it should have been an easy decision, I felt as though I was stuck in a very difficult position. Even though he was a zombie, I didn't want to be the person known for killing Eli's father...

My contemplation took too long. He suddenly lunged forwards. His huge body struck mine and I was hurled backwards, smashing through the bedroom window. It was odd...

staring at the bright blue sky, as I plummeted from the second story window to my death, I felt at peace.

Well... I thought it was my death... however, instead of crashing against the ground, I fell splashing into the pool. As my armor filled with water, I tossed my nail gun onto the nearby grass and sank to the bottom. With my armor acting as an anchor, swimming to the surface was not an option. Fully suited and strolling around the watery depths, I could have been mistaken for an 18th-century deep sea diver in training. While trying to figure out a way to resurface, an object rammed into my foot. I looked down to see that it was the Cooper's huge industrial pool cleaner. A large, rubber tube branched from the pool cleaner's base, upwards, to somewhere on land.

With my eyes stinging from the pool chlorine, combined with the onset of asphyxiation from holding my breath, I gripped the rubber tube and climbed up it like a rope. By the time I'd resurfaced and regathered my nail gun, Rufus was loudly shrieking for me to get back to the car.

As I started running towards the front gate, I looked up to see Mr Cooper climbing out the second story window. Like a crazed maniac, he suddenly leapt out and plummeted towards the ground. Unlike me, though, instead of landing in the pool, he ploughed headfirst into the pavement. His head exploded on impact, forming a raspberry slushy on the ground. It was extremely brutal to witness. "Ooooo!" I howled.

As I passed through the front gate, I realized why Rufus was shrieking so loudly. From one end of the street to the other, zombies were crowded as far as the eye could see.

Rufus noticed that I was standing in the front yard and he reversed down the driveway to pick me up. Mrs Cooper, who was hobbling across the driveway at the time, was struck by the back of the pickup. The collision snapped her disfigured leg in half making her collapse into a crawl. I stared in dismay as Rufus then unknowingly continued to reverse over her head. The pickup tilted upwards as if it was going over a speed bump. However, instead of making it over the other side, it came crushing down on her head. Similar to what I'd just witnessed with Mr Cooper, her skull exploded like a grenade. One of her eyeballs was sent rolling to my feet. Even in a panic, it was hard to believe *that in the last minute alone, I had witnessed both of Eli's parents' heads explode.*

With Rufus being completely unaware of his own brutal accident, he pointed to the back of the vehicle. "Get in!" he shouted.

Knowing exactly what he meant, I leapt into the tray and braced myself for the impending collisions.

"I'm doing it again!" Rufus shouted. He pushed the gearstick into drive and barged through the zombies like a bowling ball.

After we'd made it out of Eli's street and away from the zombies, I sat down and rested my head against the rear windscreen. Completely fatigued, I closed my eyes and leisurely waved at the zombies as they faded into the distance.

I don't know how long I was asleep, but I awoke when the vehicle came to a halt. As I got up, I looked around to see that Rufus had parked at a gas station. With no zombies in sight, he hopped out of the vehicle and started filling up the tank.

I bounced off the tray and sat in the passenger seat. Only after the tank was brimming, did Rufus hook the nozzle to the bowser and sit down beside me. "Listen to this," he said.

He changed the radio station until a distorted voice was heard. "Rufus... Tyler... If you can hear this... please come help us..." it croaked.

Even with the distortion, I could distinguish that it was Jake's voice. The vehicle's radio had no microphone and thus we could not reply. We sat quietly and waited for Jake to speak his location, however, before he could, the signal cut out.

As we sat in silence, I thought about Jake's message. The fact that he'd said "come help us," and not "come help me" meant that Eli was with him. It was pleasing to know that Jake and Eli were situated together. However, we still had the slight problem of not knowing their location. I turned to Rufus. "Where would they be with a two-way radio?" I asked.

Rufus looked at me as if I were stupid. "Tyler..." he said. "Where is the only place we know *for sure* that has a two-way radio...?"

The answer straightaway came to mind. It was embarrassing that I hadn't thought of it earlier as the location was very close to where we'd lost them. "The treehouse..." I muttered.

Rufus started the engine and headed towards the school. "Tyler," he said. "We have made a lot of terrible decisions today... Let's hope this one makes up for it..."

Chapter 7:
Liberty and Lies

It was five o'clock by the time we arrived at the school. We parked beside the police car that was stationed vertically upright against the tree. As we hopped out of the pickup we could feel that the atmosphere was nothing like this morning.

The police siren had stopped and all was tranquil. The color of the creek was no longer a crystal-clear blue, but instead a ruby red. It was brimming with blood. I gazed at it, mesmerized. It was funny to think that I found beauty in something utterly revolting.

Rufus disgustedly stared at the water. "Didn't we wash ourselves in the exact same water this morning...?" he questioned.

I gazed at the chunks of flesh that were floating down the stream, captivated. "Yep," I replied. "It looks pretty cool, don't you think?"

Rufus began jogging towards the creek. "As of now," he chuckled. "It won't be soon."

I hurried after him wondering what he meant. As we approached the creek's edge, I realized.

Up close, the water had never looked more revolting. Insects rippled over the surface like big brown waves, feasting on the never-ending supply of flesh.

I held my breath and strode across the creek. When I climbed out the other side, my pants were as slimy and smelly as the rotting meat in the water. I was the exact opposite of clean. "That has got to be the most polluted water in all of America," I said.

Rufus ignored me and dashed ahead through the forest. "It will be dark soon," he shouted. "Stop talking and keep up."

I sprinted after him. It was difficult to maintain his pace. However, my determination to rescue the others allowed me to prevail. As we ran, the sun set behind the trees casting a deep, red glow across the forest. Nighttime followed shortly after, casting us into darkness. We were closing in on the treehouse when we heard uproars in the forest.

"Stop..." Rufus hushed.

We came to a halt. The trees gracefully swayed in the wind. Moonlight shone through the tree branches illuminating a horde of zombies. They were clustered underneath the treehouse, their heads tilted upwards snarling at the stirring shadows above.

From within the treehouse, I could see humanlike silhouettes moving around. "Look up there," I said, pointing at them.

Rufus observed the treehouse and noticed the silhouettes. "Well... Eli and Jake are most certainly up there," he said. "Just how do we rescue them?"

With zombies crowded underneath the treehouse, we required a rescue plan. And for the plan to work, we required communication with Eli and Jake. "First things first," I said. "We need to get their attention somehow..."

Rufus nodded and stepped out from behind the tree into the moonlight. Standing in the clear view of the zombies, he wildly waved his arms in the air in an attempt to gain Eli and Jake's attention. Surprisingly, even though that his method was stupid and dangerous, it worked. A dark figure poked its head out of the treehouse and commenced an inept sign language to us.

"That has got to be Jake," I sniggered. "Eli would be punching the air and giving us death threats if it was him."

Rufus observed the sign language. After a few seconds, he turned to me puzzled. "Okay, reading this is impossible," he muttered.

I pushed him aside and cracked my fingers. "Let the pro work his magic," I said.

I studied the sign language and started constructing a sentence. "I... am... going... to... kill..."

"To what...?" Rufus anxiously questioned. "To what...?"

The moonlight disappeared behind a cloud, preventing any further signs from being seen.

I turned to Rufus. "Well... I'm not sure... But I think the last sign... the figure was pointing at me..."

Rufus sat down under a nearby tree. "Oh," he replied. "I am going to kill you..."

I walked over to Rufus and joined him in sitting under the tree. "Yep, that was definitely Eli," I said. "Even in a dangerous time like this, he can still be an angry idiot."

Rufus scratched his head. "How are we going to rescue them now...?" he asked. "That massive cloud blocking out the moon doesn't look like it will pass anytime soon... and frankly, I don't want to stay here all night."

Suddenly, a brilliant idea popped into my mind. "That's it!" I rejoiced.

"Tyler, keep your voice down," Rufus hushed.

"Sorry..." I replied, lowering my voice to a whisper. "I may have a plan, though..."

Rufus inquisitively stared at me. "What is it?" he asked.

I pointed up at the sky. "The cloud..." I answered. "It not only blocks our vision... it blocks the zombies' vision as well."

Rufus understood my train of thought. "Ah..." he said. "So, your idea is to perform a stealth rescue. Just how are we going to pull it off?"

The zombies were our only obstacle. With them out of the picture, it was an easy rescue. "We have got to get rid of the zombies," I said. "Since you are faster than me, I think it would be best if you lure them away with noise. To lose them, all you have to do is be silent. While you're doing that, I will rescue the idiots from inside the treehouse and together we can regroup with you at the edge of C block. Firstly, though, I will need Jake's helmet."

Rufus handed me the helmet. "Okay," he acknowledged.

Rufus was usually useless at listening to orders, so I was confused by his compliance. "Okay...?" I questioned. "Is that it...?"

He suddenly stood up and sprinted off into the dark, screaming at the top of his lungs.

A thundering sound of approaching footsteps filled the air. I jammed my back against the tree and sat motionless. The mass of zombies came tearing past me, all of them wailing with excitement.

I waited until the last zombie had disappeared out of sight before I started breathing again. "Why do I ever trust Rufus?" I asked myself.

I peeked around the side of the tree. Not a single zombie was in sight. *Now to save Jake and Eli*, I told myself.

I darted under the treehouse. "Guys!" I whispered. "It's safe to come..." Before I could finish my sentence, I was interrupted by a loud thud. I turned to my right to see Eli standing beside me, towering over me in his heavy metal suit.

I tried to smile. "Yo, Eli...?" I whispered.

He didn't reply. His lips were pursed, and his eyebrows were furrowed.

I remembered his angry death threat and started backing away. "It wasn't my fault that you guys got attacked by zombies at the creek," I pleaded.

My pleas did not stop him. He pelted his fist at my head with incredible force. I quickly ducked out of the way and it collided with a zombie behind me. The zombie's head imploded and its faceless body collapsed on the ground.

"What?" Eli laughed.

A huge wave of relief flushed over me. "Whew!" I smiled. "For a second there I thought you were going to..."

"I am not coming down without my helmet!" Jake interjected.

Both of us looked up at the treehouse to see Jake kneeling over the edge. I raised his helmet into the air. "I have got your helmet," I said.

The ladder came rushing down, followed by the slow behemoth himself. "Give it here," he whispered. I lobbed it into his chest and he clipped it over his head. "Much better," he said.

Eli gazed around. "Hold on! Where is Rufus?" he asked, puzzled.

"Rufus lured the zombies away," I replied. "We are meeting him at the edge of C block."

"Not bad, Tyler..." Jake said. "However, my plan was still better."

I shook my head. "What... your plan?" I said, baffled. "I saw Eli's sign language. Didn't he want to kill me?"

Eli looked at me confused. "Huh? Jake was the one doing charades," he said.

"Yeah," Jake agreed. "I was asking for you to toss me my helmet so that we could jump down and kill the zombies. You know, like what we did at school this morning..."

I lowered my head in shame, disappointed that I hadn't thought of his idea. "Oh..." I muttered. Jake noticed how upset I was and slapped me on the back. "Let's get moving," he enthused.

We jogged through the dark woods towards the school. Fortunately, apart from Jake falling into the disgusting creek, we made it back to C block with zero complications. Even Rufus was waiting exactly where I told him.

Eli and I jumped in the tray while Jake sat next to Rufus in the front seat. After the long day that we'd endured, we were completely exhausted and set for some relaxation.

We'd been travelling for a while and I was fading in and out of sleep when Eli pinched my arm. "Don't sleep now, Tyler," he said. "My house has got enough room for us all to rest."

Eli's remark woke me up like an alarm clock. I flailed my arms about in distress. His house was a gory crime scene and his parents were the victims. I could not let him discover the truth. "No!" I screamed.

Eli inquisitively looked at me. "Why?" he asked, suspicious. "I need to check on Bruce, anyway."

Rufus overheard the conversation between us. "Eli, you don't need to worry about it," he said. "Tyler and I have already been to your house and it is a zombie paradise."

Eli looked at me, concerned. "Is Bruce dead...?" he murmured. "Are... are my parents dead...?"

I calmly stared into his eyes. "Not from what I saw..." I replied.

"So... are they alive...?" he whimpered.

I yawned and stretched my back. "Well, your car wasn't home, neither were your parents..." I replied.

Rufus swerved the vehicle across the road. He knew that I was lying and he was letting me know. I patted Eli on the shoulder. "I checked your backyard and..."

"And what!?" Eli impatiently shouted.

"Bruce and his leash were nowhere to be seen," I answered.

Eli hugged me. "Oh, thank God!" he said. "My parents never take Bruce anywhere without his leash. They must have escaped the outbreak together."

"Yeah..." I replied, grimly.

"Wow!" Eli cheered, happily. "That is a load off my chest. My parents must be worried sick about me!"

I gave a slight smile back, thinking of how dreadful it would be if he ever found out the truth.

"Okay!" Rufus said, swiftly changing the subject. "I think we should stay at Tyler's house tonight. Jake, what's your input?"

All of us looked at Jake to see that he was sound asleep in the passenger seat, snoring like a bear. With Jake having no input, Rufus wanted my opinion. "Tyler?!" he yelled.

I didn't put any thought into the question. I just wanted somewhere to rest. "Yeah, my house is fine!" I snapped.

Rufus made a sharp turn. "Great, I was heading there, anyway," he replied.

Eli scuffed my hair. "Tyler... let's hope your mom is as lucky as mine," he heartedly said.

Rufus halted at my driveway. "Yeah, that would be terrific!" he agreed.

My face grew red hot. The conversation in the pickup was far more torturous than the tragic events that occurred throughout the day. It was bad enough that Eli had unknowingly hoped for my mom to be like his, "a zombie." What was worse, was that Rufus knew about it and agreed with him...

I forced a smile back at Eli, attempting to dim down the hatred towards Rufus's last remark.

Instead of noticing the artificiality of my grin, Eli reached around and smacked Jake on the helmet. "Wake up, Newton!" he cheered.

Jake rubbed his eyes. "What...?" he groaned. "Where are we?"

Eli leapt out of the tray. "We are at Tyler's," he answered. "We are going to sleep in his house tonight."

Jake laid back in the seat. "I'm fine just here," he moaned.

Rufus reached into his container and pulled out a packet of chips. "Okay, suit yourself," he said. "But if you want to eat this..." He shook the packet around. "You have to come inside."

Jake slumped out the door. "I'm up! I'm up!" he snapped.

After a long and stressful day, my responsiveness was poor, and I was working off basic instincts. As I was tired, sleep was all that was on my mind. I followed Eli until I was blindly standing at my front door.

Eli nudged me. "Tyler, do you have the key?" he questioned.

A shot of adrenaline rushed over me. Up until now, I had forgotten what could be waiting on the other side of the door. It was something that I would never want to see in my worst nightmare. I gulped at the thought of my mother being a zombie...

I reached into my back pocket and grasped the only object I could find. I pulled it out and admired it, before gently pushing it into the keyhole. This was a critical moment. On the other side of the door was either utopia or perdition. I hoped for the best, but feared for the worst...

I closed my eyes and rotated the key...

CHAPTER 8:
Nightmare

lick. With a spine-shuddering screech, the door gradually swung open.

Rufus shoved me aside and switched on the lights. An abrupt flicker allowed me to take in the full extent of what used to be my sanctuary.

I stared into the abyss, seizing up in shock.

Rubble covered the dirty floor. Whole sections of walls were missing. A trail of blood led from the center of the living room to the bathroom.

My heart began to race. Rufus and Jake patted me on the back, reassuring me that everything was okay.

Eli took off his gauntlet and reached for my nail gun. "Let me check," he said, empathetically. "It will be all right..."

I was stuck in a tough position, utterly helpless to the impending future.

I struggled for a moment before finally letting go. Eli glumly nodded, clicked the safety off and walked out of sight.

I was left standing in the absence of my own decision, limply holding my breath...waiting for the uproar that would devour me.

Everybody dreads the thought of their mother's demise. It's different experiencing it.

Even though I heard the terrible cries of a zombie... And the piercing shot of the nail gun. At the time, nothing arose from me. Not a single movement. Not a single word. It was as if the whole experience was a delusion.

For around five minutes I stood immobile, blankly thinking about the events that led to this defeat. That tiny spark of hope, lit like a lambent light bulb, still wished it weren't true... but in the end I had to face reality. The sullen looks of my friends as they emerged out of the dark confirmed the truth...

Within seconds I was surrounded by open arms. Eli, Rufus and Jake collectively hugged me. Although I felt like death, it was good to know others cared about me. I tightly clenched my arms around them and uncontrollably wailed in agony.

By the time I was able to speak, I'd cried so much, that I could no longer produce tears. I rubbed my dry, red face. "It's okay..." I sobbed. "I saw it coming..."

Eli took a step back and scrubbed my head. "Tyler! I think it is time we have some dinner," he said.

Rufus ecstatically pulled out dozens of snacks. "Take your pick, Tyler," he cheered. "You can have the lot, if you want."

I wiped my face with a tissue and bleakly smiled. "Thanks, Rufus," I sobbed. "It means a lot." I walked over and grabbed two packets of mac 'n' cheese and began to slowly nibble away.

After dinner, we locked all the doors around the house and rummaged mattresses and pillows into the living room. Due to the house being very insecure, we thought it would be safest if we all slept in the same room.

Rufus locked the front door and fell to sleep on a mattress beside me. Jake and Eli told me how sorry they were before they too began snoring.

I closed my eyes attempting to sleep, but no matter how much I tried, I couldn't. It was difficult to rest with a broken mind.

Every time I got relaxed my brain would impale itself with memories of my mother. Every past event, good or bad, came flushing through my head.

After hours of tossing and turning I finally accepted the truth... There is no escape from your own consciousness.

Slowly but surely... the longest night of my life ended. The sun gleamed through the window, signifying me to wake the others up.

I put on my armor. "Up and at it!" I screamed. "We have got a lot of work to do today!"

Eli arose to his feet. "Oh yeah!" he stretched "That was one fine sleep. What about you, Tyler?"

I started walking towards the door. "Oh... Yep, it was great!" I answered, blissfully.

Jake shot up in front of me. "Tyler, lift up your helmet." He said.

"What... Why?" I asked.

"Just do it!" he shouted.

I knew there was no point in quarrelling. I took off my welding mask to the sounds of loud gasps. "You look like complete shit." Rufus laughed.

Eli examined my face. "Exactly how much 'sleep' did you get?"

I pulled my mask down. "Enough for today..." I replied.

Jake patted me on the back. "Don't worry, man," he said. "The same thing happened to me when my brother Charlie died... I couldn't sleep for days... You will get through it."

Rufus got up and cart-wheeled past me. "It's easy to be happy!" he cheered. "Keep your mind off your mother by killing zombies!"

I was not in the mood for Rufus's stupid enthusiasm.

I angrily turned to him. "What the hell do you know about experiencing your own parents' death? You don't even have any!"

Rufus sat back down, upset.

"Whoa, whoa, whoa!" Eli shouted. "Tyler, we get that you are tired and angry, but even that was harsh."

"Yeah," Jake agreed. "Plus, Rufus is somewhat correct. Keeping your mind off your mother will help you rest."

I clenched my teeth together. "But she is still sitting in the bathroom! How the fuck am I meant to forget, if she is rotting in the house!"

Jake walked over and put his hand on my shoulder. "Tyler... can you even remember us last night telling you that we buried her?"

"What?" I cried, slumping to the ground. "No... how do I not remember that...?"

"Don't worry," Eli said. "We wrapped her in a silk sheet and buried her next to the rose garden. It was actually very peaceful..."

"Indeed," Rufus sobbed on the ground. "It is covered in rose petals..."

I was completely bewildered but also glad at what they had done. I would have never wanted to see my mother as a zombie.

"Thanks, guys…" I wept. "I don't know what I'd do without you."

Rufus stood up and was wiping his eyes when… *Bang!* A zombie smashed against the front door.

Eli readied his gauntlets.

"No, let me," I yelled, snatching Rufus's bat. Eli shrugged and motioned me to the door.

I swung open the door and cracked the zombie on the head as hard as I could. Its skull split like a coconut and its lifeless body collapsed on the ground. I then proceeded to bash the bat over every grain of its visible flesh. With each decisive strike, the zombie's insides became its outsides.

I bashed repeatedly until Eli screamed, "Stop!"

I turned around sneering with anger. Eli calmly approached me and yanked the bat out of my hands. "I think it's dead…?" He nudged.

I looked at the limbs scattered all over the ground, amazed at what I had done. I shut the door and sat down. "Sorry, I don't know what came over me," I said.

Eli lobbed the bat to Rufus. "It looks as if you have a new-found hatred towards zombies," he replied.

I wiped blood off my face. "But why?" I questioned.

Jake strutted over in his suit. "Well, seeing as though zombies infected your mom, I think at a subconscious level, you want vengeance."

"That's not bad, is it?"

"No," Jake answered. "To some degree, it's great. We need to kill a lot of zombies. The only difference when you do it is that it now gives you relief."

Rufus stood up and joined the conversation. "Most people know revenge as being painful and destructive," he said. "Personally, I think that's complete bullshit. Revenge has always made me feel a hell of a lot happier."

"Did that feel good, Tyler?" Jake questioned.

As disgusting as it sounded... it did. I picked up my nail gun and reloaded it. "Yeah, kind of," I replied.

Eli walked past me and opened the front door. "Good, good," he said, walking outside. "See if you can slay as many as me."

Excited by the concept of killing more zombies, I shoved Jake aside and ran after Eli.

Jake stumbled backwards and fell onto his arse. "Our job today is to secure and clean the house!" he shouted.

Instead of securing the house, Eli and I ferociously killed zombies without rest. By the time it was midday, we had slain so many zombies that our doings had induced Rufus upon cleaning up after us. He would drive the pickup to and from the dump, dropping off loads of corpses. The only person who was actually securing and cleaning the house was Jake.

I'd just finished slaying my frail, old next-door neighbor when Rufus came skidding up the driveway. "Look at this!" he cheered, holding up a twenty-four pack of Pepsi out the driver-side window.

I walked over and examined them. "Where did you get them?" I excitedly questioned.

"Check the tray!" he answered, pointing behind him.

I investigated the pickup's tray to see not bits of rotting flesh, but instead a mountain of junk food and soft drink.

"Hey, fellas!" I yelled to Eli and Jake. "Rufus has been doing some shopping!"

Both of them immediately stopped what they were doing and excitedly ran over to the pickup. Together we crowded around the tray and gazed at the heavenly food.

I snatched a box of Oreos. "Lunch time!" I screamed, running inside.

The others grabbed a snack each and ran after me. As we got inside, we started devouring the food. I ate the Oreos so quickly that my mouth became a thick whirlpool of chocolate. In one gulp, I managed to swallow six chewed-up Oreos, and by the end of the packet, I felt extremely bloated and sick.

I drowsily stood up. "I feel revolting..." I gurgled, holding my stomach.

Rufus held me up and began walking me outside. "Jake would certainly not want any vomit in this 'now' rather clean house."

I wobbled about in Rufus's grip, too nauseated to reply.

We had only been outside for a minute, when something caught my attention.

Rufus, without meaning to, brought me out the back to the rose garden. A rough stretch of soil lay beside.

Rufus realized what he had done. "Sorry," he said. "I didn't mean to..."

"Shhh," I whispered, struggling from his grip and falling onto my hands and knees. "It's... it's Mom..."

Rufus empathetically placed his hand on my back. "She is at peace," he said.

I held my finger up, averring silence for this magical moment. It was my first tiny moment of consolation.

I pulled a rose out of the garden and tossed it on top of her grave before collapsing into a deep sleep.

CHAPTER 9:
Bargain Hunting

"**R**ise and shine! It's shopping time!" I awoke in an instant, for a few seconds not knowing my current location. Only until my eyes locked onto a dusty plasma television did I realize that I was in my bedroom. I stood up and stretched. "How long was I out for?" I yawned.

Rufus counted his fingers over and over again. After a brief moment, he looked at me with a smirk. "Hmmm... Around eighteen hours all up."

I sat back down. "Wow, that's a long time," I said, puzzled.

"Yeah, but you needed it, Tyler," Rufus replied. "Yesterday, you were uglier than Eli. But today you look fresher than... ummm... than a..."

Rufus began eyeing around the room, searching for an object to finish his metaphor. The toilet flushed and Eli came strolling into the room. "Than a what?" Eli mocked.

Rufus sniffed the air and patted his chin in deep concentration. After a short moment, he shot his arms up screaming. "I got it! Today you look fresher than an air freshener!"

I tried to keep a straight face. It was even worse than Eli's disgraceful joke by the creek. "You are about as sharp as a marble," Eli cackled.

Rufus slumped on the ground, wounded by Eli's clever remark. I couldn't keep it in any longer. "Bahahaha!" I burst out in hysterics.

Jake heard the commotion and quickly came rushing into the room with a very distressed look. "Guys, I've got some bad news," he moaned.

"What is it?" I asked.

"Rufus..." he sniveled.

All of us stopped smiling and expected the worst. Rufus looked significantly more distressed than the rest of us. The quietness and intensity made it all the more dramatic.

Jake made sure we were all about to have heart attacks before shrieking. "Is a doofus!"

It came as a complete shock that he was joining us in the abuse. It was a dragged-out horrible joke. However, if Rufus got offended by it, by all means it was worthy.

"Oh, snap!" I screamed, jumping up and high-fiving Jake.

Rufus turned his back to us, not one bit amused by our witticisms. It was amazing how insulted he got by a few stupid statements. Unlike the rest of us, he was obviously not having a good start to the day.

We kept bagging him until he eventually had to change the subject. "What about shopping?" he asked. "We could be searching through an 'adult's only' shop by now..."

All of us immediately went silent. Yes, our sexual life wasn't the greatest. To sum it up, Rufus had managed to finger a drunken gorilla-like lady at a Christmas celebration one time. Eli having the highest bragging rights was the only one of us to ever have had sex. But even it was still bad as it happened to be with a relentless butterball in the year above, who stalked him every day after school.

We were eager to visit an 'adult's only' shop as our age had limited us from doing it in the past. Plus, anything that could level the boasting field always grabbed our attention.

We were armored up and strolling out to the pickup when I remembered yesterday's objective. I stopped at the driveway. "Fellas…" I sighed. "What about fortifying the house?"

Jake walked past me and sat in the passenger seat. "Oh, yeah," he replied. "With the help of your nail gun, we secured the house last night."

I climbed into the tray of the ute. "Let me guess…" I muttered. "I have no more nails…"

Rufus slammed the pickup door and began reversing. "Right you are." He smiled.

I dropped my nail gun beside me. "You guys know that there is only one place we can do all this shopping, right?"

Eli slapped me hard on the chest. "Yep," he replied. "We have already planned for the mall."

The trip to the shopping center was as joyous as our early morning jokes. It felt like only seconds before we arrived in the car park. However, it turned out we were not the only ones in the car park.

Zombies were scattered far and wide. And although I didn't have my nail gun, I was not the least bit bothered.

We all hopped out, extremely confident with our zombie-killing ability. Laughter arose as Jake went and performed a leaping body-slam on the closest zombie.

I quickly grabbed a rock and pulverized its flinching body underneath him. This was our day and nothing was stopping us.

By the time we reached the entrance, more corpses covered the ground than vehicles. The car park was a complete decimation.

Only until we noticed a metal gate blocking the front entrance did we snap out of our hysteria.

"Hmm..." Jake pondered, covered in blood. "It would have closed up when the Psyriviox warning was released."

Rufus excitedly ran off into the distance. "Don't worry!" he shouted. "I know what to do." The rest of us shrugged and sat down. A few minutes passed and all was calm.

We knew Rufus was still in a frenzy. But blaring a horn from a fast-moving truck still shocked us. "Move out of the way!" he shouted at the top of his lungs. "I'm busting the door down."

To some degree, it was actually quite comical. None of us even knew how he'd learnt to drive a truck let alone try and bust into a mall with one. We gawked at the extraordinary sight before dashing out of the way.

The truck collided hard with the metal gate. A barrage of debris rained over us like an Armageddon. Without our armor we could have all been extremely hurt.

The dust soon cleared and we were left with an open entrance. Instead of stopping at the gate, the truck had continued into the mall's central water fountain. Like a blown fire hydrant, water was streaming everywhere. Rufus emerged from the cascade of water like the Terminator. Luck was definitely on his side today as he did not have a single scratch.

Jake jogged up to him. "How did you not get hurt?" he cackled.

Drenched in water, Rufus lavishly massaged the truck. "Seatbelts save lives…" he replied.

"Too bad it doesn't prevent brain damage," Eli teased. He stretched his arms above his head, waiting for applause.

His applause never came and by the time he realized that he was not going to get one, the rest of us were already rushing ahead, sprinting up the broken escalator. Our attention was so concentrated on the forbidden 'adult's only' shop that none of us could even be bothered to acknowledge his joke.

In no time we were in the illicit store, rummaging through every nasty and weird item we could find.

Jake grabbed some beads and string and stretched them out. "What are these for?" he asked.

Eli held up a big black dildo. "Are you sure you want to try anal beads over this?" he replied.

Rufus slid his fingers inside a "Try Me!" tagged Fleshlight. "This feels like Mrs Newton," he laughed.

It just so happened that Jake's parents were on holidays for the past two weeks. And thus, them not being in the immediate outbreak and almost certainly safe in Hawaii, they were our last option for paternal puns.

I snatched the dildo out of Eli's hands and soothingly shoved it inside the Fleshlight that Rufus was holding. "And that's Jake's parents on their holiday." I smirked.

All of us began laughing at the top of our lungs. We were having a blast playing with the sex toys.

After a few more jokes and filling our minds with sex life wisdom, we left for other shops.

The three-story mall had everything you could possibly think of. We went on a rampage from store to store, trashing and picking up beneficial items. Our ideas were endless and by the time we were near finished, a brand-new dump truck was almost full with our supplies.

We had just finished unloading a couple hundred guns and ammo cartridges into the truck when Rufus detected a shop which we had completely forgotten about. It was a bottle shop.

Rufus sprinted back inside the mall. "Guys!" he shouted. "We have to get some!"

The rest of us stopped what we were doing and excitedly followed him. As soon as we saw the vast range of alcohol stretched across the bottle shop aisles, we grabbed a trolley each.

Jake pushed his trolley down the aisles, looking at the bottles as if he were about to explode with excitement. "I have never drunk alcohol before!" he said. "What do you think I would like?"

In all truth, Rufus was the only one out of us to have ever been inebriated. The rest of us tried plenty of times, but no matter how devious we were, our parents would always catch us out. It was like they had a sixth sense for underage drinking. Their consent would never come. Instead, they harassed and grounded us for doing such horrific crimes.

I pointed at the most expensive bottle in a case. "You would like that, for sure!" I said. "Look at the price tag!"

Eli smashed the glass casing and snatched the heavy bottle.

"Hmm..." he pondered, staring at it. "It is a Dalmore 62... whatever the hell that means," he said.

I began filling the rest of my trolley with every type of alcohol. "Come on, Eli!" I enthused. "Anything worth two hundred and fifty thousand dollars has got to taste good!"

Eli agreed and placed the bottle in his trolley followed by three cartons of full-strength beer. Rufus and Jake piled their trolleys with antique wines, scotches and whiskeys.

In less than a minute our trolleys were full. Jake was licking his lips looking at his alcohol. "That ought to be enough!" he said cheerfully.

"Yep!" Rufus laughed. "Has everyone got what they need from this store?"

"Yes!" Eli and I agreed.

"Okay then!" Rufus cheered. He wound back his leg and kicked the first aisle.

Our mouths dropped as it slowly fell and struck another. Like a domino effect, every aisle fell on the next, shattering every bottle on the ground and creating a tremendous flood. We all gripped our trolleys as a wave of alcohol swept across the floor, drenching our feet.

It was one of the few spectacular events we had witnessed today. All of us pinched our noses to avoid the potent, burning smell of ethanol and using our one free hand, we pushed our trolleys out the door.

The sun was setting as we piled the alcohol into the truck. We tried to leave. However, all four of us could not fit into the truck's two-seat cabin. It was at this point that we realized that we had completely missed a task.

Eli, Jake and I exchanged glances before leaping out and running around the car park. Rufus agreed to drive the truck while we find our own vehicle.

The massive car park allowed us to be very choosy with our selections. The only gadget that our vehicles required was the keys in the ignition, which to our surprise was actually quite easy to find.

In the end, we were tailing one another out the exit comprising of Rufus's dump truck, Eli's Lamborghini, Jake's 4wd and my Chrysler. It was obvious that Eli and I had the least safe transport. But still… we regretted nothing.

After the slow, tacky drive and unloading of supplies, we sat down in my house for some relaxation.

I rested on the couch. "It's been a good day," I said.

Rufus got up and walked over to our mountain of alcohol. "Do you know what would make it better?" he said.

"What?" Eli asked.

Rufus picked up a Styrofoam cup and tossed one to each of us. "After a long day of hard work, I think we deserve a little drink," he said.

Jake half-crushed his cup with anticipation.

I sat up ready. Rufus opened the Dalmore 62 and walked around the room pouring it into our cups. He filled my cup up halfway. "That's about a shot," he assessed. "I know… because my adoptive parents had them all the time."

I examined the bottle of Dalmore 62 to see that it was almost empty. "If you say so!" I replied.

"Recreation is better than rest!" Jake sniggered.

Everyone had high spirits. We all stood up and smashed cups. "Cheers!"

Chapter 10:
Hangover

"Cheers!" was without a doubt the wrong saying. The alcohol's horrid taste was almost as bad as its extreme burn.

I placed my cup down and shook my head, attempting to rid of the awful sensation.

Jake looked more offended than myself. "That is disgusting!" He spat, hurling his cup against the ground.

"Why is that shit so expensive?" Eli agreed.

Rufus poured himself another shot. "It could be worse." He smiled, sculling it and wiping his chin.

All of us goggled in disbelief. *How could he drink another so easily when the first cup was torment?* "

It's not that bad..." Rufus chuckled. "Anyway, it can only get better from here on out. Just go try some other drinks."

"How do you mean 'better'?" Jake questioned.

Rufus, completely oblivious to Jake's question, took a swig and hurled the bottle against a wall.

"That actually does taste bad," he laughed. He grabbed a bottle of vodka and poured us each another shot. "Trust me, drink vodka and you will have the time of your life."

Believing Rufus was telling the truth, the rest of us gripped our noses and gulped heavily.

As soon as we finished our first shot of vodka, Rufus handed us another three more different shots of alcohol. Rufus's determination to get us intoxicated was unfathomable.

Once having accomplished the three shots, we were onto beer. And by this time, we were starting to feel something.

We usually hated the taste of beer, but tonight it was satisfying. Even Jake enjoyed it.

As I cracked open my second can, Rufus came past with a pitch-black bottle. He held it up to my eyes to ensure that I saw the full extent of its potency.

I extended my cup towards him. "Seventy-four percent doesn't sound that bad," I said.

Rufus was about to pour one of his oversized shots when Jake stood up. "Come on now," he simpered, requesting for the bottle. "We shouldn't..." With great disappointment, Rufus slowly passed it over.

Jake held it high in the air and screamed. "We shouldn't, unless I'm pouring!"

All of our eyes, especially Rufus's, glowed with happiness. We were starting to have fun. Jake smashed off the bottle cap on the table and poured us each a round.

Together, we took two huge mouthfuls, attempting to down his so-called shot.

Somehow, I managed to finish first. "That's how it's done!" I yelled, jumping up in the air and accidentally tripping over the table.

Rufus slapped me on the back. "You think you are drunk now?" he said. "Wait until that last one kicks in."

I brushed myself off and regathered my misplaced beer. I couldn't comprehend what he meant... I thought I already was inebriated? Nevertheless, an hour passed and the night became a blur.

Largely consisting of joy riding, gunpowder and sex toy impersonations, from what I recall it was a great night. The only downside was Rufus getting sick and going to bed early... that and the fact that the alcohol left us feeling the exact opposite of "great" the following morning.

I awoke with a splitting headache. "Urgh..." I muttered. "I feel dead."

Rufus stood in front of me, a slice of cake half-hanging from his mouth. "Funny that!" He laughed. "You look and sound like a zombie, too."

"Yeah..." I moped, struggling to a stand. "Where are the others...?"

Rufus pointed to my feet. I looked down to see Jake and Eli tossing and turning beneath me. It turned out we had all slept under the same blanket. What made matters worse was that we had all stripped down to our underpants.

I gazed down in bewilderment. "What the... Why are you guys...? Never mind..." I muttered.

I got dressed and walked out of the room. I was lumbering past Rufus when he held a cup that we'd used for alcohol under my nose.

Straightaway, the smell of the vodka made me violently retch and spew. I tried to cover my mouth, but that only led it to circulate out through my nose.

I ran to the bathroom, leaving a thick path of repugnance behind. All that was in my gut was transferred into the toilet. Most of it being bile.

After ten long minutes, I washed my mouth over the sink and walked outside. Rufus was busily laughing and mopping up my mess as I walked past him. He knew exactly what he did.

With the stench of puke inside the house, Jake and Eli stumbled outside to get some fresh air. In the sunlight they both looked as obliterated as me. Rufus finished mopping and started rummaging through the kitchen for food.

My stomach was empty and sore. I wasn't hungry, but I knew that I needed something to fill it. "Cook us up some breakfast!" I screamed at Rufus.

"Yeah!" Eli and Jake agreed.

Rufus stopped rummaging and peered at us through the front door. "Cook... what?" he said. "Can you guys not remember the blackout?"

We all exchanged confused expressions as none of us had any idea what he was talking about. For all we knew, it was just an escape from cooking us breakfast.

"It's the reason you guys slept under the same blanket..." Rufus said. "You all got scared of the dark."

"Wait!" I laughed. "Even Eli?"

Rufus walked outside and flicked the light switches on and off to no response. "Yes!" he smirked. "Even Eli..."

It was unnatural for Eli to be remotely scared of anything, apart from deep water. "Poor snookums," Jake teased Eli.

Eli had been pestered so much lately that instead of being embarrassed, he shrugged and joined in the laughter.

"Don't forget," he grinned, pointing at Jake and me. "You two were with me."

Rufus gazed past us and grabbed a pistol from the stack of weapons. A zombie had found its way into our front yard.

"Hold on a tick," he said. He aimed the gun at the zombie and fired. *Bang!* The zombie collapsed in a heap.

With the zombie dead on the ground, Rufus then unexpectedly lobbed the pistol at me. "Heads up!" he laughed.

Instead of landing in my lap, the gun sailed short. I attempted to dive for it and catch it, but missed. The gun hit the ground and fired. *Bang!* The bullet narrowly missed my head, hitting an object inside the house.

"Phew!" I picked up the smoking gun. "That was a close one!"

Jake rested back in his seat. "Rufus, make sure you put the safety on next time," he said. Eli walked inside and searched for the bullet.

Moments later he returned with the canister that I'd built for Rufus in the industrial room. "Hahaha!" Eli laughed. "It cut a clear hole right through Rufus's prized possession."

"Whatever is in Rufus's canister is probably broken," I chuckled.

Eli tried to open it, but couldn't. "Why is it locked?" He mumbled.

"Maybe so that he doesn't lose anything important," Jake answered, disparagingly.

Rufus strolled over and peered through the hole. "It's chock-a-block full of ammunition, anyway," he said. "I don't think anything would be broken."

Eli sat back down. "Oh, okay," he said. "Now back to an important question. What are we supposed to do with no electricity?"

Rufus tossed the canister aside. "I guess we are going to have to live without it," he replied. "There is plenty of fun stuff to do!"

"You are kidding me?" Jake questioned in disbelief. "Look at the roofs around us..."

I attempted to stare outwards but got dazed by the reflection of numerous solar panels around the neighborhood. "I'm sorry, Jake," I said. "The solar panels make it impossible for me to concentrate on the roofs..."

Jake slapped me across the face. "Congratulations, genius, you just figured out the answer..." I understood what he meant. Solar power was our key to electricity.

"Just one question..." I queried.

"I don't know," Jake replied. "We can deal with that later. First thing's first, though. Let's collect some solar panels."

Eli and I were absolutely wrecked, even more so than Jake and we weren't going to climb roofs and scavenge solar panels without incentive. To motivate us, Jake promised to cook us all a big feast. A promise which we could not pass up.

We walked from house to house, dismantling the solar panels and placing them in the dump truck. Eli and I would tear the panels off the roofs while Jake and Rufus would load them into the truck. Stray zombies would occasionally show up. However, with our pistols in hand, they were killed the second we saw them. We collected over fifty solar panels from three separate streets and after four hours we were finally finished.

I slid off the roof onto the ground. "Wooo hooo! Last panel!" I cheered, lobbing it to Rufus.

Rufus lobbed it to Eli who gently placed it in the truck with all the others. Jake honked the horn and began driving back to the house. He poked his head out the window. "One more thing," he shouted. "You now have to set them up on the house! You won't need more than two people."

I sprinted after the truck and gripped onto the back of it like a fireman. "Eli..." I groaned. "He is talking to us."

"Yeah, I know..." Eli replied.

When we arrived home, although we did not want to, we both climbed on the roof and started installing the solar panels. To ensure that the solar panels received maximum sunlight, Jake directed their positioning to us from the front lawn. As Eli was about to install the final solar panel, Jake signaled him to stop.

"You have to move it higher!" he shouted, pointing upwards. "It needs to have direct sunlight!"

Eli swore under his breath in frustration and walked to the topmost part of the roof. I followed him up and helped him attach the solar panel to the roof. We were cabling the panel when Eli suddenly turned to me with a concerned expression.

I looked at him confused. "What is it?" I asked.

Eli reached into his pocket and pulled out his mobile. He pressed a few buttons and gaped at the screen.

"What's going on?" I queried. "You didn't receive another photo of Mrs Newton's nudes, did you?"

He held the mobile to my face. A message from "Little Dick Nick" read: "At hospital! Need help!"

Chapter 11: Familiar Face

This was our second sign of outside communication since the outbreak began. I was pleased that someone had managed to contact us, but also quite worried about the tone and urgency of the message. "Which hospital is he at?" I asked. "For all we know, 'Little Dick Nick' could be in Paris..."

"He is definitely in our city," Eli replied "I will message him right now to confirm which of the three hospitals he is stuck in." He quickly texted a message and sent it.

It wasn't long after the text was sent did he receive a notification.

"You have got to be kidding me..." Eli said. "You deal with it, Tyler." He tossed his mobile to me.

I squinted at the reply. "Message not sent"

Hmm, I thought. *How was Eli able to receive texts, but not send them?* I checked the connectivity bars and began climbing higher up the roof.

"Where are you going?" Eli asked.

"To the location you were at when your phone vibrated," I replied.

I kept climbing until I stood at the topmost peak of the house. To my luck, the phone's connectivity raised one bar. I smiled and re-sent the message.

"I'm guessing it worked?" Eli laughed.

I ignored Eli and anxiously waited. After a short moment, another response came through. The message read: "Southport Hospital!"

I winced at the name of the hospital. For even though Southport was located in our city and renowned for comprising of some of the best doctors in the world, it also happened to be the largest hospital with an unnecessary scary complex. I had only ever entered the hospital once and within a mere moment got lost in the maze of corridors. It happened to be one of the few places any of us would ever willingly venture to... Besides Eli, of course; his parents had worked there.

"Eli!" I shouted. "You still know your way through the catacombs of Southport, don't you...?"

Eli smiled and leapt off the roof. "We have got a new mission, Tyler!" he excitedly answered.

Before long, we were explaining the situation to Jake and Rufus. Both of them looked as baffled as me. Jake sat on the couch and opened up a packet of chips. "Why did the person message us now?" he asked.

"We can sort that out when we save him," Eli replied.

Jake had promised to cook us a big meal and as he was no longer directing us with installing the solar panels, I found it odd that he hadn't started cooking. "Wait!" I shrieked. "Why aren't you cooking anything, Jake?"

"Cook?" Jake laughed. "With what electricity?"

I realized that he had played Eli and I for fools. "You lazy bastard..." I muttered.

Eli slammed his fist down on the table. "Stop talking and let's go fetch Nick!" he shouted.

"What... at this time...?" Rufus moaned. "It's sooo dark..."

Eli gritted his teeth. "Get some flashlights, before I break all your fucking necks..." he growled.

Our disinterest in rescuing Nick had infuriated Eli. To stop him from having an outburst, we promptly nodded in agreement and started assembling our equipment. We knew that rescuing Nick at night-time from the labyrinth of Southport Hospital was an extremely dangerous task, thus we thought we'd try and use the best equipment that we had at our disposal.

After half an hour of preparation, we were ready to go. Jake slung an assault rifle over his shoulder and unhappily gazed at his exposed hands. "It feels weird not to wear any gloves," he said.

I was dual-wielding two small, but powerful submachine guns. "Don't worry," I soothingly replied. "I will protect your fingers."

Eli slammed his gauntlets together. "That's one thing I don't need to worry about!" He chuckled.

"There is one thing you should worry about," Jake said, pointing at Rufus.

Rufus pumped a little flame out the end of his flame-thrower. "Where's the party at?" he said cheerfully.

Eli marched outside with a huge grin. "Let's start at Southport."

Due to our horrid circumstances, we thought it would be best to use one source of transport.

Rufus's dump truck, being the largest and most powerful vehicle, was the one that we planned to use.

As we knew that we were heading to Southport, all of us except Eli, hesitantly climbed into the truck.

The trip was relatively smooth and before long we were standing outside the hospital. The trees swayed violently in the cold wind. A single beacon of light could be seen flashing from one of the top-most windows. We were certain that it was Nick signaling us with a flashlight. All of us double-checked our weapons and flashlights and followed Eli inside.

As we passed through the entrance, our flashlights became our only source of light. However, venturing down the first hallway, I was tempted to switch mine off. The hospital was more nightmarish than any of us could have ever imagined. Every step was an obstacle. Whether it be dangling wires, blood-bathed wheelchairs or a corpse, everything seemed to be alive. Our flashlights illuminated the shadows like a depraved puppet play. Every slight movement made us falter with fear. It was unbelievable that Nick was located at the top of the building. I couldn't imagine why anyone would want to be inside this hell hole.

We were walking towards the stairs when movement was heard in the room beside us. Rufus climbed over a blood-stained bed and walked out of sight.

"What are you doing?" Eli wailed, waving his flashlight around like a maniac.

Rufus did not reply. All of us stopped and stared as his light disappeared around the corner. "I can't handle this," I said. "Let's get out of here."

"I agree," Jake said.

Jake and I were both walking back to the front exit when a high-pitched screech resonated behind us. We started to sprint but it was too late. An object hit us sharply in the back and toppled us over.

We were face-down on the ground when a low growl echoed through the hallway. A loud thudding followed by a crash, indicated that something was moving towards us. I turned around and quickly raised my flashlight.

To my horror, Eli's nose was less than an inch away from mine. His owlish-sized eyes and furrowed brow portrayed a nightmarish amount of anger.

"Okay..." I trembled. "We aren't leaving..."

Eli gripped us both and even with our armor equipped, heaved us to our feet.

Jake dusted himself off. "I get that you want to find Nick. But there is no need to shove a bed at us," he said.

Eli ignored Jake and stormed off down the hallway. "Run-away then," he retorted. "You will not be able to find your way out."

Jake and I gazed around in confusion. He was right, we weren't in the first corridor anymore... Both of us sprinted after him.

After proceeding up two staircases and tunnelling through a mountain of dark passages, not a single zombie had been seen. It was like a ghost town. The hospital had killed off every patient.

It was also funny that no one was worried about finding Rufus. In truth, we felt safer without him.

We were proceeding through the fourth floor when we began hearing subtle noises. *Murmurs, grunts, cries.* Like eyes adapting to darkness, our ears adapted to the quietness.

As we neared the final stairway, Eli halted us to a stand-still. Jake and I immediately switched off our flashlights. The atmosphere was intense. Thudding and crashing could be heard through the ceiling. We stood motionless, listening for anything that would allow us to estimate the situation above.

Twenty seconds passed in complete darkness. "What do we do now?" I whispered.

Jake slapped my ass.

"Dude..." I whispered. "I didn't mean for you to get erotic..."

"What?" Eli laughed. "Who are you talking to?"

"Jake," I replied.

"Huh?" Jake questioned. "I thought I was standing beside Eli..."

"Yeah," Eli agreed. "I'm pretty sure Jake's standing beside me."

"Wait..." I whispered. "So none of you slapped my bum?"

"Nope," they replied.

A cold sandpaper tongue gently stroked the back of my neck. "This is not good..." I shivered.

Eli prodded his arm into the figure beside him. "Yeah," he laughed. "Jake seems to have gotten a bit fatter than what I remember."

"You aren't touching me..." Jake replied.

"Oh..."

All of us went dead quiet. It was one of those times where we knew what was happening, but we didn't want to confirm it.

"Don't make any sudden movement," I whispered.

"Yes...very quiet..." Jake agreed.

Eli punched the figure beside him. "Yuck!" He screamed. "It tried to lick me!"

Suddenly all of the hospital lights flicked on. As predicted, multiple zombies had surrounded us. One zombie had grasped my waist from behind as if it were about to give me a slow dance, and another with both of its legs missing was gripped onto my ankle. A morbidly obese zombie was collapsed on the ground beside Eli, its fat head bashed into a pulp. It was a total fiesta.

I pushed back the slow-dancing zombie and darted towards Eli. "Help!" I squealed, dragging the one attached to my ankle along the ground.

Eli did not help as he was too busy laughing at me. Jake being just as scared as myself attempted to shoot the zombie off my ankle.

"Don't close your eyes, Jake!" I shouted, accidentally somersaulting over a bed and hurling the zombie like a catapult. Jake opened his eyes to see the legless zombie flying directly at him.

"Ahhh!" he screamed.

Eli stopped laughing and raised his arm in front of Jake. The zombie, unable to change its impending collision, collided into Eli's gauntlet with a loud *thwack!* It fell to the ground lifeless.

The other zombie that had been gripping my waist was stuck behind a chair clawing at us like a house cat. I aimed my gun at it and shot it in the head. "That is how you do it," I said to Jake.

Jake was holding his chest as if he were having a heart attack. "Yeah, no problem," he replied, breathing heavily.

Eli rubbed his forehead, both disgusted and bemused by how badly Jake and myself had handled the situation. I forced a smile to try to appear brave. "Time for the top floor to meet its makers," I nervously enthused.

We continued down the hallway and were walking up the final set of stairs when we saw the awful situation that was concealed in the top floor. There was a reason why we'd only met three zombies in the hospital so far. The majority were crammed within the top floor. They populated the hallway from one end to the other. A lot of them were crowding around a room in particular. It was definitely the room that Nick was trapped in.

I held out a submachine gun for Eli to use. He smirked, removed his gauntlet and grabbed it out of my hand. "Okay," he said. "Seeing as we don't have Rufus to screw things up, this should be easy."

Jake reloaded his gun. "I will try to aim better," he said.

"Let's hope so..." I replied.

We marched up the stairs like terminators. As we stepped into the hallway, the zombies started charging towards us. The differing speeds between the disabled, fat and skinny zombies caused the horde to tumble over one another like a wave.

We continued our steady march and opened fire. The shower of bullets ripped apart the approaching zombies. Their frontlines fell to the ground where they were then trampled to death by the masses behind them.

We marched forwards, cutting down every zombie that got in our way. By the time we'd reached Nick's room, we were trekking over mounds of flesh.

Eli bashed his fist against the door. "Little dick Nick!" he screamed.

The door swung open and a huge figure stepped out. I tried to get a glimpse of their face. However, I was cut short by the sound of a distant chime. I curiously stared down the hallway. "What the hell is that?" I asked.

"Don't know, don't care," Eli said. "It's time to get out of here."

We turned around and proceeded back down the hall-way. We'd almost reached the stairs when yet another noise came into hearing. This noise was resonating from the stairs. A stampede of feet. "Oh shit..." Jake said. "Run!"

All of us turned and started sprinting in the opposite direction. As we ran, I glanced behind us to see hundreds of zombies race up the stairs.

We'd almost reached Nick's room when an elevator at the end of the hallway opened with a loud *ding!* We stared in bewilderment as Rufus stepped out. "You have got to be fucking kidding me!" Eli screamed.

All of us continued running towards Rufus. Rufus strode towards us holding his flamethrower out in front.

We ran past him and leapt inside the open elevator. "Rufus! Get in!" Jake shouted.

Instead of returning to the elevator, Rufus blasted the flamethrower. An intense flame lit up the hallway inciner-ating every onrushing zombie into ashes. The heat was so intense that we all had to cover our faces. We had no idea how Rufus was withstanding the temperature and we didn't care. It was dangerous and we wanted to leave.

The cindered hallway started to crumble under its own weight. "Rufus, run, you idiot!" I screamed. Jake repeatedly pressed the button to the bottom floor and the elevator door started to close. Rufus tossed the flamethrower into the fire and sprinted towards us. He dove through the narrow gap in the door with no time to spare. A thunderous boom erupted from the opposite side of the door. It was the sound of the flamethrower's fuel canister exploding in the fire.

The elevator shook and the lights flickered. I thankfully exhaled as the elevator music commenced and we started to descend. As we stood in the calm ambience of the elevator, I was able to examine Nick's face. It was a face that looked awfully familiar. I was unable to pick it out though as my mind was still racing from the blaring mayhem that happened in the top floor.

The elevator arrived at ground level and we raced outside. As we neared the truck, we turned around to see the hospital slowly collapse. From top to bottom, each floor consecutively crashed into the one below. The building's final impact with the ground created a dust cloud which filled the entire street.

We brushed ourselves off. "That was epic!" Rufus laughed.

Eli sat in the truck. "Remind me to never involve Rufus in anything that remotely matters."

"Agreed," Jake said.

Eli pointed at Nick. "You come drive this thing," he said. "Rufus will hop in the back with Tyler and Jake."

As we drove away, I could make out the shadowy figures of two zombies running out of the wreckage. I laid back beside Rufus who looked awfully angry.

I grinned at him. "What's up?" I asked.

"Nothing," he replied. "I'm just pissed off that I didn't get those last few zombies."

"Hahaha," I said. "You are just jealous that Nick stole your driving position!"

Rufus sneered at me and curled into a ball. "Whatever," he muttered.

Nick was a far more sensible and experienced driver than Rufus. The speed in which we returned to my house was phenomenally fast.

After hopping out of the vehicle and walking inside, we all found a comfortable spot in the house and went to bed.

I was searching for breakfast the following morning when I stumbled upon Nick peacefully lying asleep. Wondering where I had seen him before, I grabbed a Krispy Kreme donut, sat in a chair beside him and examined him. After a minute's evaluation, I recognized who he was. "I know you!" I screamed, throwing my arms up in the air. A piece of my Krispy Kreme donut flung out of my hand and struck his chin, accidentally waking him up. "You are the 'unknown massive student' that tried to fight Jake a few days ago!"

Jake walked into the room and sat down beside me. "I'm glad you're awake, Nick," he said, sarcastically smiling at him. "You have some explaining to do."

Chapter 12:
Psyriviox

Before long, everyone in the house had gathered around the dining room table. Rufus and Eli were busily tapping their fingers on the table wondering why there was a house meeting.

Jake crossed his arms and stared at Eli. "So..." Jake said. "Why did your Russian friend 'Nick' bully me at school the other day?"

"You call that bullying...?" Nick interjected.

"I'm not asking you, Nick!" Jake spat.

Eli rolled his eyes. "Okay," he sighed.

"Hopefully this will stop your sulking, Jake. My parents and Nick's parents have been close friends for many years as well as colleagues in separate medical teams.

With our families working together as well as both Nick and I having a similar interest in boxing, over time we have become good friends."

"That doesn't explain anything..." Jake muttered.

"Please let me continue... The Russian epidemic forced Nick to be evacuated to our country. While over here, it was intended that he went to the same school as me. In the middle of the holidays, we made a bet. 'The winner of the bet was allowed to make the other look like a pussy at school…' Judging by this ridiculous meeting, you can already tell that I won…" Eli contently smiled and rested back in his seat, expecting the whole conversation to be over.

"But why did you let him bully me?" Jake questioned.

"I was never going to hurt you," Nick interrupted. "Ell-yee told me who you were, and we planned the whole thing out."

The rest of us smirked at Nick's humorous pronunciation of Eli.

Rufus inquiringly raised his hand. "But Nick," he said. "Why did you cry when Eli, *ahem*, Ell-yee hit you?"

Eli playfully slapped Nick on the back. "My Russian pal has great crocodile tears." he answered.

The whole explanation was fine. However, there was still a detail that did not make sense. *Why was it so important to rescue Nick, a single teenager from a contaminated country?* Jake must have been thinking the same thing, as his next question instigated an unexpected conversation. "Eli, exactly what do your parents work on?" he asked. "Better yet, what about Nick's?"

Eli shrugged. "I don't know," he replied.

"It wouldn't have to do with a drug that ruined the world?" Jake questioned.

"What are you talking about?" Eli said.

Nick hesitantly looked away.

Jake noticed Nick's hesitation and stared at him, interrogatively. "Tell us what you know about Psyriviox," he said, sternly.

Nick sighed. "Okay…" he said. "This had to come out sometime. You guys did save me and I mean here we are now…living in the aftermath of Psyriviox destruction… It's probably best that I tell you everything straight up... I'll start from the beginning."

"First off, my full name is Nikolai Richton, and yes, I'm from Russia. The drug you guys are talking about, 'Psyriviox', when first created was known as 'Z14'. It first appeared in a small town north of Moscow and my parents being one of the most qualified medical researchers in the world, they were required to investigate it.

"At first it seemed great. Every time I conversed with my parents they would go off on a tangent saying they had 'found the miracle drug.' I recall them mentioning that it could manipulate cells and have something to do with cell regeneration. But after the first negative effect appeared, 'aggression', it was immediately barred from society.

"After a thorough investigation within the town of the drug's first appearance, there was no evidence found of how it was discovered or developed and as quickly as it appeared... it vanished... The minuscule amount that remained, but still the clear majority in general, was given to doctors to study.

"Z14 was informally accredited to be five times more addictive than methamphetamine, its users were left to go through withdrawal.

"In rehab, as usual, the addicts were violently attacking one another. It was only until they were restrained did the doctors realize that it wasn't a typical withdrawal. This was the time when the drug went into silence. From what I read: the restrained addicts, did not drink, eat or sleep."

"Wait... doesn't that mean they died?" Jake questioned.

"Well, yes… Eventually… After a week of retainment, most of the addicts had their organs exposed swaying beside their beds, blood oozing from their eyes and pussy growths extruding from every extremity. Due to the unknown manipulation in human cells, it took another two weeks for the addicts to pass away."

"Well, that's good!" Rufus cheered. "We only need to wait out another two weeks!"

"Hold on, I'm not finished…" Nick said. "A small sample of 'Z14' was transported to the esteemed Cooper Medical Research Labs in America where they were supposed to find a cure for the drug's negative effects."

Eli jumped up in shock. "What?" he screamed. "How come my parents didn't tell me they were studying Psyriviox?"

"I don't know," Nick smirked. "They are your parents."

"Let him speak," Jake shushed.

Nick cleared his throat. "The Cooper Medical Team saw the same benefits as my parents and instead of finding a cure, they set out to develop the drug to maximize its positive effects.

"It didn't take long for them to establish a new 'Z15', referred to nowadays as just simply 'Psyriviox'. Its testing on monkeys cured every known disease, virus and physical abnormality. If the same worked on humans, what they'd re-engineered was built to change the world.

"The mutual sharing of the drug enabled Russian doctors to retrieve 'Z15' from the Cooper Medical Team as soon as they requested. Which regrettably was right away…

"Completely astounded by its enhancement on monkeys, the Russian doctors desired human subjects for experimentation. Initially, three terminally ill people accepted the offer. No matter the state of their condition, it was determined that a dosage of 0.05 milliliter (better known as a metric drop) given at a seven-day interval, was, and still is the only amount that a person could take without having a withdrawal.

"At the time, it was assumed that a human 'Z15' withdrawal would be similar to that of a human 'Z14' withdrawal, and thus it was illegal to induce a withdrawal, especially without a developed cure. What was remarkable with the periodic dosage was not only did it completely heal the three terminally ill patients, but it gave them phenomenal strength and cell regeneration as well."

"Wow, that's awesome!" I yelled in amazement.

"Why a drop a week?" Jake questioned.

"Z15's intense euphoria lasted a week from a single drop," Nick replied.

"Jesus!" Eli laughed. "My parents sure can create effective drugs!"

"Yes, now back to the story. Russia was the first country in the world to test it on human subjects. The doctors were so exhilarated with the results that they wanted to expand their experimentation. As crazy as it sounds, they were speculating whether they could bring the deceased back to life.

"One remaining Z14 withdrawal subject was as close to death as one could possibly be. From the reading of my mother's description, he had no nails, no hair and almost no muscle or fat attached to his leather-like body. Blind, deaf, and thoughtless, the disfigured creature was brought to a research facility in Moscow and injected with a drop of Psyriviox Z15.

"Unfortunately, the drop had no effect. Dissatisfied with the outcome, the doctors gathered all the Psyriviox in the laboratory and illegally injected every last bit of it into the subject.

"Miraculously, the test subject's flesh instantly regenerated. Regaining his senses and strength in under thirty seconds, the doctors were able to have a fluent discussion with him."

"What was he like?" Eli questioned.

"At first, his enjoyment was remarkable. Vividly expressing all the best moments of his crazy life, the doctors could have sworn he was the happiest man alive. However, as the conversation continued, the tone slowly changed. From well-structured Russian sentences, to irritated English words, the man progressively began demanding for Psyriviox."

"'More,' he whispered. 'I need more...'

"His euphoria did not last long and with no Psyriviox to spare, they were unable to organize any further injections. With each passing minute the subject's frustration and utterance became increasingly violent. Targeting particular doctors, he began expressing torturous ways in which he was going to murder their families... In under an hour, the man that was once so happy had become the most hateful person in existence."

"Wow, that's creepy..." I mumbled.

"It gets worse. Whilst screaming in rage, the subject was confirmed dead by every medical device known to man.

After a few hours of tirelessly listening to his shrieks, the doctors decided to terminate him."

"Did they shoot him in the head?" Jake asked.

"That was the first thing they did... After that, they tried to drown, euthanize and electrocute him. As expected, all the executions failed."

"Whoa! So, he was like superhuman." Rufus grinned.

"No... he was subhuman. Even after all the executional procedures, he still looked fine. The doctors knew that the only recognizable way to kill him was through incineration. The subject was cloaked, chained to a stretcher and transported towards a furnace.

"Unfortunately, one of the doctors transporting him was one of the three terminally ill patients which had been saved through the use of Psyriviox. While transporting the subject out of the facility, massive amounts of blood guzzled out from either side of the cover. The doctors, confused about what was happening, immediately ripped off the cover and to their amazement saw the subject's chewed off hand come rapidly, scuttling towards them. With no time to react, the hand fell to the ground where it gripped a doctor's leg, instantly breaking their ankle."

"Aren't you lucky, Tyler?" Eli grinned.

"The weight of the doctor's leg compounded in on itself and the doctor staggered onto the test subject. With their faces less than an inch apart, the subject sadistically laughed in hysteria."

"Is this the part where he gets bitten?" I sighed.

"Oddly enough... no. It was when the commotion was over, while the stable Psyriviox user was fixing his glasses, did he realize that his syringe of Psyriviox was missing from his lab coat. By the time he could warn the others, it was already too late. The subject's animated hand, in an attempt to inject itself, accidentally slipped on some blood and plunged the syringe into the stable Psyriviox user's leg. The incorrect dosage corrupted the doctor into becoming the same as the subject: a violent, undying maniac. Unrestrained, he mercilessly tore apart his fellow colleagues..."

"That story..." I murmured. "It was on world news... 'The Moscow Massacre'..."

"Yes," Nick said. "However, the news got it wrong. It was not a massacre... It was worse. The Z15 user's withdrawal was far more dire than predicted. No one knows why, but there was a mutation within Z15 which created something completely hostile and infectious... the zombie contagion.

"The 'Moscow Massacre' was the start of the Russian pandemic.

"The test subject having the highest recorded dosage of Psyriviox as well as beginning the pandemic, got a name for himself that day. Alpha Z15."

"Wait up..." Eli said. "Wasn't your uncle Dr Alkaev involved in the Moscow Massacre?"

"Yes," Nick blankly replied.

"Wait... how do you know all this information?" Jake asked.

"In the hospital, the room that you guys rescued me from was a Cooper laboratory that contained almost all known evidence about Psyriviox. Being trapped in it, gave me time to look over the videos and files."

"Rufus just had to burn the entire fucking building down!" Jake said. He angrily pulled out some paper and began recording. "So... Alpha Z15 cannot be killed, has incredible strength, is in search for Psyriviox and from your description, looks like a normal human being...

"Correct," Nick agreed.

"I wonder where the one in America is hiding out..." Jake muttered.

"What makes you think Alpha Z15 is in America?" Rufus questioned.

"I'm not saying that Alpha Z15 boarded a plane over to America," Jake answered. "I'm saying that there may be others like it in America.'"

"Why would you think that?" Rufus asked.

"Nikolai said 'Americans created Psyriviox Z15'," Jake replied. "It just stands to reason that we'd be stupid enough to experiment on humans as well."

"Yeah," Nick agreed. "Stupid Americans."

Jake, Rufus and I stared at Nick disgustedly; utterly offended by his foreign remark.

Eli quickly broke the tension. "But what about the Z14 withdrawal? Didn't that have something to do with the creation of Alpha Z15?"

Completely oblivious to the intense atmosphere, Nick unconcernedly answered Eli's question. "The subject's Z14 withdrawal had nothing to do with what happened. The Psyriviox that America created, 'Z15' was the source of the alpha anomaly. It is now officially known that any deviation from a metric drop of 0.05 milliliter and or failing to be inoculated at a precise seven-day interval will cause a person, regardless of age, weight or gender, to go through withdrawal and become a crazed maniac. Its nonsensical dosage is what has made it impossible for doctors to find a cure or understand its subsequent zombie contagion."

"Do you know how the contagion is spread?" Jake asked.

"I assume through the transfer of saliva," Nick answered.

Eli scratched his head in confusion. "How could Z15 cause such a different withdrawal to Z14?" He said, baffled.

"I don't know how the Z15 contagion came to be..." Nick said. "However, there is a reason to why the withdrawal was different. For you see... when you Americans reengineered Psyriviox, you did not remove any of the negative effects. All you did was concentrate the drug. My parents' testing confirmed that Psyriviox Z15 was at minimum a thousand times more powerful than a drop of its original."

"That's ridiculous!" Rufus laughed.

"The equivalent would be to having one shot, or a thousand shots of vodka. You guys have had vodka before?"

"Yeah," I grinned. "We got drunk yesterday."

"You get a hangover," Nick asked.

"Yep, all today," I replied.

"You know this then: one shot would not give you a hangover."

"Correct!" I exclaimed.

"The original Psyriviox users all suffered and died from a single shot. Now imagine a stupid person having a thousand shots at once."

"That's putting it in perspective," I shivered.

"Alpha Z15 was already dead from one shot. Having a couple thousand times that, is why he became what he is."

"What has he become?" Jake questioned, intrigued.

"An undead creature with an awful hangover," Nick sniggered.

The amount of disappointment on Jake's face was comical. All of us burst out laughing at him.

"Hahaha!" Eli laughed, collapsing on the ground in hysterics. "Nick gets his wit from me!"

"Sorry," Nick said, extending his arm out to shake Jake's hand. "No hard feelings."

Jake angrily walked out of the room. "Nope, that is all the information I need," he muttered.

After the laughter quietened, Eli continued with another question. "So 'Little Dick'," he wiped tears off his face. "Does that mean that the terminally ill users of Psyriviox including the doctor that got stabbed in the leg with his syringe, became as powerful as Alpha Z15?"

"In a way," Nick replied. "Any person who had direct contact with the Z15 drug became a dominant carrier of the contagion and far more difficult to kill. They are referred to as just alphas. However, Alpha Z15's extremely high dosage still made him predominantly tougher and unique."

"Wait up," I questioned. "If the users took their correct weekly dosage, could they survive forever without any withdrawal?"

"It was not tested, but if I were to guess... I would say yes," Nick answered. "Within the first day of the outbreak, the drug was perceived as a direct threat to our nation, which as a result, set our military to a red alert. The remaining two terminally ill patients that were using Psyriviox were dragged out of their homes, drenched with gasoline and set alight. At the time, you Americans thought it would be funny to call Russia a 'nation of damnation.' I bet it's not so funny now..."

I didn't know if Nick was deliberately trying to offend us, but Rufus unintentionally fed him some of his own medicine. "I still call your nation that!" He laughed. "But tell me now... Is your uncle still alive? Dead? Or in-between?"

Nick plucked out a biscuit from a leftover Oreo packet that was sitting on the table and ate it. "No, my mother killed him," he replied calmly.

All of us paused for a moment. "So, you are telling me that your mother had to kill her brother...?" I questioned.

Nick shoved another biscuit into his mouth. "Yes, my mother sacrificed herself in an attempt to save her fellow doctors from her very own brother."

All of us went silent. The only thing we could hear was Nick's loud chewing. We were surprised at how emotionless he was about all of it.

"It was a Molotov," Nick continued speaking. "Hey, is there anything better to eat?"

Jake must have overheard the conversation as he instantly came rushing out with a sponge cake. Nick grabbed a slice of sponge cake and ate it. "Wow!" he exclaimed. "This is good."

Jake winked at me. "Come on, guys," he jostled. "Enough chit-chat, we need to finish installing the solar panels."

"You mean 'Eli and I install the solar panels while you laze about'?" I laughed.

"Correct!" Jake replied.

Chapter 13:
No Shame

Solar panels were good at creating electricity but not good at storing it. The main reason why we required electricity was to power the lights and refrigerator at night. Without a solar battery, the electricity could only be used throughout the day, which evidently was not useful. It was the following morning and Jake had forced Nick and Rufus to accompany him in finding a solar battery. With the three of them out working, Eli and I decided to finish cabling the solar panels.

The day was a particularly hot one and working on the roof made it all the hotter. After two hours of sweltering labour, we had finished cabling the solar panels so that all were functional. With the roof perfectly fitted, we slapped each other a victorious high-five and proceeded down the ladder.

I had just walked through the front door when Eli came rushing past me. "Shotgun first shower!" he shouted.

Before I could even reply, his bare bum disappeared into the bathroom. The door locked behind him and a low rattle murmured through the walls as the shower turned on. In the thick humidity, I slumped on the ground and waited for him to finish.

Ten long minutes passed by and Eli was still singing loudly in the shower. "How long are you going to be in there for...?" I moaned.

Eli stopped singing. "Close to an hour," he replied.

"No..." I whined. "That will be enough time for the others to get home and take my spot after you..."

"Tyler," he replied. "There are plenty of other showers in your neighborhood."

What the hell? I thought to myself. *How could I forget that we were now free to do anything?*

Straightaway, I grabbed a towel and rushed to the next-door neighbor's house. My enthusiasm to have a shower was far more important than the headaches I was feeling while running.

Entering the neighbor's pristine bathroom, I dove through the shower curtains. What I saw next was as humorous as it was shocking. I stumbled backwards in disbelief. "What in the hell?" I screamed.

Beside me in the shower stood a completely naked, female zombie. With its long gross hair waving around like a model, I tossed the shower curtain over its head and pushed it through the glass.

The glass shattered over the floor, slicing through the zombie like razor blades. I was about to bash the zombie with a shower head when I noticed yet another figure standing at the bathroom door. It was the most disgusting, dangerous and downright dirty creature on earth... It was a butt-naked Rufus.

I scoped him up and down. "Oh... my... god..." I muttered.

Rufus, completely oblivious to me staring at him, smashed the zombie's head with a blow dryer. Bending over to ensure that it was dead, he gave me a memory that I will never forget.

"Ahem... Rufus," I murmured.

"Don't worry," Rufus answered, stepping into the shower next to me. "We finished installing the solar battery, so I'm good for a shower now."

I stood speechless. He was facing me with a clear view of his penis. I had to be careful, in case I bumped into it.

Just as I was about to step out, Rufus revolved around and slapped his dick against my leg. "What temperature do you want it at?" he asked.

In a complete panic, I dove out of the shower. I was cut by a few shards of glass, but it was a lot better than staying in the shower. As I stood up, blood dripping from my elbows, I noticed yet another creature in the bathroom. It was Nick. He was sitting on the toilet.

In utter disgust, I covered my eyes. "Are you all gay?!" I screamed.

Nick farted and a splash sounded from the toilet bowl. "We are men with penises," he laughed.

I didn't understand how all of us being males made the situation any better. "Is that supposed to make me feel better?!" I shrieked. "The only two dicks I haven't seen today are Eli's and Jake's!"

"Ha-ha!" Rufus sniggered. "You just called 'them' dicks..."

I could not believe that after all this time, I had still not been able to have a shower. I raised a middle finger at both of them. "Fuck you, Rufus!" I shouted. "And fuck you, Nick!"

I exited the bathroom a lot worse than when I'd arrived, both physically and mentally scarred. As I walked back to my house, I noticed that Jake was sitting on the couch with a towel wrapped around his waist. It was good to see that he at least had some decency.

"Thank Christ…" I muttered. "At least you aren't naked."

Unfortunately, he assumed that I was mocking his weight. "What, just because I'm fat, I can't be naked?!" he shouted.

"Huh…?"

He bitterly examined my body up and down. "You are standing fully naked in front of me and you still think that it's fun to make fat jokes?!" he shouted.

Oh shit… I thought to myself. I had completely forgotten that I was naked.

"Well, guess what?" Jake sneered. "You have a small cock."

My penis wasn't big, but it certainly wasn't small. Infuriated with his hurtful comment, I acted the same as any other displeased person would do. I gripped his towel and tore it out from underneath him.

To what I saw next, was one of the funniest things I'd ever seen. Tucked under his huge belly, were two gigantic testicles, and squished between them was a near-impossible-to-see penis. I pointed at it and began laughing.

Eli walked into the room and shook his head. "I always knew you were gay. Tyler…" he muttered.

I immediately stopped laughing. *Out of the whole situation, how did I end up the gay one?* I thought to myself.

Without thinking, I bluntly replied. "Go get your girly, little nose fixed…"

As soon as I said it, I regretted it. My remark was very personal and uncalled for. Eli grew as red as a tomato and stared at me, gritting his teeth.

Jake pulled his towel back over himself and smiled at me. "You better start running," he chuckled.

Eli was faster than me, but fortunately I knew a place where I could lose him. It was not far. I just had to make it there without him catching me. I booked it out the door and over to the neighbors. Eli trailed one step behind, his towel falling off along the way.

I halted in the bathroom. Luckily, both Nick and Rufus hadn't moved. The room smelt like feces and for once, Rufus was cleaner than his surroundings.

Eli did not notice the others. He barged me against the sink and lifted me into the air.

Nick flushed the toilet. "Ell-yee," he laughed. "Are you and Tyler having a shower with Rufus?"

Eli turned to Nick and seized up in shock. The situation immediately got worse for Eli when Rufus stepped out of the shower. "Ooooh!" he moaned, stretching his back. "That hit the spot."

Eli let go of me and stumbled back in fear.

"Well, now that all four of us are here," Nick said. "We have some business to attend to."

Eli was more than ready to leave. However, the poor choice of words by both Nick and Rufus caused him to sprint out of the room quicker than when he'd arrived.

My escape plan had worked. I rubbed my throat and slapped Rufus on the back.

"What was that about?" Rufus questioned.

I covered my eyes and walked out of the bathroom. "Eli is more homophobic than me!" I laughed.

After an hour-long cold shower, I put some board shorts on and sat down for a late lunch. Now that the microwave and fridge were running, we were able to cook up numerous amounts of fantastic food. Lasagna being everyone's favorite, it was the agreed meal.

Eli still couldn't fathom the amount of "homosexuality" he had witnessed and it was taking him a while to adjust back to normal.

"So umm nice food…" Eli smiled.

Nick finished his meal off with no leftovers. "Great food!" he said, rubbing his tummy. "Hospital food is sickly! That lasagna was the first satisfying meal I have had in a week."

Jake stopped eating and placed his knife and fork on his plate. "That reminds me," he said to Nick. "How did you get trapped in the hospital?"

Nick rested back in his seat and stretched his back. "After our little play at school, I caught a taxi to the Southport Hospital," he replied.

"But it was your first day of school…" Jake mumbled. "You weren't hurt… so why would you leave…?"

Nick smirked at Jake. "I would prefer to learn from qualified doctors than America's B-grade education system," he answered.

"Okay…" Jake said, ignoring Nick's rude remark. "And…?"

"And what…?" Nick answered. "You want to know how patients got infected by the dozen? Or how the doctors had to slaughter thousands of undead just to survive? Or how…"

"Wait…" Jake interjected. "There were no doctors in the hospital when we entered."

"Correct," Nick replied. "No living doctors…"

"What happened?"

"Jake, I've heard you are smart. What happens to rotting flesh?"

"There are many things," Jake answered. "Maggot infestation, leakage from orifices, discoloration, bacterial colonization, gaseous release…"

"What type of gas?" Nick interrupted.

"Methane, of course."

"Precisely," Nick replied.

"What does that have to do with anything?"

"I will explain. After the Russian pandemic, some doctors understood how to deal with an outbreak. At Southport, the first thing they did was lock down the hospital. After that, they rounded up the remaining survivors and wiped out the zombies inside the hospital. From there, they began working in the Cooper laboratory in search for a Psyriviox vaccine."

"Good on them!" I grinned.

"There was only one problem… The methane buildup made it extremely difficult to survive. The oxygen tanks allowed us all to breathe. However, it didn't stop the fact that if a spark were to happen, the entire building would blow up."

"Why is that?" Rufus questioned.

"Because methane is flammable, you idiot," Jake muttered.

"Anyhow. On the third day, to prevent a potential explosion, the doctors switched off power to the hospital and disposed of the bodies."

"Where did the rotters get placed?" Eli questioned.

"The doctors were intent on getting them as far away as possible. Right beside the hospital, the creek was their designated spot to drift away."

"Ohhh!" I burst out. "That's why there was so much flesh floating down the river the other day!"

"Oh, yeah!" Rufus laughed. "That was a gross time!"

"Not as bad as today..." Eli said, rubbing his eyes, as if he was picturing us naked all over again.

"Let him continue," Jake shushed.

"I was considered 'too young' to be included. The doctors made me gather supplies while they disposed of the dead. They had only been gone for a few minutes when I sensed something was wrong. My sense became fact when they returned as zombies... They chased me to the top floor where I locked myself in a laboratory. I was stuck in there until Ell-yee rescued me."

Eli slapped Nick on the back. "I would do it all again," he said.

Rufus who looked to be completely bored by Nick's recount sat up and tossed a towel over his shoulder.

"Wait, haven't you already had a shower?" Jake asked.

Rufus picked up a pistol. "It's still a stinking hot day," he enthusiastically replied. "I think it's time we went to the beach!"

Before the Psyriviox outbreak, we'd often visit the beach. Rufus was a remarkably good surfer. Jake and I always had fun bodysurfing beside Rufus, and even though Eli was an incompetent swimmer, he always found pleasure in splashing in the shallows or knocking over little kids' sand castles. The beach was always enjoyable.

Nick had no idea what a beach was and it required a dragged out, descriptive explanation for him to understand. "Okay. So do you know what a beach is now...?" Jake questioned.

"Yes!" Nick valiantly smiled.

Rufus fitted on an old pair of my board shorts. "Let's surf!" he said cheerfully.

Chapter 14:
Coastline

Before heading to the beach, I always monitored a Coastal Watch website to determine the safety of the oceanic conditions and from that, which beach we would visit. Since the internet was no longer working, we did not have the luxury. Instead, we had a brief discussion. The safest beach, "Crystal Cove" was the final choice.

Crystal Cove was a secluded coastline enclosed by rocky cliffs, caves and lush, beautiful landscape. The fine white sand, combined with perfect barreling waves made it a beach which could not be overlooked. On a day like today, it was a wonder why we hadn't left earlier.

As the weather conditions were terrific, we decided to drive our separate vehicles. Since Nick did not yet own one, he was to ride with Eli in the Lamborghini.

On the way to Crystal Cove, we had to make two stops. One at Sam's Surf Shack Essentials and another at a gas station. By the time we were walking down to the dunes, we were shirtless, wearing sunglasses and board shorts, carrying surfboards, umbrellas, towels, guns and a carton of Coke. If Jake weren't so overweight and if the rest of us were tanned, we could have been classified as beach models.

I jumped up and peered over a bush to get a brief glimpse of the ocean. As expected, it looked flawless.

Following the trail down to the beach we dropped our items on the sand and gazed at the marvelous crystal-clear waves. They broke in unison creating an array of thick, white crumbling foam. Nick gazed at the waves as if he had just seen an angel.

"Are you okay?" I asked him.

Nick stared into the distance. "I have just... I have never seen waves up close before," he replied.

"Just wait until you get out there!" Eli chuckled. "It is a lot bigger than what it seems..."

Rufus picked up a surfboard and sprinted out into the ocean.

I squirted some sunscreen into my hands and generously applied it to my face. "Nothing worse than getting burnt!" I shouted.

"Too true," Jake agreed, picking up the bottle of sunscreen. "Tyler, you do my back and I will do yours."

Normally, rubbing sunscreen into another male's back was embarrassing. As we were the only people on the beach, though, I had no problem with it.

"Yeah!" I replied. "Eli and Nick can do each other."

Nick rushed over to Eli with an overflowing amount of sunscreen cupped in his hands. Eli signaled him to stop. "No, thanks," he laughed. "I can do it myself."

After Jake and I had finished lathering each other up, we slapped each other a greasy high five and jogged to the ocean shore. By the time we had reached the water's edge,

Rufus was already out past the second break waiting for a decent set of waves.

A small wave rolled over our feet. The water was icy cold. On a day like today, it was desired. I smiled at Jake. "Let's do this!" I roared.

Both of us dove into the shallows. To avoid plowing into the sand we dove outwards, belly flopping into the water.

We resurfaced and began paddling out. It wasn't long before we reached the first break. Although the waves were small, they were quite powerful. We paddled through them and eventually reached the second break. Unlike the first break, these waves were quite large. We watched in awe as Rufus paddled onto his first wave.

It was magnificent. He skimmed down the front of the wave gaining momentum. The wave grew larger and larger, forming a thick foamy cap at its lipping peak. As he neared the flat depression of water below, he leapt to a stand, swiftly cut back up the side of the wave and surfed across it horizontally. The wave proceeded to break over the top of him, enclosing him in a barrel and blocking him from our view. As the wave ended, he shot out the end of the barrel and somersaulted into the water.

Jake and I clapped. "Woo-hoo!" We cheered.

Rufus hopped on his board and rapidly paddled back out. It took us a while to realize why he was in such a hurry. A monster set was approaching...

The deep blue, breaking crests could be seen in the horizon. Luckily, Jake and I weren't far enough out for them to be dangerous. We watched as Rufus narrowly made it over the top of them.

The huge waves created five-foot-high white-water, which we had to repeatedly duck under.

We continued to swim further out to sea until we were beside Rufus. As we trod water, I was quite surprised by how little energy I had lost. Surviving in a zombie apocalypse had clearly improved my fitness.

We waited for a wave that we could all catch. It wasn't long before one large enough came through.

All of us aggressively paddled onto it. Multiple people on a single wave were considered in our beach slang a "party wave." This wave in particular was a perfect party wave.

I stopped paddling as the forceful grip of the breaking surge pushed me down the front of the wave. I skidded downwards, glancing from side to side to see Jake and Rufus on either side of me, giving me a thumb's up. It was a joyous moment.

Rufus curved off to the side while Jake and I embraced our relentless fate. The wave curled up behind us and crashed down, heaving us around like a washing machine.

As it turned out, getting smashed by waves was not unusual for us. Jake and I were notorious for getting wiped out by heavy waves. While under water we would always count the seconds to relax.

Ten seconds was the longest time we had ever been held under and that was in freakish-sized surf. "One... Two... Three... Four... Five... Six..."

My head broke through the surface and I took a deep breath. I looked around to see Jake treading water beside me.

"You get six?" I asked.

He shook his head. "Five..." he replied.

"I came up a little before you."

"Ha-ha," I laughed. "I would expect a dugong to remain underwater!"

Jake smiled and splashed me. "I wonder where Eli and Nick are..."

I gazed back into shore. Neither of them could be seen on the beach.

"Oh wait." Jake pointed towards the shore. "There's Eli splashing around in the shallows."

"Yep, that'd be Eli," I sniggered. "But where is Nick?"

A long board abruptly surfaced over the first break. The dorkiness of the individual paddling on the board was amusing. Nick was untimely moving his arms around like a ragdoll while his legs were completely spread out on either side of the board trying to balance himself.

"Do you think it's safe for Nick to come out this far in the ocean?" I asked Jake. Rufus came scooting past us on another wave.

"Who knows?" Jake laughed. "He is caught in a riptide anyway..."

I examined the water that Nick was paddling in to see that it was surging out towards us. "No wonder his terrible paddling technique is actually working..." I muttered.

Rufus curled off the wave and ecstatically paddled over to us. "Guys," he staggered. "The waves are the biggest things I've ever seen!"

"They aren't that big..." I replied.

"Would you count twelve-foot-high being big?"

It sounded too big to be true. However, his face was stern with confidence. "No... they can't be..." I stammered, worriedly.

Jake turned and tried to head back to shore. He paddled for a couple of seconds before realizing that he was moving further out to sea. "What!" he shouted, staring at the murky water around us. "We are in a riptide as well!"

I looked at the shoreline to see that we were rapidly drifting outwards. "Oh god..." I muttered. "It's going to be difficult to get back to shore..."

Nick floated over the first set of waves and rested beside us. "Wow those first couple of waves were scary!" he shouted, excitedly.

The first set of waves were roughly three-foot high. I smiled grimly, knowing that he was about to face much larger waves.

Rufus sat upright on his board. "Guys, this is one mean riptide and there is no way we are paddling out of it without dying from exhaustion first. Our only option is to follow it further out to sea. Riptides go in circles and therefore if we keep calm and float in it for long enough, we will eventually return to shore."

As Rufus wasn't the most intelligent being, I wondered if what he was telling us was the actual truth. I turned my head to Jake who validated it with a nod.

I gazed back into shore to see that Eli was no longer splashing in the shallows. "Where is Eli?" I asked. "Last time I saw him he was just..."

"I'm beside you!" Eli squealed. He was hidden behind Nick, attached to the longboard like a stray dog.

"Thank god!" Rufus cheered. "That's a relief. Now we can all face it together!"

"Face what?" Eli anxiously replied.

"Have you ever dreamt about huge waves?" I asked.

"Ahem, they are called nightmares..." Eli answered.

"Well... I think we are all about to experience it..."

Eli's face filled with terror. I thought his terrified expression was because of what I'd said. However, he was staring at a large approaching wave behind me.

Rufus jumped on Nick's longboard and pushed the nose of it under water. "Dive!" he shouted.

All of us ducked under the wave. Even whilst swimming underwater, I could feel the riptide pulling us further out to sea.

When I resurfaced, I quickly looked around to see that everyone had made it under the wave. It may have not been the largest wave, but like a parent caring for a toddler in a swimming pool, I felt the need to confirm Nick and Eli's wellbeing. To my relief they were floating beside me, stuck to the longboard like glue.

"Okay, keep doing the same dive under each wave and we should be good," I said, comfortingly. "Just remember not to panic."

"Under!" Rufus screamed.

We continued the routine until we were past the final breaks. Out in the open water, all was calm. We floated beside each other in the riptide, powerless to its surge.

"Those waves weren't twelve-foot..." I laughed.

The waves may not have been as large as what Rufus had told us, but for Eli and Nick they were gigantic. They huddled silently together on Nick's longboard, too scared to move.

Five minutes passed by and we were no longer at Crystal Cove. The view of the sandy, white beach was replaced with an enormous dark cliff side. Waves pummeled against the rocks, smashing large pieces of driftwood into splinters. The riptide was dragging us across to the next beach.

"What now?" Jake asked.

"One thing's for sure," Rufus replied. "Don't go near the cliff." Eli and Nick immediately stopped their profuse paddling. "We will have to circulate onto the next beach. It's just around the other side of the cliff face," Rufus assured.

Next to Crystal Cove was Falrip Beach. Due to its openness to strong winds and large swell, it was a location which we always avoided. However, with the position that we were in, it was our only option.

I looked ahead to see a hurricane of flying foam. As predicted, Falrip's breaking waves were much larger and messier than Crystal Cove's. The waves formed chaotically and clashed together, creating thunderous booms. The raging, murky waves looked like they would drown even the most experienced swimmer and the riptide was taking us right towards them.

I pointed at the crashing waves. "Okay, guys," I said. "As you can see, we are heading directly into this... no matter what..."

In a panic, Eli jumped off his board and tried to paddle away. I quickly swam in front of him and calmly directed him back to the board.

"Don't worry, Eli," I reassured. "We can get out of this riptide and back to shore. We just need to catch one of the waves in. Please... whatever you do... don't panic..."

Eli rested still on the board, too terrified to reply.

After two minutes of floating in the riptide, the cliff face was behind us and we were fixed in the strong humid breeze of Falrip Beach. The waves were crashing less than fifty feet in front of us. It was time to get prepared...

Rufus paddled over to Eli and Nick and set them up so that they could catch a wave together on the longboard.

He placed them so that they were laying down in front of each other with Eli's chin resting on Nick's ass. "You two look hilarious," Rufus chuckled. "Just remember to slide real far back when you are about to catch a wave. Otherwise, you will nosedive."

Eli looked at Rufus with sad, puppy dog eyes. "Could you just give us your board so that Nick and I have one each...?" he pleaded.

"Get bent!" Rufus laughed, paddling further out to sea towards the third break. "These monster waves out the back are a rarity and I'm not missing out."

It was lucky that we weren't further out to sea, as the third set of breakers that Rufus was heading towards were monstrous.

Jake and I steered Eli and Nick into the violent white-water. We gripped each other tightly as the chaotic swell thrashed us around like ragdolls. The swell thankfully settled for a bit and together we waited for a small cresting wave to catch.

As we waited, I noticed that the sweep had stopped. It was good to know that we were no longer caught in the riptide. Rufus was correct in telling us not to fight against it.

Staring out into the approaching swell, the receding sun forced Jake and I to use our hands as hats. Nick and Eli positioned themselves facing towards the shore, readying themselves for a wave.

We had only been waiting for a few seconds when Rufus started paddling further out to sea.

With Eli facing towards the shore, he had no idea what was happening behind him. "What's going on!" He screamed, almost slipping off the board as a small torrent of white-water collided into his side.

"The set is coming!" Rufus shouted back to us.

"What does he mean by set...?" Eli moaned.

Rufus disappeared over a huge mountain of water. At our current location I could assess that it wouldn't break before reaching us.

"There is a big one coming," I said, through gritted teeth. "But don't worry, we are safe here."

The wave approaching us was becoming thicker and taller with each passing second. The surge of the wave pushed us ten feet high as we floated over the top of it. Moments later the wave crashed with the sound of thunder, back-spraying thousands of droplets of water over our exposed faces.

Jake wiped his eyes. "See? That wasn't so bad," he said.

For some reason, Eli felt as though it was a good time to act tough. "Yeah, I'm not even scared of this stuff..." he said.

I was about to tease him when something caught my attention. A set of gigantic waves were racing towards us. Their dark blue peaks blocked out the setting sun. They were a distance away. However, the speed at which they were moving was that of a tsunami. They were by far the largest waves I'd ever seen... From my guess at least twenty feet high. My heart began to race as I saw one of them start to peak. Jake saw it too and shook his head in dismay.

"I'm glad these waves don't scare you, Eli," I said. "Otherwise, you wouldn't like what I'm seeing."

Eli turned his head and glimpsed at the approaching set of waves. Instead of trying to act tough, he started to quietly whimper. Nick noticed Eli's whimpering and shuffled to the back of the board.

"Yeah, good work!" I encouraged. "Catch it just like that."

Nick gripped the sides of the board. "Ell-yee whimpering is making me uncomfortable," he muttered.

I rushed up and jokingly twisted Nick's head towards the massive crashing wave.

Nick's face became as pale as a ghost. "What is that...?" he staggered.

I gazed at the wave to see Rufus surfing down the side of it. Rufus hadn't even made it halfway down when his board flew out from underneath him. I watched in horror as his helpless body got sucked up to the top of the wave and pulverized back down. It was a scary wipe out.

I turned back to Nick. "On the bright side... I think we are better off than Rufus..." I laughed nervously.

Nick started to sob. The approaching white-water from the wave which Rufus had wiped out on was at least fifteen feet high. I knew that it was going to be near impossible to body surf, but I had no other choice. Ducking under it wasn't an option as it would take too long to resurface. The roaring water grew deafeningly loud, foreboding us of its immense power. As it closed in on us, I closed my eyes and tensed my entire body, readying myself for the impact. "Let's do this!" I screamed.

The white-water smashed into my back with such force that it almost knocked me out. I shook my head to regain my senses all the while being violently tossed about, completely powerless to its wrath. All my muscles winced under the turbulence of water, draining me of energy.

Side flip, back flip, front flip, I could not tell which direction was up. I closed my eyes, relaxed my muscles and counted each passing second.

I tumbled around. "...Thirteen... Fourteen... Fifteen... Sixteen... Seventeen... Eighteen... Nineteen..." Asphyxiation was amassing inside my chest and I started to panic.

"Twenty, twenty-one, twenty-two." *That's it!* I told myself. I opened my eyes and frantically waved my arms in an attempt to resurface.

Swallowing water, my heart was racing at a million times a minute. It was only until I noticed Rufus standing casually beside me with his thumbs up, did I realize that I was no longer in the wave. I shot my legs into the sand and leapt out of the water, coughing profusely.

As I looked around, I could see that I was the last one to resurface. Nick and Eli were cheering at the top of their lungs. I had never seen them so happy. They were high fiving one another and shrieking about how epic the wave was. It seemed as though they'd actually caught it...

Jake was lying on his back in the water like a starfish. He looked to be as exhausted as me.

I kept coughing and rinsing my nose. Rufus walked over to me and patted me on the back. "That was crazy!" he shouted.

"How long...?" I spluttered. "How long were you under?"

"Erm." Rufus pondered. "Just over two minutes."

"Damn, that's a long time," I coughed.

"Yeah, it is, isn't it?" He laughed.

I smiled and lethargically hobbled out of the ocean onto the soft, dry sand. It was late in the afternoon and I wanted to get back home before nightfall.

"Let's go guys..." I said.

The walk back to Crystal Cove was enjoyable. Eli and Nick were non-stop chatting about the wave. Whether it be busting out the front of it like a bullet or riding the wave standing up, both of them detailed it very differently. The only similarity between the stories was that it was the most exhilarating thing they'd ever experienced.

It was great to see friends overcome their worst fears. Even if they were denying the fact that they cried. I was pleased to see everyone happy. The experience had left our minds full of vigor and we felt unstoppable.

After a twenty-minute walk, we reached our vehicles. I hopped in my Chrysler and comfortably sat in the leather seat. We revved our engines and sped out of the car park.

The sun had gone down by the time we'd got home. As we parked out the front with our car lights on, we could clearly see that we had forgotten to close the front door. Shadows could be seen moving inside. The trespassing victims brought a smile to my face. *Time to kill again!* I told myself.

Chapter 15: Cleansing

I stared at the flickering shadows and reached over the passenger seat for my gun. I felt around for it before realizing that we had left our belongings at Crystal Cove. It may have hindered us in our killing efficiency, but it was never going to stop what we did best.

All of us hopped out of our vehicles with the same deducing expression. "How do we go about this?" Jake questioned.

"It should be simple," I replied. "We leave the car lights on, pick up any stray items like 'sticks or rocks' for weapons, and get Rufus to lure them out."

"Wait! Why do I have to lure them out?" Rufus shouted.

"Because you are the quickest..."

"Oh, fair enough," Rufus replied, forgivingly.

All of us scrounged around the yard for potential weapons. After a five-minute search, we came to the conclusion that rocks were the only option.

"A stoning." Nick chuckled to himself.

"Let's just hope one of us is a good shot," Jake smirked.

Standing side by side in a linear formation with rocks piled at our feet, Rufus ran to the front door and began making monkey noises. It took longer than expected, but eventually the first zombie came stumbling out. Rufus jogged towards us while the rest of us attempted to kill the zombie behind him.

Crack! Smack! Thud! If our goal was to try and miss the zombie, we couldn't have been more perfect. Nick and Eli were damaging the house more than the zombie. Me on the other hand, I could barely lift the oversized stones, let alone throw them... However, I still wasn't as bad as Jake. He was girlishly underarming rocks as small as pennies. As I watched the zombie come charging towards us like it was making a homerun, it made me remember why none of us ever played baseball...

We hurled and tossed stones as quickly and as hard as we could. Eventually it came down to Eli riskily bashing its head in with a rock. As it collapsed, I could hear Rufus laughing his head off.

"Ahahahaha..." he cried. "We now have established something that we are all bad at!"

All of us shrugged. It was true, a five-year-old would have a better arm than all of us combined. Jake eagerly ran inside. "Let's go get some dinner," he said.

He walked through the dark door and squealed like an oversized mouse. "Eeeeeeeeeee!"

I ran inside and switched on the lights. The next thing I saw was Jake getting chased around the living room by two zombies. They were extremely slow, but Jake himself was still not much faster.

Eli and Nick charged past me and synchronously kicked a couch into the zombies, toppling them.

I dashed past them, picked up a loaded assault rifle and wildly fired at the zombies. The sound inside was intense, like someone had just let off a hundred fireworks. Everyone covered their ears and watched as I lost control of my weapon. The kickback on the gun was so powerful that I ended up firing at the ceiling.

"Let go of the trigger!" Jake screamed.

I dropped the gun and stood on it. The firing stopped but the barrel was still smoking.

I looked around at the mess of the house. The lounge and walls were shredded, food was scattered everywhere and there was a dirty great hole in the roof. The zombies lay bloody and lifeless on the ground.

"Check your bodies," Jake said.

All of us drastically searched ourselves to ensure that we hadn't gotten wounded by any stray bullets.

Luckily, we were all okay.

Jake stared at the ceiling and shook his head. "Guys," he said. "We have got to make this place more secure, even if it requires some effort. Look at what we have done over a few stupid trespassing zombies..."

I loved my house and I didn't like seeing it in ruins. "I agree with Jake," I said, approvingly. "We will start by putting up a barrier outside. We have a variety of options. Just grab some excavators and we will see what we can accomplish."

Eli turned the lounge back over and sat down. "Yeah, I'm keen," he replied. "Just let me go to my house in the morning. If we are going to use your place as our haven, I think it's best that we grab a few home essentials of our own."

If Eli went back home, I thought to myself. *He would discover the brutal truth about his parents and Bruce. I could not allow it. I had to stop it. I had to clear his parents' bodies before morning.* "Yeah, sounds good!" I awkwardly replied.

"Why are we staying here?" Nick questioned. "We could just find a safer place in general."

"Ha-ha Nick," Rufus retorted. "Any place can be as safe as you want it to be."

"Yeah, and why would we want to leave our newly set up electrical system?" Eli argued.

Nick sneered at Eli and dragged a zombie corpse out the front door.

"Dinner, Xbox and bed," I ordered. "We will get started in the morning. Rufus, can you clean up this mess a bit while Eli, Jake and I make dinner?"

Even though it was a poor deal, Rufus was hungry and responded with a salute.

After thirty minutes, apart from the shredded walls and roof, the house was relatively clean. We were sitting down in the living room eating dinner and watching a zombie movie on a large, flat-screen television.

Eli stretched to his feet. "Why are we watching *Dawn of the Dead* when we can just go outside and live it?" he asked.

Rufus fumbled around on the bean bag in front. "Because Nick hasn't seen it!" he excitedly replied.

With a mouthful of food, I spluttered. "We would never live like these people, anyway! I mean who sees a zombie as a predator? We sit at the top of the food chain around here!"

Jake reached over and high-fived me. "Damn right!" he shouted.

Eli looked at me and raised an eyebrow. "Fair enough," he said. "But just so you know... they are the ones that eat us..."

"Just shut up and watch the movie," Nick requested. "It's humorous watching these pathetic actors die."

Eli stood up. "I'm going to go play Xbox. If any of you want to join me, you can..." he said.

My eyes were fixated on the screen. "Yeah, no worries," I replied.

In the end, none of us joined Eli on the Xbox. Even though we had seen *Dawn of the Dead* plenty of times, it was fun to compare our survivability. None of us had died yet, so therefore we were superior.

Eli was still mashing the Xbox controller buttons when we decided it was time for bed.

I walked into his room and tossed a pillow beside him. "We are waking up early, so get a good night's rest," I said.

Eli switched off the Xbox and rested his head against the pillow. "No worries," he yawned. "I wasn't getting anywhere in that game, anyway."

I switched off his room light. "I am sleeping in the living room," I said. "Please don't constantly wake me up by going to the toilet."

"I should be fine," Eli laughed. "Just shut the door behind you."

I walked out of the room and kicked the door closed behind me. Lying on the couch, I still knew what I had to do. I had purposely set myself up in the living room so that I had easy access to sneak out of the house and dispose of Eli's loved ones before sunrise.

Even though I saw myself as a predator amongst zombies, there was no way I was ever going to risk my life for a late-night sanitary task. Before we had even made dinner, I had gathered my armor, a flashlight and a weapon and hidden it under the veranda out the front. As it was a stealth mission, my weapon of choice was a solid wooden baseball bat.

I waited until everyone was sound asleep. Snoring was my way of knowing for sure.

After hearing the bellows of Eli's and Jake's annoying snores, I tiptoed outside and equipped my armor. I then slowly closed the front door, crept down the driveway and hopped in my Chrysler. I turned the ignition on and softly pressed my foot against the pedal. The Chrysler rolled down the street with a low purr no louder than the snoring inside. I then flicked the lights to low and steadily drove to Eli's house.

On the trip, stray zombies could be seen aimlessly wandering in the streets. It was funny to watch them stumble after the vehicle. I would tease them by changing my speed. I would wait for them to reach full sprint and then slam on the brakes. Every time at least one zombie would crash hard into the rear of the vehicle, fracturing its limbs.

My little game prolonged my trip to Eli's house. However, as it was four o'clock in the morning, I still had at least two hours to clean up and return before dawn.

The last time Rufus drove down Eli's street, it was riddled with zombies everywhere. I found it odd but helpful that this time, apart from several zombie carcasses, the road was completely bare. Since there were no zombies around,

I casually parked the vehicle out the front of Eli's house and walked inside.

As I stepped through the front door, a subtle chill ran up my spine. It was eerie to think that I was about to clean up Eli's parents' corpses without him even knowing. I walked into the kitchen and grabbed a towel. The nail-ridden and blood-streaked walls were the first to get cleaned. I scrubbed them multiple times to ensure that the level of cleanliness fitted with the rest of the house.

Walking upstairs I went through each room and ensured that there were no signs of death or struggle. This included no blood, no flesh and, of course, no untidiness. Eli would instantly discern the happenings within his house if he merely managed to find a single piece of clothing on the floor.

After an hour, I had almost finished cleaning the inside of the house. The last remaining place was Eli's room. As I was cleaning around, I remembered where Mr Cooper was hiding before he shoved me through the window. I opened up the cupboard to find a maggot-infested, partially rotted jaw. Mr Cooper had a chin on him like a superhero. I distastefully tossed it into a plastic bag and scrubbed the floor where it had been sitting.

Wiping sweat off my forehead, I got up and walked downstairs. Knowing the entire inside was spotless, I strolled out into the backyard and began cleaning. The fur and skeleton of Bruce was still sad to see when I heaved it into a plastic bag. I knew it would have been better to bury him, but my time frame was too tight to take any chances.

I knotted the bag and tossed it over the next-door neighbor's fence. Fortunately, it landed in an overgrown hedge where it could not be seen. I was about to try and drag Mr Cooper's splattered body into the rear seat of my Chrysler when I heard a creepy noise. The sound itself was not scary. I had been hearing ghastly sounds all night. It was the direction in which it came from.

The sound appeared to have come from within the top floor of the Cooper mansion. The main thing that bothered me was that it was a single clatter. If it were a zombie, its uproar would be a lot easier to distinguish. *Maybe it was just a book falling off the shelf,* I told myself. *Maybe it was just an animal...*

I shone my flashlight towards the window of where I thought it'd sounded. I kept my flashlight still for a bit before shining it to the other windows. I dragged the light from one end of the house to the other before switching it off. If someone was up there, they would have known I was looking for them. With my torch switched off, they would have no idea where I was.

In complete blackness, a cool breeze brushed over my skin, making my hairs stand on end. I started to shiver. Not because I was cold, but because I was scared... It was weird to think that a few hours before this I gave a heroic "top of the food chain" speech. *How could an odd noise frighten me like this?* Eventually, I forced myself. *Oh, what the hell. One last look.* I shot my flashlight at the same window that I did before to see a pair of eyes staring back at me. "Oh fuck!" I screamed, stumbling backwards in terror.

I readied my baseball bat over my shoulder. "If you don't tell me who you are," I screamed. "I am going to fucking rip your intestines out through your mouth!"

Suddenly the backdoor swung open and a person strolled out. I shone my flashlight on their face. It was Nick. He raised his hand in front of his eyes to block the light. "I'm sorry!" he laughed. "I didn't mean to scare you..."

"What the hell!" I shrieked. "How many of you followed me?"

Nick abruptly stopped, a puzzled look on his face. "Huh?" he questioned. "You and I are the only ones here..."

I raised my flashlight back at the window. "Then who the fuck is that!" I questioned.

The light shone into a blank room. Nick stared at the window, wondering what I was going on about.

"No one is there...?" he replied.

I blinked a few times. There was no way I imagined it. Eventually I came to terms with what was happening. "Ha-ha! Good one, Nick!" I laughed. "You are as witty as Eli."

Nick looked at me, confused.

"You had me there for a bit!" I said. "I don't care if you brought Rufus or Jake with you. I just don't want Eli here while I'm doing this..."

Nick ran inside and shortly after poked his head out of the second story window which my flashlight was fixed on.

"As I said..." he answered. "You and I are the only ones here..."

I knew he was lying. "As you love jokes and dead people so much," I said. "Can you come down and help me clean up this zombie?"

Nick left the window and moments later came walking out the backdoor. He leant over and gripped the corpse's ankles with a very concerned expression on his face.

"What are we doing with Mr Cooper?" he questioned.

I immediately stopped what I was doing. Even with a crushed head showing zero resemblance to Mr Cooper, Nick could still identify the body. I couldn't believe I had forgotten that Nick actually knew Eli's father in person.

"Erm… You aren't going to tell Eli? Are you…?" I mumbled.

Nick started heaving the body across the ground. "Nope. If he still thinks that his parents are alive, I will leave him with that."

He dragged the corpse across the grass and out the front gate.

I strolled behind him. "You knew them…" I said. "Aren't you sad that they are dead?"

The mass of Mr Cooper was beginning to show. Nick was struggling to drag the corpse. He was now jerking it along the grass, one step at a time. "You have not experienced death…" he said.

I scrunched up my face in confusion. "Of course, I haven't…" I replied. "I'm still alive, aren't I?"

Nick dropped the corpse at the car and turned around to me. "Death is a perception," he muttered. "To the majority, it is perceived as a figment of something that's more than what is. I have seen it for what it is. And my perspective is that it's a lot worse than the bitter end to the degradation of life."

"What do you mean?" I questioned.

Nick lifted the corpse into the backseat of the car. "Do you fear sinking into an imminent abyss?" he asked.

"Yeah," I answered.

"From my perspective, that abyss is only but an escape from death," he replied. "And only until you cheat it will you ever understand the terrifying simplicity of it."

I scratched my head. Nick's concept of death was very puzzling. To be perfectly honest, I didn't understand any of it. "Nick, if death is so bad," I replied. "Why do you find it so funny?"

Nick squished Mr Cooper's corpse in the car and shut the door. "Simple!" he answered. "I am a glorious cheat..."

I raised an eyebrow at him. I wasn't sure if Nick was crazy or wise. Was he speaking in riddles? Or was he speaking sense? Either way, I was as bad as Eli at understanding the conversation. And in the end, there was no point in reasoning with the little time we had left.

"Nick," I asked, pointing at Mrs Cooper's ruptured corpse on the driveway. "Could you be a pal and toss that body into the car as well? I'll clean up whatever 'your friend' knocked over upstairs."

I walked inside and up the stairs to the room in which I saw the dark figure. Everything inside the room seemed to be intact. The only object that was out of order was a cheerful portrait of Nick and Eli's family in Russia. I straightened it up so that it met the firm composition of the rest of the house.

By the time I walked downstairs, Nick was already set to help. Together with a mop in hand, it took us thirty minutes to tidy up the minced brains of Eli's parents.

I grabbed the mops and threw them on top of the corpses in the backseat. All the evidence had to be destroyed.

Nick walked down the street and hopped in Eli's Lamborghini. I figured he must have stolen it in order to follow me.

We turned on our lights and proceeded home. On the way back, we picked up some gasoline and burnt the evidence inside a random house. Staring into the roasting flame, both of us were pleased with our accomplishment. Eli would never know the horrible truth.

"So…" I asked Nick. "If you took Eli's car, whose did your accomplice take?"

Nick worriedly stared at me. "I told you, I was by myself…" he answered. "No one would ever be able to tail me without me knowing…"

His expression was serious. "Well, if that's true…" I replied. "Who was the figure that watched me clean and followed you here without you knowing…?"

"How do you know that I was being tailed?" Nick replied. "For all I know, you were just imagining it…"

"Let's hope," I sighed, walking back to my car. "Because if not, you are indeed traceable…"

Chapter 16:
Haven

Nick and I arrived back home ten minutes before six o'clock and went straight to sleep.

It felt like I had only just closed my eyes when I was rudely awoken... Jake pulled back the curtains and let the morning sunlight shine on my face. "It's seven o'clock!" he cheered. "The sun is up and we have work to do!"

I sighed and rolled over. I was about to fall back to sleep when I felt a heavy weight press against the side of my chest. The weight was so heavy that it hurt. I looked to my side to see Eli sitting on top of me, a big smile stretched across his face. "Sorry..." he laughed, "I didn't see you there." I attempted to move, but couldn't. "You're a slut..." I groaned.

Eli pointed at his striped underwear that he was wearing. "Yeah, these are pretty slutty," he said cheerfully.

It took me a while to notice that the underwear that he was wearing was new. "Where did you get those?" I asked.

"Duh..." Eli replied. "Obviously from my house..."

Even though he'd stated that he was "planning to retrieve his belongings from his house early in the morning," it still came as a surprise to me that he'd done so before I'd awoken. It was pleasing to see him cheerful though, as it meant that he still had no idea about his parents' or pet's demise.

"Shit-stains appear to be the only thing holding your underwear together," I teased.

"That was so funny I forgot to laugh..." Eli replied, wittily.

"Yeah, the joke was pretty rotten," I smirked. "You know, rotten egg."

Eli knew exactly what I meant. "I'm going to go make a coffee," he smirked. "Do you want one?"

I struggled under his weight. "Get your fat ass off me and I'll go make one myself," I replied.

Eli let out a fart so loud and forceful that it shook my entire body. "You are right," he said. "Rotten eggs aren't funny."

He got up and walked into the kitchen. I instantly ran out of the living room in an attempt to escape the putrid smell of rotten egg. I held my nose until I had a steaming hot coffee directly under it. The strong smell of the Arabica coffee beans surpassed Eli's dreadful fart. As I sipped the coffee I thought about our mornings over the past few days. Sunrise seemed to bring out the best of us. Stupid jokes were a great way to start the day.

Everyone woke up and started discussing the day's plan. After an hour's conversation, we had finalized the improvements.

Nick's objective was to mount a machine gun on the roof of the house. It wasn't a necessity, but it would certainly come in useful if zombies tried to overrun the house.

I mean... how are they meant to win against a rain of high caliber bullets?

Rufus's ideas had no potential, so instead, he had to pursue one of mine. I may have stolen the idea from various zombie apocalypse movies, but hey... modifying our vehicles into indestructible tanks seemed appropriate for our lifestyle.

Jake's idea was the main fortification. A deep trench similar to that of a castle's moat was to be excavated around the house. A heavy duty, electric fence was to be constructed within the confines of the trench to act as a second layer of protection.

All of us went to work straightaway. With Jake, Eli and I designated to constructing the trench and fence, Eli set out to retrieve an excavator from a local construction site while Jake and I set out to retrieve a suitable electric fence from a nearby Walmart.

After a thorough search through the store, Jake and I decided on a Volte 3000. It was a three-meter-high, stainless steel electric fence with thick cables and a heavy base. It also happened to be the most expensive fence in the store. Jake and I had to make several trips in the truck to amass all the parts required. As we were unloading the final parts of the fence, Eli arrived home in the driver's seat of a heavy-duty excavator. He parked it beside us and climbed off.

"Do you guys need a hand?" he asked.

"Yeah, sure," I said, tossing a fence piece onto the road.

Eli picked it up and stacked it with the rest of the pieces on the front lawn. "What's Rufus and Nick doing?" he asked.

Before I could respond, Rufus came running over to us ecstatically. "I have finished!" he said joyfully.

"Finished what?" I questioned.

"Spray painting Eli's car, of course!"

"Wait..." Eli said, "I didn't ask for..."—he looked at his Lamborghini parked down the street and became lost for words. Even from where he was standing, he could tell that Rufus's spray paint was one of the worst jobs in human history. It was as if a squirrel had sprinted through multiple trays of different colored paint and attacked his car.

Eli confoundedly stared at his ruined Lamborghini, baffled by Rufus's hopelessness. "You have got to be kidding me..." he said, rubbing his forehead in disappointment. "Lucky that it's only us alive to see your putrid work, Rufus..."

"Thank me later," Rufus said, blissfully ignorant of Eli's hurtful remark.

Aside from Rufus ruining Eli's vehicle, work continued and with the excavator at hand, we got to work on excavating the trench. The trench was to be six feet wide and ten feet deep. We had to ensure that zombies could not climb out after falling in. I spray painted lines across the ground for Eli to dig out. Eli was a decent driver, but when it came to excavating, he was like a kid in a sand pit. Eventually, after a couple hours of him flicking dirt across the yard I had to take over.

We worked late into the night and went to bed. By the time the day was over, Nick's search for a mini-gun was predictably unsuccessful and the vehicles had not been armored. With only the trench completed, we went to sleep knowing that it would take a lot of time for us to complete our tasks.

Waking up and following the same routine, it took us another three days of hard labor for us to near completion. I was securing the last section of the fence when Nick came rolling into the driveway.

He leapt out of a large Hilux pickup which he happened to be fond of. "We found it!" he cheered. "We finally found it!"

I stopped working and ran over to him. "Bullshit..." I said in dismay. Nick grinned and swung open the vehicle's door. Inside was a M134 minigun.

I stared astonishingly at the jet black minigun and the long belt of bullets beside it. "How the... Where did you get it from?" I stammered.

Nick heaved it out of the vehicle and carried it down the driveway. "I got it from an old military vehicle parked down a street called Minton Avenue. Pretty luck, aye!" he said ecstatically.

Nick walked across the lawn with an awkward strut. "How much does that thing weigh?" I questioned.

He placed it at the front door. "Around ninety pounds," he answered.

"Dearie me," I said. "No wonder they get mounted on vehicles."

Rufus strolled up to us spiritedly. "Since I've already completed my vehicle stuff, I'll help you get that thing mounted on the roof," he said.

Nick shook his head. "No, thank you."

A gloomy frown spread across Rufus's face. His high-spirited stroll changed to a disappointed slouch.

"Don't worry, Rufus," I said sympathetically. "You can come help us finish the fence."

Rufus half-smiled. "Fair enough..." he said. "Nick will probably regret not having my help, anyway."

I picked up a section of the fence that was lying on the ground and proceeded towards the gate. "Yeah... I'm sure he will..." I lied, attempting to make him feel better.

Rufus picked up a section of the fence and followed me towards the front gate. We got to work installing the final sections of the fence. As expected, Rufus's help was a hindrance and every fence piece that he set up had to be replaced.

The day's work took twice as long as expected, but thankfully by sunset both the fence and trench were complete. With our work at an end, I happily closed the front gate and locked it.

Jake skipped along the fence's edge, running his hand across the wire. "Woo-hoo!" he cheered, grinning ear to ear. "With this barrier sorted, no zombies will ever be able to enter the house. Testing it will be fun!"

I sympathetically smiled and walked across the front lawn towards the house. "Come get a drink!" I said. "For tomorrow, it will be tested!"

As I reached the veranda, Nick came sliding down a ladder off the roof. He landed beside me, dripping with sweat. "Give me some vodka," he puffed.

Rufus overheard the conversation and sprinted across the lawn to us. "And me a drink as well!" he shouted.

"Coming right up!" I cheered. I turned and walked inside the house, returning a couple of seconds later with a juice box for Rufus and a bottle of vodka for Nick.

Nick opened the vodka and sculled it like water. He managed to down a third of it before pulling it away from his mouth. "Ha-ha that hit the spot!" he said, patting his tummy, satisfied.

Rufus looked at the juice box and then back at me, confused. "What the hell is this shit?" he questioned.

"It is 'a drink'," I mockingly answered, trying to hold in my laughter.

Rufus punched a straw through the top of the juice box and began slurping up the juice. "Good one!" he said sarcastically, spluttering juice all over himself.

An abrupt crackle of electricity sounded off as Eli switched on the electric fence. "Yo, Tyler!" he yelled. "Fetch me a drink as well!"

"Yeah, okay..." I muttered, knowing that I had made myself a waiter for the night.

With the house fortified and safe, all of us decided to lie back and get drunk. As I was the designated waiter, it was my job to fetch drinks for everyone. I still had no idea which type of alcohol was the best. I would just grab bottles at random and toss them around. It was easy to tell which ones were the best tasting, though, as the ones that we didn't like were smashed on the ground.

At first, I was becoming annoyed at the mess that we were creating. However, after my sixth beer my care disappeared and just like last time, I became a drunk, sloppy mess.

The following morning, I awoke on the front lawn, sitting in a wheelbarrow wearing only but my underpants.

The morning sun was blazing down, heating up the wheelbarrow like a stove. Even though I was reluctant to move, I was quickly forced out of the wheelbarrow by the heat.

I stood up and inspected the trench. To my joy, four zombies were trapped. They were groaning loudly and scratching at the dirt in an attempt to climb out.

"Jake!" I screamed in excitement.

"Up here!" a voice replied.

I turned around and shielded my eyes. To my surprise, both Jake and Rufus were sitting on the roof, groggy and shirtless. Beside them, on the downward slope of the roof, the minigun was fixed. A leather seat was secured behind it with a long chain of bullets amassed on top.

Yesterday I hadn't paid any attention to Nick or his effort. It was my first time seeing the minigun setup and it was impressive.

It was surprising that he'd managed to install it in a single afternoon. What was more surprising, though, was the fact that all the tiles he had removed were neatly stacked beside the ladder. It was apparent that he was the only one out of us that cared about tidiness. I mean... Eli's house was the definition of cleanliness and yet somehow, he was just as dirty as Rufus.

I pointed at the zombies stuck in the trench. "It works!" I cheered.

Jake stood up and blearily stumbled back and forth trying to maintain his balance. He shielded his eyes and stared at the trench. After wobbling back and forth for a minute, he said, "Oh, now I see!"

Rufus leapt from the roof and tumbled across the ground to a stand. He strolled over to the fence and inspected the zombies in the trench.

Jake stumbled down the ladder and sat down on the veranda. "Where's Eli?" he questioned.

"Probably having sex with Nick," I replied jokingly, completely unaware that he was standing right behind me.

Eli tapped my shoulder causing me to jump in fright. "Get some pants on before you say that shit," he chuckled.

His playful response showed that he wasn't offended by my remark. I sighed in relief and slapped my ass.

"This is probably a turn on for you," I said, cheekily winking at him.

"You definitely wouldn't want that," he replied, shaking his head.

I was about to go put on a pair of pants when I saw Nick pull up in his vehicle. He hopped out and walked through the front gate holding up two cans of gasoline. The zombies in the trench clawed and swiped at his legs as he passed through the gate.

"What are they for?" Jake questioned, inspecting the gasoline cans.

"We will use these to burn the zombies in the trench," Nick replied. "We should incinerate them daily. Go fetch the other cans out of the vehicle."

"Use some manners and I will," Jake spat back, provocatively.

Eli walked up to Jake and slapped him over the back of the head. "Nick has gone out of his way to fetch the gasoline cans for us and yet you still treat him with no respect. Stop being a child and just do it..."

Jake clenched his fists and gritted his teeth in anger. "Nick treats us like shit!" he shouted. "And Eli, if you can't see that, you are just as much of a jerk as him!"

Nick and Eli started laughing in hysterics together. "Awww... Poor little Jake..." Eli teased. "Cranky because Nick is smarter than you."

Jake crossed his arms in frustration.

To avoid conflict, Rufus and I rushed over to the pickup and started carting gasoline cans into the house. We were on our final trip when Jake angrily snatched one out of my hands.

He walked over to the trench, twisted off the cap and poured the gasoline over the zombies that were trapped within the trench, drenching them entirely. "Is this what you want?" he questioned.

Eli looked at him, confused and curious.

Jake suddenly picked up a metal rod off the ground and tossed it at the zombies so that one end landed in the trench and the opposite end on the fence. The electricity from the fence shot through the rod and ignited the gasoline. The zombies caught ablaze and scrambled around in the trench. No matter how hard they tried, they could not escape the fire. All of us watched in awe as the zombies disintegrated into ash.

The smell of burning carcasses and gasoline filled the air. I inhaled deeply through my nose as I knew that it was a smell that I would have to become accustomed to.

Eli held his nose and stared at Jake. "What was that...?" he questioned.

Jake screwed the lid back on the gasoline can and placed it behind the fence. "It was to prove that this place can actually be a haven."

I knew that he was lying and that he'd done it out of pure frustration. But hey, if he was willing to stop the argument that he'd started, I was fine with it.

"Whatever." Eli shrugged, having the same acceptance as myself.

Nick waved Jake off as being an idiot and walked back to his pickup. "I'll go get some more," he said, hopping in his vehicle.

With everyone calm again, I stared at the drifting smoke. It floated above the fence and dissipated into the blue sky. It was unusual to think that the zombies' only escape from the trench was through incineration. As I stared at the entrance, I realized something was missing. My house was now an actual sanctuary. It needed a name that would fit its significance... I grabbed a sheet of stainless steel and cut it into large, crooked capital letters. After welding it to the fence's entrance, I stood back and gazed at the shimmering silver sign atop of the gate. In large glimmering letters read the word "HAVEN."

Chapter 17:
Tedious Routines

After the Psyriviox outbreak and before the final completion of our haven, every day had been an exciting struggle. Now that normality had been established, we were able to return to our ordinary existence.

With nothing to reinvigorate my life, I was left with only my mind. After the first month of reminiscing about our epic experiences, my thoughts decided to take a huge turn. It was little at first, but eventually memories of my mother pierced my mind. At the end of the first month of living in our Haven, the shrieks of her final utterance had become so real, that the only way I could silence them was by killing zombies. To account for this, I created a routine.

The routine was to search the city for survivors every afternoon. Well... that's what I convinced the others we were doing anyway. In truth, the chances of finding someone alive was so incredibly slim, that we would have honestly had a better chance of winning the lottery.

On the bright side, most of the time we would just go to the densest undead area. The logic behind this was the fact that zombies were drawn towards survivors. It wasn't solid evidence, but with the group I was with, persuasion wasn't needed.

We would ram through hordes of zombies while raining gunfire. By this time, our vehicles had been fortified with thick, plated steel armor and murderous wheel spikes like that used by charioteers in colosseums. In combination with our unlimited weapons and ammo, we were able to massacre zombies by the hundreds.

After our daily exterminations we would have to stop at a carwash. We would rip fleshy chunks off the wheel-spikes and rinse gallons of blood off the car with high-powered hoses. In our minds, what we saw as a total water party, was in fact a gut-wrenching blood bath.

One day a bad thought crossed my mind. A thought that *at some point there'd be no zombies left to kill.* However, with the overcrowded trenches needing to be set ablaze every night, it was obvious that that would never happen.

On windy days, zombie ashes would sail out of the trench, creating a smoke screen. Initially, it was funny. Only until we breathed it in did we realize that it could quite easily suffocate us. To prevent this, we would regularly have to clear out the remains in the trenches and transport them anywhere away from our Haven.

After two months of living like this, overgrown flora was now a part of our lifestyle. With inch-long thorns and sharp rubble at every step, all of us adapted to wearing thick steel-capped boots. Unlike the rest of us who had relatively small feet; Nick wore big ugly size fifteen boots. He would always make jokes about the size of his feet and how they relate to having a huge penis.

However, with all of us having already seen it, it didn't really seem to work...

Being all boys, walking in on one of us masturbating became a common occurrence. At one point, I managed to walk in on Rufus three times in one day... It was disgusting enough to find one of us "slaying the cyclops," but to not stop when another saw you belonged only to Rufus's area of infamy... Ultimately, he gave us nightmares which I don't think we'll ever forget.

By the end of the third month, food throughout the city had degraded. Bread was now stale, dairy products were expired and the only foods left, which were safe and edible, were either canned or dehydrated.

Markets were infested with rats, maggots and cockroaches. The smell from being near a supermarket stunk like the carcass of a rotting whale. We used to love fetching great-tasting supplies from food outlets, but now it was considered a horrible chore.

Wearing breathing masks, we would have to bury our arms shoulder deep into decomposed sludge to search for food. Upon entering a market, it was amazing how little we could see. Flies would crowd together in the millions, blinding us with their little black bodies. With millions of wings beating together, they would also create a roar like a barge horn.

On top of this, being deaf and blind while carrying the food outside, we would constantly trip over loose wires and rubble on the floor. Embarrassingly enough, what I thought could never happen, a common grocery run now took as long as what my mother used to. When it came around to Rufus and I having to do it, I nearly always came close to crying. Despite how time-consuming it was, whether it be crashing the car, or nearly drowning in sludge, Rufus always managed to prolong the shopping.

No matter how dull our existence became, our daily routines persisted. Every morning Jake and Eli would climb to the top of the roof to check their mobiles for messages. Each day they would attempt to contact their parents... and each day they'd fail. Every morning Eli would return more miserable than the last. I was unsure whether mobile connection still worked, but I could see that having no contact with his parents was slowly eating away at him.

Conversely, Jake didn't seem to care in the slightest. His affection resembled that of a guinea pig: occasionally pedantic, but most of the time emotionless. I remember Jake's distraught reaction when his brother Charlie got diagnosed with leukemia. It was one of the saddest moments I had ever witnessed. Crying and screaming in frustration, he was now the complete opposite... I knew Jake for a long time and there was only one reason why he was impassive. His interest was clearly in something else...

In the end, I never bothered to ask because I didn't want to instigate any sort of drama. For me, less drama meant more time for killing zombies. It was a win-win situation.

By the fourth month, life as we knew it had become extremely tedious. Our endless amount of freedom had allowed us, up to this point, do anything. We did stuff that wasn't even imaginable. It was hard to believe that nothing could excite us.

Drifting around the streets in fast vehicles and blowing up buildings became a thrill of the past. Our communication also became as dismal as the experience. "I'm hungry," "That was okay..." or "Let's go home..." were now the only sentences we'd ever utter. And even that was rare...

Playing video games and surviving became our lives. With four high-definition, seventy-inch LED flat screens and an Xbox attached to each one, we would play a wide array of games. In fact, we could play any game available, as long as it didn't require internet.

Living through fantasy worlds may sound lame, but it was actually rather fun. Teaming up to slay a dragon or levelling up to kill one another, the virtual life provided us with enjoyment that was impossible to receive from reality. Gaming also gave us a stimulant which proved that we were still somewhat human. It caused arguments.

It was always funny to watch one another argue. The amount of anger the video games would create was tremendous. Thankfully, as Eli was the best gamer out of us, he never got into arguments. Nick, on the other hand being the worst, he would never shut up. Whether it be breaking a controller or smashing a television screen, we had to replace his entire gaming setup multiple times.

From the time that we had lived together, I estimated our total money consumption to be over one billion dollars. Still, with no people alive to drive the green paper value of economics, money meant nothing.

Another benefit of being the only ones alive, was that apart from the occasional food poisoning, we never got sick. With everybody dead, apart from the Psyriviox contagion, pathogens were unable to spread. As long as we wore safety equipment and kept hygienic, the chances of us requiring chronic medical attention were minuscule. In the end, if worse came to worst, we agreed that since Nick was the most experienced with medicine, he would be our surgeon.

From the date specified on our mobiles, five months and five days had passed since creating our Haven.

We were sitting in the living room in a state of boredom. The coolness of winter could be felt and we were rugged up in warm clothes.

"I'm sick of this!" I burst out.

"Sick of what?" Rufus replied.

I waved my hand around the room. "I'm sick of living like this!"

"Well…" Rufus stretched. "You better get used to it, because we are stuck like this."

Eli got up off the couch and walked over to the cupboard. "We could always go on a holiday," he replied, scavenging through a few old maps.

None of us were quite sure what he meant about a holiday. I mean, where would there be a place apart from our Haven which was safe? Most of the holiday destinations around the world would probably be more trouble than they would be enjoyable.

Eli found a map and walked back over to us with his finger marking a location in what appeared to be the middle of nowhere.

"Where the hell is that?" I questioned.

"That's a hundred and fifty miles away from here!" Rufus shouted.

Eli sat down and stared out the window. "It was a holiday spot which my family and I used to go to," he replied. "It is in the middle of a thick, lush rainforest and is known for having the third longest zipline in the world. However, I enjoyed the cliff jumping and waterfalls."

I held up my hand to pause him. There was no way a high-class family like the Coopers would ever go on a thrill-seeking camping trip without Western essentials like power and toilets... "Wait, wait, wait... Hold on... So, you are telling me that you and your family used to go camping?" I questioned.

Eli stared at me, confused. "What's that?" he replied.

"Ok..." I laughed, knowing he had just answered my question. "Was it a resort...?"

"Was it a resort?!" Eli stammered excitedly. "It was a five-star paradise! Spars, pools, great food. You name it, Golden Willow Resort had it!"

"That sounds pretty good." Nick nodded.

"Yeah, that does sound like my cup of tea," I agreed.

"But Tyler..." Rufus mumbled. "You don't like tea."

Eli turned around and slapped Rufus on the forehead. "Rufus, your stupidity makes me sick. Oh, and since Tyler is completely homesick, I have just made the joint decision that we are all going to Golden Willow Resort."

Jake raised his hand. "But... but... what about...?"

Eli squinted at Jake forebodingly.

"Okay..." Jake groaned. "Just remind me to tell you 'I told you so' when this holiday turns to shit."

"Come on, Jake!" I enthused. "Have some confidence!"

Jake stared at me, trying to maintain a frown. I stared back at him with a huge grin.

Eventually a slight smirk spread across his face. "Fine..." He laughed, rolling his eyes. "Just please stop looking at me like that."

In under ten minutes, I managed to gather all my supplies in my car. It had been a long time since I was this excited.

Just as I sat down in the driver's seat, the others came busting out the front door with Eli pointing at the Hilux. "We all have to go in Nick's pickup!" he shouted. "None of the other vehicles will make it through the shitty dirt road!"

I bent down and examined the three-inch gap under my Chrysler. Eli was right. My car could barely make it over a speed bump let alone an overgrown dirt road. I walked over to the pickup and shoved my gear in the tray.

Nick, Jake, and Rufus crammed their supplies on top of mine and hopped in the vehicle. Eli and Nick sat in the front while Jake, Rufus and I sat in the back.

When packing for a holiday I would almost always forget something. Today was different, though. All of us seemed to have remembered everything.

Eli pulled out a GPS and began typing in coordinates. I found it funny that after all this time, the satellites were still perfectly functioning around the Earth.

Nick checked the fuel gauge, started the engine and began driving towards Golden Willow Resort. Travelling at a hundred miles an hour, it only took ninety minutes to reach the rocky dirt road that led into the forest.

"Left in five hundred feet," said the monotone voice of the GPS.

"Oh my god!" Jake shouted. "Shut that piece of shit up! It's driving me nuts!"

"Left now. Left now," it repeated.

"Eh…" Eli shrugged. "It's better than listening to you complain, Jake."

"Yeah!" Nick laughed, jerking the steering wheel sideways and smashing through shrubs and tree branches.

"What are you doing?!" Jake screamed.

"Following the GPS of course, not you," Nick replied.

Jake lunged out of his seat and pulled up the handbrake. The vehicle came to a grinding stop. Nick angrily turned to Jake. "You are going to destroy the brakes, you idiot!" he screamed.

Jake pointed out the front windscreen. In front of the car stood a humungous fig tree. "The GPS lags, you Russian moron. You are not even on a road."

Nick gritted his teeth in frustration. He jammed down the handbrake and reversed the car back onto the dirt road.

Jake sat back, satisfied. "I am right... You are wrong..." he said.

After travelling another forty feet, Nick took another sharp turn. Thankfully, this time he ended up on the correct road. I didn't think it was possible, but the actual road was denser in branches than the off-road track that we had just taken.

We travelled for a further thirty minutes before we reached our destination. All of us hopped out of the Hilux and looked around intriguingly.

"Golden Willow Resort..." Jake laughed. "I thought it would be fancier..."

A large golden gate could be seen down the road. A rusted, blood-smeared sign hung above it. Past the gate, weeds and vines crawled up the walls of every visible building, making them appear alive with vascularity. *It was funny to think that after five months of no human interference, Mother Nature was beginning to take back what was rightfully hers. A decade more, and this place would no longer exist.*

I walked over to the tray and equipped my armor. I stared in awe at the vibrant green and brown surroundings. *Nature is beautiful...* I thought to myself. *Nature is scary...*

CHAPTER 18:
Golden Willow Resort

Even though we were completely isolated in an unfamiliar area, I couldn't have been happier. Golden Willow Resort may not have been as safe as our Haven, but it was certainly an exciting change from our tedious routines.

As we stood together lock-and-loading our guns, we looked like bikers about to go on a raid on a rival gang.

Over the past five months of living together, leaving the house and venturing through the city was an everyday task. Wearing our metal armor was essential for all inner-city expeditions. However, the lengthy time required to equip it was of great annoyance.

It didn't take long for us to establish that leather motorcycle clothes were more beneficial than metal. The thick, black outfits were lightweight and could withstand high-speed accidents.

Zombie teeth could barely scratch the leather, let alone pierce through it. Nonetheless, as we were in a completely new location, I took the liberty to equip both my chain mail and leather jacket.

Rufus stretched his neck from side to side. "It's like the good ole times!" he cheered.

Nick raised his hand and motioned Jake to the front. "Ladies first," he said with a smirk.

Jake sneered at Nick and walked ahead of us into the resort. Eli fetched a large, shiny machete out of the vehicle and together we followed after Jake.

It was a short walk to reach the inner complex of the resort. Standing in a large garden at the resort's center, we were surrounded by several tall bamboo buildings, pools and spas. Apart from all the water being dark green and algae infested, the gold slides that entered each pool still looked gleamingly new. The odd mix of colors between the burgundy hardwood buildings and gold recreational areas was as unusual as it was exquisite.

As we entered a building, we could straight away discern that Golden Willow Resort would have been an extremely luxurious place before the outbreak. The gold-veined marble interior, combined with the huge fluffy beds and expensive commodity, contradicted the resort's location entirely. No one would have ever thought that this upper-class place could exist in an isolated jungle.

After testing out the apartment's toiletries, we all rushed out to explore the rest of the resort. I darted from room to room inspecting and looting along the way. Whether the rooms were completely spotless, bloody crime scenes, or crawling with insects, each one told a different story. The resort gave me an overwhelming feeling of exhilaration. Something that the city had lost a while ago.

Just as I was nearing the end of the apartment block, I came to a door which was heavily padlocked... "Yo! Guys, come check this out!" I shouted.

My voice echoed throughout the resort. The others heard my call and within moments were standing beside me.

Nick bashed on the padlock repeatedly with the butt of his gun. With it having no effect, Rufus attempted to pick-lock it. Eventually, after ten minutes of Rufus saying "I've nearly got it!" Eli pushed him aside and started cleaving at the door with his machete. He relentlessly hacked pieces out of it until a man-sized hole was formed. Eager to get inside, Rufus hurriedly shoved Eli aside and squeezed through the hole. As the rest of us were about to enter, a loud gun shot fired off inside.

All of us stopped moving. "Rufus, are you okay...?" Jake anxiously questioned.

After a few muffled seconds, we got a response. "This bitch tried to shoot me!" Rufus shrieked.

The rest of us glanced at one another excitedly and dashed inside. What we saw next was exactly what we'd hoped.

"Jackpot!" Eli cheered.

In the dark, dirty room, Rufus was kneeling on top of a woman, pinning her to the ground with his knee. The woman had a small, lean figure. Her untidy, brown hair was spread over the floor like a dirty mop.

Her huge hazel eyes, thick black eyelashes and small button nose looked perfect on her tan, muddy face. She looked to be in her mid-twenties. As nefarious as it sounds, I found it humorous watching her sob and struggle under the weak strength of Rufus.

"I shot you!" she cried, in a high-pitched voice. "I shot you!"

Rufus wiped his nose. "I find it funny that you could miss with a shotgun," he laughed.

I walked over and picked up a double-barrel shotgun lying beside her. I clicked it open and looked at the shells. One of them was smoking.

"Hahaha! That's so pathetic," I laughed.

Nick walked over and pulled her out from underneath Rufus. He stood her up and examined her ears, nose and eyes. He was about to examine her mouth when she abruptly spat on his face.

Nick wound back his arm and fiercely backhanded her across the jaw. "Don't do that," he muttered, sternly.

She started to cry loudly.

Jake ran over to her. "Oh, look what you have done now!" he said, sympathetically placing his hand on her shoulder.

The girl appeared to want no physical contact because as soon as Jake's hand touched her shoulder, she wound back her leg and kicked him in the testicles. He fell over and squirmed around on the ground in pain. "For fuck's sake..." he muttered.

"Dear god!" I laughed in amazement. "She is something!"

Eli strutted over to her and smacked her on the forehead with the handle of his machete. She fell over completely unconscious.

Nick looked at her unconscious on the ground. "Now let's have our way with her," he said, not even joking in the slightest.

The rest of us turned and stared at Nick in disgust. In the violent apocalyptic environment that we lived in, it was one thing to backhand and or knock out a female, but to have sex without one's permission was still unquestionably wrong. We may have been without females in our lives for five months, but we still had our morals.

"So... No sex?" Nick puzzlingly questioned.

I blinked a few times trying to comprehend how Nick could perceive rape as sex. "Yes... no sex..." I scornfully replied.

After briefly searching the room for other survivors, Eli tossed the unconscious woman over his shoulder and exited the building. The rest of us being utterly fascinated by the female, we quickly followed behind.

As we got outside, the sun was setting over the forest. The receding light filtered through the tree branches, creating a vibrant mist of deep red. Everywhere around us was glowing like a ruby. It was a stunning sight to see. All of us took in the surroundings without saying a single word. To me, the sight evoked our valiant efforts at the treehouse. I gazed at the dazzling ruby glow, pleasantly reminiscing our early adventures. Together, we watched the sun set behind the trees and before we knew it, we were surrounded by gloomy shadows in the darkness of the night.

"Okay, time to go," Eli said. "I have been holding this lady for too long."

"You could always pass her to me," Rufus replied, cheekily winking at him.

"Rufus..." Eli said sternly. "That would be worse than killing her..."

Although Eli was joking, a level of emotion could be heard in his voice. He sounded as if he'd already fallen in love with the woman. We all burst out laughing at him. Eli smiled at us, thinking we were laughing at his joke.

"Eli the comedian is back in town," I teased.

Eli skipped towards the resort's exit with the woman still wrapped over his shoulder. "That's what I'm here for!" he replied, happily.

He had only skipped a few meters when he stopped and screamed. "She's biting me!"

We watched in amusement as she struggled out of his grip and fell to the ground. She attempted to crawl away. However, Nick stepped in front of her, blocking her path. Eli rubbed the bite-mark on his wrist. "What is your problem?!" he shouted at the woman.

"What time is it...?" she whispered.

"What?" I questioned.

"What time is it...?" she repeated.

Nick grabbed her throat and lifted her to her feet. "It's time for you to get up before I bash your dumb skull in," he muttered.

In a heroic attempt to defend the woman, Eli rushed forward and tackled Nick. Rufus, amused by Eli's efforts, stood in front of the woman like a bodyguard. "Don't worry," he said. "I'll protect your sweet little ass."

The woman rubbed her throat and smiled at Rufus. Jake, unable to see the facade of her smile, thought it would be a terrific idea to make a similar move. He rushed over and pushed Rufus to the ground. As he turned to look at the woman's admiration, she raised her leg and once again kicked him hard in the testicles.

Jake collapsed on the ground and writhed around in pain. "Not again..." he moaned.

Rufus and I burst out laughing. Eli and Nick were too busy wrestling on the ground to notice Jake's dumb mistake. However, it wasn't long before something did catch our attention. All of us heard it. It sounded off in the distance like the terrified shriek of a hundred dying rabbits.

I stopped laughing and stared at the girl's worried expression. "What is it?" I questioned.

"Time for us to leave..." she replied.

Eli walked over to her and gripped her arm like a vice. "I was thinking the same thing!" he said.

Unlike what we were expecting, she did not struggle. Something was obviously wrong. We all started pacing towards the pickup, both fearful and excited by the pandemonium. The shrieks became louder and more ecstatic the closer we got to the vehicle. It was as if we were walking towards the uproar.

We were almost at the pickup when we came to a halt. The dreadful noise had suddenly stopped. All was quiet, and we felt as though we were being watched.

"Don't move," the woman whispered.

Rufus ignored her and switched on a flashlight. He swayed the light back and forth along the tree line illuminating hundreds of red, beady eyes.

"What are they?" I whispered.

"They are spawn from hell," she replied, fearfully.

As she said it, the eyes started to move. We shuffled backwards as hundreds of small black creatures hobbled out from the tree line and carpeted the road ahead of us.

"Do not take your eyes off them," the girl whispered.

We crept backwards, keeping our eyes directed at the creatures.

We had only retreated a couple of steps when something clutched my leg. "Guys!" I shrieked.

Rufus aimed his flashlight at my leg. "Umm, Tyler..." he whispered. "You have a friend..."

I glanced down to see one of the creatures attached to my calf like a parasite. Up close I could see that it was not spawn from hell, but a monkey... or what I assumed to be a monkey... Apart from having bright red eyes, it had huge, bear-sized claws and coarse blackish fur like a wolverine. It made small grunting noises and foamed at the mouth as it attempted to ravage through my leather pants. It was as if it had contracted rabies and was in the crazed, final stage of brain necrosis before death.

I was breathing heavily. "Guys..." I whispered.

Nick, Rufus and Jake immediately kicked it to the ground and stomped on it. The final blow was from Rufus. His boot came down so hard on its head that its skull exploded like a water balloon.

Rufus looked at me with a satisfied smile. "I think that ought to do it," he cheered.

I smiled back, but only momentarily for I noticed the monkey's arm twitch. "Hey... did you see that?" I questioned.

Rufus shone his flashlight at the monkey. "See what?" he replied.

The monkey violently jolted, snapping its broken leg back into place.

"Oh..." Rufus chuckled.

Nick saw it and started to back away. "Let's move," he said, worriedly.

"Yeah, good idea," the woman agreed.

Suddenly, the monkey started spasming on the ground as if it was having a seizure. With each convulsion its splattered brain slithered back inside its skull.

It was interesting and revolting at the same time. "What's going on...?" I questioned.

The monkey unnaturally jerked from side to side. Loud whip-like cracks could be heard as its mutilated corpse became whole again. After its brain had fully receded into its skull, it twisted its head back around a hundred and eighty degrees and glared at us.

"Yep, it's time to run," I muttered in disbelief.

We all turned and ran. The revived monkey proceeded to stretch to a stand and howl at the top of its lungs. The rest of the monkeys that had gathered in the distance came rushing after us. We sprinted through the resort with the monkeys tailing close behind. By the time we'd reached the opposite end of the resort, the woman was so tired that Eli was dragging her along the ground. Our physical fitness was clearly better than hers.

"Where are we running to?" I puffed.

Eli picked up the girl and tossed her over his shoulder. He pointed to a dirt track leading deep into the forest. "Follow me," he said.

We rushed behind Eli progressing through a series of connected trails. From left to right, then right to left, the rapid changes in directions made it near impossible to know where we were at any point in time. This combined with the cold, howling wind, shadowy trees, and ear-piercing shrieks of monkeys, it felt like we were being chased through a horrifying maze.

After five minutes of running, Jake was almost out of breath. He wasn't going to last much longer, and we needed to know if Eli was leading us somewhere close and safe.

Jake stumbled over a branch but luckily regathered his feet underneath him. "Where are you taking us?" he heaved.

The trail ahead of us split in two. Eli pointed to the trail on the right. "In ten feet, jump as far as you can!" he shouted.

By the time I realized what he'd said I had already tumbled off the edge of the cliff. As I plummeted through the air, I embraced my body in the form of a pin-drop and waited for a splash. Watching the spiraling flashlights below me and hearing the terrified screams of Jake, it felt like forever. I fell faster and faster until I eventually connected with the water.

I shot through the water, plunging into darkness. I tried to swim upwards but was pulled down by the weight of my chainmail. I sank deep beneath the surface. Descending into the overwhelming blackness, I was freezing and suffocating. With no idea of the waterhole's depth, I had to take off my chainmail. And I had to do it quick.

I pinched my nose and popped the gas out of my ears. It took five seconds of hysterical fiddling to release my leather jacket and another ten to release my chainmail. Deep underwater with no light to guide me to the surface, I noted the gravitational pull on my chainmail and let it go. I swam in the opposite direction as it was my best hope to resurface.

Breast-stroking through the blackness, I powered through the water for twenty seconds. By the time I saw the familiar glow of Rufus's flashlight, I was almost out of breath.

As I neared the surface, Rufus dove down and pulled me upwards. It wasn't much effort for him, but for me it was the potential between life and death.

My head shot out of the water and I took a huge gasp of air. I looked around to see the others beckoning me out of the water. Monkeys had gathered in the trees around the waterhole and were shrieking at us ferociously.

Rufus grabbed my arm and pulled me out of the water. "We have to go," he said, urgently.

Wet, cold and exhausted, I pulled myself to a stand. Before I could regain my breath, Nick tossed me over his shoulder and sprinted down an overgrown track leading away from the waterhole. "Let's move!" he shouted.

Even while carrying me, Nick weaved through protruding branches and vines, nimbly avoiding all obstacles. The others followed close behind. As we were moving, I glanced backwards to see Jake sprawled over Eli's shoulder like a sloth. Although it was difficult to see, I could still make out an indolent smile on his face.

We continued moving until we reached a small opening in the forest. The muddy terrain gradually formed into a rocky climb ahead of us. At the end, a massive tree could be seen towering over the jungle canopy.

Having regained my strength, I leapt off Nick's shoulder onto the ground. Nick smiled and stretched his back in relief.

Eli saw me standing and immediately tossed Jake onto the ground. "Jake, carry your own weight," he said, sternly. "It's not much further now."

Jake struggled to his feet and we started our ascent up the rocky track.

Although it was a short climb, the large, jagged rocks were deceptively unstable. Every so often one of us would grab a loose rock which would dislodge and tumble down the track. Anyone standing behind would have to quickly dodge to the side. Luckily none of us were hit. As we neared the top, the track became so steep that a fixed chain was required to climb up. The toll of having to continually recover our grip from the loosened rocks made the final climb tremendously strenuous on our forearms.

We reached the end of the track utterly exhausted. Hunched lethargically underneath the massive tree, a large sign fixed to its trunk revealed why Eli had led us to it. Golden Willow Resort had the world's third longest zipline. At the top of the tree was its starting point. A golden ladder ran to its top. A box of harnesses sat on the ground next to the tree. Eli grabbed a harness and dashed up the ladder. "Climb up!" he yelled, excitedly.

All of us took a harness and climbed up the ladder. When I got to the top, I gazed around in awe. Above the trees, the brightness of the moon enabled a full view of the forest. The trees swayed calmly in the cool breeze. The waterhole glistened like a diamond amongst the thick of the forest. At the edge of the round wooden platform that we were standing on, a thick golden cable stretched three thousand feet down towards the resort.

All of us equipped our harnesses and tightened them against our waists. I peered over the edge to see that monkeys had gathered underneath the tree. Some of them were even climbing up.

Eli walked over to the cable and attached a carabiner to his harness. He pulled out his machete and readied it in front of him. "I will get rid of any small branches in front of us," he said. "You guys just have to clip yourself in and you're all set to go." He leapt off the platform and sailed along the zipline.

Nick grabbed the girl and tightened her harness to the point of suffocation. He then clipped her to the cable and abruptly kicked her off the platform. Her terrified shrieks echoed through the air.

Nick clipped himself in and went after her. Rufus followed close behind. I was set to leap off when I noticed Jake fiddling around with his harness.

"What are you doing?" I questioned. "We have got to go."

Jake frantically shook his harness. "This son of a bitch is torn!" he shouted.

"Come on..." I moaned. "Hurry..."

Suddenly, a monkey toppled onto the platform.

"Watch out!" I yelled.

The monkey rushed towards Jake; its claws outstretched. Jake turned around and kicked it clean off the platform as if it were a football. He then resumed trying to fix his harness.

I grabbed hold of the cable. "Get a move on, Jake!" I screamed. "There will be hundreds here any second!"

As I said it, a dozen monkeys climbed onto the platform and came rushing towards us. Instead of turning around to attack them, Jake ran towards me.

"I'm not wearing any armor!" I screamed. "Don't lead them to me!"

Jake kept his pace. "Let's hope you can hold me!" he shouted.

I didn't want to do it. But I had to. I stood still and embraced his leap of faith. The force at which he hit me, flung me straight off the platform. Clinging on for dear life, Jake wrapped his legs tightly around my waist. Face to face, both of us squealed like babies as we plunged down the zipline.

We glided through the air at a tremendous speed. The grinding noise of the trolley against the cable was all I could hear. For an activity that was meant to be enjoyable, the ear-splitting sound, combined with Jake's gonads squished against my stomach; I was extremely uncomfortable.

We continued down the zipline, my entire body aching under Jake's weight. I found it bizarre that *for someone who'd survived on canned food for the past five months, he'd somehow managed to stay fat...*

Being sore and fatigued wasn't even the worst part, though. It was when we shot through the last stretch of trees that I discovered the true meaning of pain.

As we neared the finish, our combined weight made the zipline droop closer to the trees. The branches that Eli had missed with his machete succeeded in colliding with my legs. Luckily for Jake, his legs were wrapped so high around my waist that they could not be struck.

At the end of the zipline, Eli was standing on a long strip of grass, pointing at us, laughing. His cheery expression quickly changed to terror as he realized how fast we were moving. We shot towards him like a bullet, forcing him to dive out of the way. As we shot past Eli, the cable proceeded to incline which slowed us down drastically. We decelerated, coming to a stop on an elevated, wooden platform at the end of the grass strip. As soon as my feet touched the platform, I shoved Jake to the ground and unclipped my harness, eager to get back in the vehicle.

Eli ran over to us and noticing my heavily bruised legs, he tossed me over his shoulder.

"You get to ride everyone tonight!" he laughed. "Nick, Jake and myself!"

"Hey!" I snapped angrily. "Jake rode me!"

Eli slapped my leg joyfully. "Yep. It wouldn't be the first time either!" he joked.

Even though I was in agonizing pain, his joke made me smirk.

Jake stumbled beside us. "Where are the other three idiots?" he muttered.

Eli pointed at the resort's exit. The pickup was parked behind the gate with its high beam lights on. "They are ready to go," he answered.

It was relieving to see the vehicle so close. As we approached it, I climbed off Eli's shoulder and peered into the side window. Nick was sitting in the driver's seat while Rufus and the female were in the backseat. Jake spotted the female and climbed in next to her. The pickup had five seats in total and now that there were six of us, there wasn't enough room for us to have a seat each. One of us was going to have to squeeze into the back with the others. I groaned at the thought of being squished next to Jake for a second time. "Umm... there isn't much room back there..." I muttered.

Eli chuckled and excitedly dove into the backseat. "Don't worry," he said. "Your legs look sore, so I'll let you have the front."

I smiled, knowing full well that he only gave me the front seat so that he could sit closer to the female. "Thanks," I replied, delightedly.

I hopped in the front seat and stretched my legs, pleased with the vast amount of leg room. Nick started the vehicle and headed back towards our Haven.

CHAPTER 19:
Beauty and the Beast

The journey home was a riot. With the female squished in the backseat, Eli attempted to seduce her. From "Are you a religious? Because you're the answer to all my prayers," all the way to, "Do you live on a chicken farm? Because you know how to raise a cock," he used every pick-up line in the book.

However, that wasn't the worst of it. Jake being shy, he occasionally made yelping noises to get her attention, while Rufus being an idiot, he non-stop stared at her the entire way home... Conclusively, through all the creepiness towards the poor girl, we only managed to receive one piece of information from her. We discovered that for such a violent female, she had a very gentle name. Her name was Bella.

It was late at night when we arrived home. After a small argument about where Bella was going to sleep, we tucked her in on the couch and we went to bed. After all the drama from our one-day holiday at Golden Willow Resort, I was able to have a very relaxing sleep.

I awoke the next morning and sat down for breakfast. Nick sat beside me and watched as Eli, Rufus and Jake attempted to gather the finest canned food for Bella. Whether it be canned peaches or chunky beef stew, what they thought would impress her was comical. Before the zombie apocalypse, she undoubtedly would have been on romantic dates filled with lobster and caviar. It was going to take more than a few old cans of food to impress her. I knew this much.

After finishing some baked beans, I went and had a shower. While in the shower, I shaved off the little stubble I had on my face and thoroughly washed myself with some expensive soap. After drying myself off and brushing my teeth, I put on dress clothes and sprayed myself with cologne. Smiling and winking at myself in the mirror, I looked impressively handsome.

I walked outside and pushed Jake off his chair and sat down in his spot beside Bella. Jake looked at me shocked. He was probably more shocked at the fact of what I was wearing rather than what I did to him. Anyhow, Bella was all that was on my mind. Watching her demolish off a can of salmon, she couldn't have looked any sexier...

I stared into her eyes and brushed her hair over her ear. "Vous êtes, belle," I said, soothingly. She let out a deep burp. Chunks of salmon and trickles of saliva splattered over my face.

I smiled and lightly kissed her hand. "Nothing can break this moment," I replied, smiling happily.

All of a sudden, Rufus rushed out and jumped in between us. It was obvious that he didn't want me to make a move.

I was unshaken to Rufus's sudden disruption. Even with him trying to block me, I maintained my deep stare into Bella's eyes. "Je parie que vos pets odeur aussi bon que vous regardez," I uncaringly continued.

Bella looked at me confused while Rufus looked at me in amazement. "Tyler!" he staggered. "I never knew you spoke Spanish!"

Jake laughed in hysterics and walked out of the room. "I'm done!" he cackled. "I'm done!"

I was about to say my next romantic line when Bella excreted a deep, rumbly fart. The smell was so toxic that it stung my nostrils and made my eyes teary. "I hope that satisfies you," she giggled.

I jumped up off the seat. "That does it!" I screamed in frustration. "I'm done with this! Jake can keep his fancy French pick-up lines!" I angrily marched off back into the bathroom.

After washing my face and calming down, Jake laughingly explained that one of my French pick up lines translated to, "I bet your farts smell as good as you look." This may have clarified why Bella farted, but it didn't explain why she continued with her grossness over the following days.

Five guys cramped together in a single house. An average person would think that we would be used to gross stuff. Well... the truth is "we were...." Day in and day out, we thought we'd familiarized ourselves with every disgusting thing in existence. We were clearly wrong, though. A girl habitually living like "us" still seemed incredibly revolting.

A week had passed and Bella maintained her repulsiveness. Whether it be not flushing the toilet, hacking up globs of mucus or having an awful odor. Through her strategic method, she was able to repulse everyone except Rufus away from her. It was quite comical as no matter how hard she tried, she could not get rid of him. Rufus was attached to her like a fly to a steaming pile of manure.

By day eight, Bella was beginning to crumble under her own grossness. Up until now, she had not taken a bath. Her beautiful thick hair was now stiff and dreadlocked. From head to toe, her delicate skin was patched with dirt. Her tattered clothes dangled from her body like a blanket and her tiredness made her look completely drunk. Conclusively, she looked like a withered, old prostitute.

I was sitting on the couch playing the Xbox when she sat down beside me. Without saving my game's progress, I got up and walked outside. Out the front past the fence, Eli was relentlessly bashing a zombie with a mallet. I walked up to him to see if there was anything to do.

"Yo, Eli!" I shouted. "Want to go do something?"

Eli stopped his slaughter and wiped blood off his mallet. He turned to me. "What, where and why?" he answered.

"I don't know," I said. "I just want to get away from Bella. She makes me sick."

Eli tossed his mallet on the ground and wiped his hands on his shirt. "Yeah, she is ratchet," he laughed. "She even makes Rufus look hygienic."

Bella's thick repugnant odor was still stinging my nostrils. I wiped my nose. "To be perfectly honest, I wish we never found her," I replied. "You should have let her die by the monkeys."

Eli smiled and pointed behind me. I was wondering why I could still smell Bella's odor. I turned around to see both Rufus and Bella standing a couple feet away from me. Rufus was looking appalled at what I had said and judging by the tears streaming down Bella's face, she wasn't pleased either.

Rufus grabbed me by the scruff of my shirt. "Say sorry!" he shouted.

I know I should have apologized. But I just didn't care. I was sick of Bella's attitude and she needed to grow up. I pushed Rufus away and shoved past Bella with my shoulder. "Sorry doesn't fix the truth," I muttered.

For the rest of the day Bella was crying. Rufus tried to cheer her up, but nothing, not even flowers or food was working. Bella's tantrum was the first I had seen in close to six months. For some reason, it evoked a memory of a particular female when Jake's brother died. A memory which was difficult to forget.

The news of Charlie Newton's death spread throughout the school like wildfire. A popular girl in our year, Debra, admitted to having a relationship with Charlie. Overwhelmed with apparent grief, she wrote a poem about Charlie and posted it on his Facebook wall for all to see. It spoke of how brave Charlie was and how lucky she was to have had him in her life. Hundreds of people encouraged and supported Debra's poem. People told her that "she was an incredibly strong woman" and that "she had a beautiful soul." Jake seemed to be the only one who saw the complete opposite.

Jake used an anonymous Facebook account to post a quiz about Charlie in the comments of Debra's poem. It was a simple quiz. It consisted of a few minor details about Charlie. You would have only needed to have talked to Charlie once, to get them all correct.

Funnily enough, Debra could not answer a single question. The quiz only received abuse. Both from Debra and her supporters.... Jake's post was depicted as vain and uncaring.

Ultimately, Jake knew that Debra did not even remotely know his brother. The death of Charlie was only a source of attention and she was clever enough to extract every little bit of it. It was fortunate that her followers weren't as clever. Regarding the abusive comments, Jake discerned that the girl's followers were nothing more than a bunch of mindless zombies. He recognized that they would make stupid assumptions based on only hearing one side of a story. Jake established that the followers' dimwittedness would allow him to enact his vengeance.

The girl had belittled the death of Charlie. It was inexcusable, and Jake understood that abusing Debra would not fulfil his desire for her unhappiness. Instead, he ensured to make her life a living hell. Jake researched and discovered details about Debra, finding cracks in her apparent flawless character. Once he had gathered enough cracks, he formed a crevice and pushed her into it.

The humiliation Debra finally received was undeniably the worst someone could ever experience. The dispersal of nudes accompanied by doctoral information about sexually transmitted diseases came first. The exposure of explicit conversations about Debra's friends and the publicized hilarity of Debra's poverty-stricken household came next. Like blind sheep, Debra's followers never questioned but only accepted the new information. Jake plummeted Debra into a place of no return. He demolished Debra's relationship with her friends and family and assured that everyone who knew her, ended up despising her. By the end of it,

Debra truly needed counselling. Jake was able to achieve the destruction of her reputation with only me knowing that it was his doing.

Conclusively, this memory was profound not because it was the destruction of a girl's reputation, but because I learned something from it. I learned that using someone else's predicaments in order to gain attention for yourself was evil. I learned that to satisfy vengeance, people need a punishment equal to the severity of their actions. And I learnt that Jake's grudges will inevitably lead to someone else's hell...

Living in a house full of young tough males, emotions and attention did not run rampant. From the violent and emotionless female that we met on the first day, Bella was now the opposite. I understood that she actually had a reason to be upset, but if she was going to survive, she had to toughen up.

It was night-time and we were trying to watch a movie. It was difficult to enjoy with the whimpers and moans of a woman in another room.

We were nearing the climax of the movie when Nick stood up. "That does it!" he shouted. He stomped out of the living room.

Eli, Jake and I waited. The noise of what we heard next sounded as if a cougar had been let loose in her room. Nick came sprinting out, bloody and terrified. Bella followed close behind him, her arms outstretched ready to attack. "She's got fingernails!" he screamed.

Jake sprinted into the bathroom and locked the door. "What did you say to her?!" he shrieked through a crack in the door.

Nick rushed into the living room and did a commando roll over the couch. He landed beside me. "I just told her to get off her rags," he replied.

"That ought to do it!" I laughed.

With everyone frantic, Eli leapt forward and swung his arm out sideways. Bella swiftly ducked under his arm. Rufus who was following close behind was not quick enough. He ran into Eli's arm like a blind bull. The impact was so hard, that it made Rufus do a backflip. To what happened next seemed impossible... I would never have believed it unless I saw it with my own two eyes.

Rufus fell on his face and slid along the ground. The speed at which he was sliding enabled him to become a self-propelled bowling ball. Rufus uncontrollably collided into the back of Bella's legs. Bella tripped backwards, cracking her head on the ground and knocking her unconscious.

Nick was hiding behind me. "Thank you, Rufus!" he screamed in joy. "You saved me!"

Rufus scratched his head and looked at Bella unconscious on the ground. "No!" he sobbed. "It wasn't me!"

Eli walked over and patted Rufus on the back. "Great work!" he rejoiced. "Now we can watch the movie in peace!"

Jake came rushing back out of the bathroom. He looked at Bella lying unconscious on the ground. "What happened?!" he questioned, excitedly.

We knew it wasn't Rufus's fault, but ever since Bella had joined our group Rufus had been more annoying than usual. It was about time we got some revenge. I winked at Jake. "Rufus saved us," I cheered.

Rufus looked at me with watery eyes. It was obvious that he did not like being responsible for her injury.

Jake recognized my wink and applauded Rufus. "Awesome job!" he cheered. "It was about time you showed some initiative!"

Rufus looked at us distraught. "But... I didn't. It wasn't... my fault," he stammered.

It was funny to see how sad Rufus was getting over something he didn't do. He couldn't even understand that it was all one big joke.

My amusement was shortly stopped by Nick. He pointed at a red trail leading away from Bella's head. "Whoa guys," he said. "Look at that."

Rufus drastically dove on top of Bella. "Oh my god!" he shrieked. "She's dead!"

Eli stepped forward and pulled Rufus away. Nick bent down and tilted Bella's head to the side. Blood was drizzling out through her weedy hair. Nick placed his hand on Bella's neck to check for her pulse. After a moment, he stood up. "Bella's all right," he said. "However, she does require medical attention."

With that, Rufus dashed out of the room.

Eli crossed his arms. "What needs to be done, Doctor little dick Nick?"

Nick laughed and closely examined the laceration. "It needs stitches. I'm not sure how many, though. It's difficult to see," he replied.

I bent down and pulled her hair back to get a better look. My dumb action made blood seep out at a much faster rate. Nick slapped my hand away. "Don't do that," he said. "We need to shave her head."

Rufus came rushing back into the room with a medical kit. "Please save her..." he muttered.

Nick carefully lifted Bella up and carried her into the bathroom. He stripped off her clothes and laid her in the shower.

All of us crowded around and stared at her naked body. "Why does she have to be naked?!" Rufus screamed.

Nick ignored him and grabbed the electric shaver. "The quicker we do this the better," he said. "I need some chloroform. It's best that she doesn't wake up while I'm working on her."

The use of chloroform in the medical profession was entirely unprofessional. However, Nick was so confident in this particular medical emergency that everyone including Jake was afraid to question him. Rufus may have been interrogative at the beginning, but as the treatment got underway, he stopped.

Rufus rushed out of the room. Moments later, he returned with the chloroform. "I got it!" he shrieked.

Nick yanked the chloroform out of Rufus's hands and emptied it on a towel. He placed the towel over Bella's mouth so that she would inhale the chloroform. After a couple of seconds, Nick pulled the towel back off her face and tossed it in the sink. "That should do it!" he said.

With Bella being completely sedated, Nick switched on the electric razor and combed it over her hair. Bella may have had sticky, dreadlocked hair, but the expensive razor was able to sheer through it with ease. Huge brown clumps fell onto the shower floor. When there was no hair left on Bella's head, Nick turned on the shower. He washed the blood off her head and examined the three-inch split in the back of her scalp. For a small fall, it was a brutal result.

While the rest of us were busily staring at Bella's privates, Nick cut a strand of thread and began weaving it through her scalp. Through each forward and back motion, Nick pulled on the wire and tightened the skin together. After a delicate five minutes, Nick cut the thread and knotted it to her scalp. Apart from a few droplets of blood oozing out between the stitches, the laceration was completely sealed.

Nick washed his hands in the shower. "I think we are done here," he said.

Eli stepped into the shower with Nick. "Not yet!" he replied. "Bella needs a full wash."

Jake jumped into the shower as well. "It's true!" he excitedly agreed. "I don't think she's had a wash in the last week!"

I knew what Eli and Jake were up to. They just wanted to have a feel of Bella's boobs while she was unconscious. It was utterly revolting...

I stepped into the shower and joined them. "You guys do have a point," I approved.

Nick shrugged at us and climbed out of the shower. "You kids can have your fun with her," he said. "If it's not sex, it's not for me... Rufus shook his head in shame. "I can't believe you guys would do this," he muttered. "A knocked-out girl and you feel you should take advantage of her... It's sickening..."

Eli turned on the shower and pulled back the shower curtain. "Relax!" he laughed. "It's not like we are all getting naked together."

Jake stopped pulling off his pants and looked around to see if anyone had noticed. "Yeah... ha-ha!" he awkwardly agreed. "What do you take us for?"

Rufus pulled back the shower curtain. "You are a bunch of animals," he shouted.

I smiled at him. "Rufus!" I laughed. "I remember you when you fingered that semi-conscious Sasquatch at that celebration last year."

Rufus gave me a troubled look. My ruthless comment gave him no moral ground to stand on. "Okay," he muttered. "But please don't do that to her." He hopped in the shower with us.

Jake bent down and squeezed Bella's breasts. "Yep, no problem," he beamed. "I'm happy with where this is at."

In all, the shower was fantastic. We not only played with Bella's boobs, but we actually washed her. We also avoided her downstairs area like Rufus had insisted so we didn't perceive our actions as "that invasive." Apart from blood-stained stitches in her head, by the end of it, Bella was sparkling clean. Even with no hair, when Bella was hygienic, she was stunningly good-looking. We dressed her in warm clothes and laid her in bed. I glowered at her sleeping with an overwhelming sense of calmness. It was nice to see how such a ferocious monster could change into a sleeping beauty. We walked out of the room and flicked the light off.

With Bella fast asleep and Rufus quiet, the rest of us were at peace.

For the rest of the night, I played through the campaign of my video game. It was a rather easy fantasy game. It didn't frustrate me nor did it surprise me. For once, it was exactly what I needed to escape from reality.

The game's captivating storyline kept me amused for hours. By the time I finished, it was midnight. I rubbed my bloodshot eyes and went to bed.

I wasn't sure how long I slept for. But it wasn't long enough. Everyone in the household was awoken by terrible screams.

At first, I thought a zombie had broken into the house. But I soon realized why there was so much noise.

All of us burst through the door into my old bedroom. Bella was in front of my wardrobe mirror, looking at her head in horror. "Where is my hair?!" she screamed. "And what the fuck did you do to my head?!" She pointed at her scar. "I look like Frankenstein!"

Eli started to snigger. "You look a lot better than what you did before," he laughed.

Bella turned and gave Eli a look of pure hate. It was as if she was killing him with her eyes. "You tried to coat hang me!" she screamed.

Eli took a frightened step backwards.

Nick calmly walked over and examined her scalp. "Oh, yeah, I forgot something..." he said.

"What is that?!" Bella shouted.

"To sterilize your laceration." He pulled a bottle of spirits out of his pocket and poured it over her head. Bella screamed at the top of her lungs as it soaked into her wound.

Rufus rushed forward and tried to calm her down. It was too late, though. What Nick had unleashed was beyond measure. The beast inside Bella had once again been released.

Bella lashed out with her claws. Rufus got struck three times and fell to the ground. With Rufus down, the rest of us rushed out of the room. As I slammed and locked the door behind me. An uproar of thudding and scraping could be heard from the other side of the door. I kind of felt bad for leaving Rufus in there with Bella. But it had to happen.

The rush of adrenaline we all got from the incident kept us wide awake. As the sun ascended into the morning sky, slowly but surely the uproar died away.

I sat down and ate breakfast. I wondered what my room would look like next time I see it. Probably not good. Anyhow, Nick agreed to repair any damages. He told us that he had intentionally forgotten to sterilize Bella's wound until she had awoken. He also said that he specifically used alcohol to induce pain on her. For Nick, it was just payback for Bella being gross.

To be truthful, for someone whom I earlier "wished were dead," it was still somewhat mean. Bella had been through a lot over the past twenty-four hours and she needed a break.

I went and got some canned food out of the cupboard. I walked to my bedroom and swung open the door. To what I saw next, I never thought I'd see it in one hundred years. My jaw dropped. Bella and Rufus were sitting on my bed, kissing...

I dropped the canned food on the ground. "Oh my god!" I shrieked.

Bella ran over and placed her finger on my lips. "Shh..." she whispered. "If you tell the others, I will never wash myself again."

"What is it?" Eli and Jake shouted.

I looked into Bella's large, worried eyes. It was mesmerizing. I sadly caved in to her allure. "Argh..." I replied, trying to think of something. "I accidentally dropped a can on my foot."

The sound of their rushing footsteps came to a halt and they began to laugh. "You are a little bitch!" Eli chuckled.

Bella happily nodded at me and sat back down on the bed. "Umm I got you guys some food," I murmured. I rolled the cans to them.

Bella picked up the cans and looked at them in disgust. "Not these awful things," she muttered.

I walked out of the room. "Too bad!" I shouted. "That's all we got!"

My angry outburst was a surprise to myself. I tottered outside and slumped on the veranda. *Rufus's persistence actually paid off...* I thought to myself.

I had only just begun pondering my defeat when Rufus and Bella came strolling past me, smiling and holding hands. I looked at them, miserably. "Where are you guy's off to?" I moaned.

They skipped out the front gate and hopped in a car. "Bella thinks she can find better food," Rufus giggled. "We will be back later."

I sank my head in misery. "Have fun on your date..." I muttered under my breath.

Bella cutely scrunched her face and pinched Rufus on the nose. "Rufus, you are so wonderful!" she said loudly as they drove off.

I unhappily walked inside and played my video game. Today, the video game was not providing the same enjoyment as what it was yesterday. I was too caught up contemplating what I should say to Bella when she returned. "I love you" or "Rufus and you are not meant to be" was far too absurd. I needed to express my feelings towards her without tearing apart her relationship with Rufus. Furthermore, I didn't want to portray myself as a desperate asshole. It was an impossible task.

After five minutes of playing, I smashed the controller against the ground and walked outside to kill some zombies.

Zombies were piled up in the trench. I slaughtered for hours on end. Every time a thought about Bella crossed my mind, I killed a zombie. The splatter of blood and splitting of bones took my mind off it. As always, zombie slaying was satisfying.

It was midday when I stopped. The reason being was that there were no more zombies left in the trench. With my entire body aching and drenched in sweat, I walked inside and cracked open a fresh, icy beer. As I was about to take my first sip, Rufus busted through the front door.

His clothes were torn and dirty. He hobbled over to me and sat on a seat. He looked as if he had just run a marathon.

I handed him my beer and grabbed another one. "What happened to you?" I said, calmly.

Rufus lifted the beer to his mouth and sculled it. He crushed it up and asked for another.

I went to the fridge and retrieved a six pack of beer. I sat it on the table in front of him. Rufus reached out and grabbed another. He cracked it open and sipped it. "She's gone," he muttered.

I intriguingly sipped my beer. "You are talking about Bella, right?" I replied. "What do you mean by gone?"

Rufus started to sob.

I placed my beer down on the table in disbelief. "No..." I said. "You can't mean it..."

"Yes, she ditched me!" Rufus shouted.

"Oh..." I muttered, grateful that she wasn't dead. "What happened?"

Rufus started to cry. "I thought she loved me!" he shrieked. "Instead, she was just using me!"

"Using you how?" I replied.

"We went out to go shopping for some tampons or maxi-pads," Rufus said. "Whatever it is that women get for their vagina. She advised that I go in and get some. Since I thought we were dating, I did what she asked."

"Ha-ha," I laughed. "How would you know what size to get her?"

Rufus frowned. "When I got back out," he sobbed. "She was pointing a pistol at me. She told me that I was the ugliest person in the world and that she'd rather die than live another moment with me."

I raised my eyebrows in surprise. That had to be one of the harshest things a person could ever say. Rufus may have been profoundly ugly, but to call him the worst person in the world was just plain cruel.

Rufus cracked open another beer. "She held the gun to my head," he muttered. "She asked for the maxi-pads. I tossed them to her and she drove off..."

I laid back in my seat and stared at the ceiling. Rufus's story was amusing. I found it funny that Bella could miss with a shotgun at point blank range, but wind up scaring Rufus off with a pistol. I also found it funny how Nick was actually correct with his joking assumption the night before. Bella really was on her period.

As bad as it was, Rufus's story made me feel good. It turns out that I wasn't in love with Bella at all. I was just jealous of Rufus. "Where do you think she's off to?" I questioned.

Rufus ran out of the room crying loudly. I smiled and drank my beer. *Breakups are tough,* I thought to myself. *But it's true. Bella over the last ten days had been kidnapped, forced to make herself unbearable, knocked unconscious twice and molested in a shower. I'm surprised she didn't kill Rufus, let alone the rest of us... For such a vicious monster, it was nice of her to leave us in one piece.*

CHAPTER 20:
Conspiracy

Breaking the news to the others about Bella's departure was one of the easiest consultations ever. Apart from Rufus, everyone was thrilled that she had left. We didn't care that she'd stolen our supplies. We could plunder the equivalent in five minutes. We were just happy that she was gone. Our only regret was that none of us got the privilege to have sex with her. After my announcement, Nick poured us each a cup of vodka and we drank to our hearts' content. That was the last thing I remember.

For being so drunk, we awoke the next day perfectly fine. We found out why, though. Nick explained that he had spiked our drinks with antibiotics. Apparently, the combination of alcohol and antibiotics work against each other. The end result is that a person can get intoxicated from a single drink. It didn't pose any concern to me. I actually found it quite amusing. Jake, on the other hand, did not.

Jake shoved Nick in the chest. "Why did you spike my drink?!" he shouted.

"Stop your bitching," Nick replied, irately. "You aren't hung-over."

Jake repeatedly tapped his foot on the ground, contemplating what he should say. He reminded me of a parent about to punish their child.

Nick teasingly patted Jake on the head and walked out of the house. Nick was off to go on a supply run with Eli and Rufus. With them out of the house, it left Jake and me alone together.

Over the past few days, Jake had been really eager to tell me something. Though, he said he would only do it when it was safe. I didn't quite understand what he meant. But now, with only him and myself in the house, he was ready to tell me.

I made a coffee and sat at the dining room table. Jake sat down opposite me, pulled a crinkled piece of paper out of his pocket and placed it on the table. From the looks of the paper, it was the same piece he'd used to record our conversation with Nick about Psyriviox.

"What is this?" I questioned.

Jake gave me a very stern look. "Promise me you won't tell anyone."

"What?" I replied. "What are you talking about?"

"Just promise..."

I rolled my eyes. "Cross my heart and hope to die..."

Jake sternly looked at me. "You better be," he said. "Anyways, here it goes..." Jake pointed at Nick's name on the paper. "Nick, formally known as Nicholai Richton, I am certain... has been lying to us..."

"Okay?" I uncaringly replied.

"Hear me out," Jake continued. "From what he told us, it seemed that Psyriviox was 'no more' than an unknown drug that was being traded between Russia and America. Doesn't that sound a little bit odd?"

"Well... Kind of..." I replied. "What's your point?"

"My point is..." Jake said. "Is that it was more than that. Let's start from: 'hey... I don't know...' the part where America and Russia suddenly become allies and casually share the most dangerous substance on the planet..."

I took a sip of coffee. "Well, if you put it that way, it sounds worse," I replied. "But anyway, keep going."

Jake turned over the page. I stared at it in shock. The entire sheet was covered in tiny words and connecting arrows. Jake moved his finger across the paper until it was sitting on top of a name.

"Igor..." Jake said. "It's a recurring name throughout these documents."

"So..." I replied. "What does that have to do with anything?"

Jake slid his finger along an arrow and stopped at another name. "Ivan Alkaev, formally known as Doctor Alkaev, owned a pharmaceutical franchise in America," Jake said. "Do you know which company I am talking about?"

"Of course, I do," I replied. "I always bought Panadol from Paramaxima. It's a well-known fact that Alkaev owned it."

"But that is where you are wrong," Jake said. "Ivan actually shared the company Paramaxima with his colleague Igor. Apparently, they were the leading two facilitators of the entire industry."

"Did this Igor have a last name?" I asked.

"Nope," Jake replied. "If he does, it never gets a mention. Igor is a doctor, though."

It seemed very peculiar that Igor did not have a last name. "Hmm..." I muttered.

Jake stared at me. "Okay, so you understand what I just told you?" he questioned.

"Yeah." I replied. "Doctor Ivan and Igor owned the company 'Paramaxima' in America."

Jake nodded. "Correct," he said. "But calling them 'doctors' seems a bit degrading..."

I raised my eyebrows in disbelief. I found it impossible for the term doctor to be seen as degrading.

"From what I've read," Jake continued. "Igor and Ivan were extremely intelligent people. A step above genius. You and I would be as brainy as a two-year old in comparison to them. Everything they did, they did for a reason..."

"Ha-ha," I laughed. "Nick mentioned that Ivan died. That's not smart."

"Very funny..." Jake said. "Now can you please shut up?"

I smiled at him and sealed my lips.

Jake cracked his fingers and flipped the paper back over. "From what Nick told us, I don't think the drug appeared in a small town near Moscow. I think Igor and Ivan created it. You may think this sounds crazy... but hear me out."

My smile faded and I motioned him to continue his explanation.

"From my research, both Igor and Ivan were terminally ill with cancer. Both of them wouldn't have wanted to die and both being as powerful as they are, they would have done anything to prevent it. Being the owners of the Paramaxima franchise, I think that they constructed a drug that would stop cell mutation. I think that they created 'Psyriviox'."

I squinted at Jake, confused.

"With the creation of a new substance," Jake said. "Testing is needed. And what a better way to do it, than round up the homeless and poor to use as test subjects. Nick said that 'drug addicts were the first to use the drug', I think that the test subjects were turned into drug addicts."

I took the final sip of my coffee. The cold dregs were intensely sweet. I cringed at the taste. "Go on..." I said.

"Nick is correct about one thing," Jake said. "The Psyriviox subjects did all die a most brutal death. Igor and Ivan would have quickly discerned this and known that they were running out of time. Without a stable substance, Psyriviox was of no use. Cancer was winning... they needed more medical researchers. As you know, Nick's parents, the Richtons, were family with Ivan Alkeav and they were the first to join the search for the cure for cancer. However, it wasn't enough. Weeks passed by and they were making zero progress. Eventually, Igor and Ivan figured out that without additional skilled doctors, they would die before altering Psyriviox into a cure for cancer. And so as much as they didn't want to collaborate with us Americans, the Coopers were asked to join the search."

I rubbed my chin. "This doesn't sound that bad," I replied. "Where are you leading with this?"

Jake quickly turned the paper back over. "The Cooper medical team were recognized as having some of the finest high-technology equipment around the world. Within a couple days they managed to produce Psyriviox Z15. A drug that through testing on monkeys could cure cancer.

"At the same time in Russia, Doctor Igor and Ivan were overrun with cancer. They were surviving on oxygen tanks and an excessive number of medical conduits. With the possibility of dying at any second, they needed the drug right away. And as the Richtons were good partners with the Coopers, the Coopers were obliged to hand it over. Which, according to my research, they evidently did."

"Hmm..." I nodded. "Wouldn't handing the Psyriviox Z15 over to the Russians cause a lot of controversy with the media and general public? I mean... it was the cure to cancer, for Christ's sake."

"Yep," Jake replied. "That's why it was all done in secret."

I shook my head. "Fucking secrets..." I muttered. "They always lead to nothing good."

Jake looked at me puzzled. "Anyhow..." he continued. "Ivan and Igor were in dire need of Psyriviox Z15. They were given the precise 0.05 ml amount to use. I'm unsure how it happened, but Ivan was accidentally injected with more than one drop. Much more..."

I picked up the piece of paper and began to read it. "How much?" I questioned.

Jake snatched it back out of my hands. "More than five times the recommended dosage," he replied.

"God damn..." I muttered. "He sounds like Alpha Z15."

Jake looked at me, grimly.

It took me a moment to understand the meaning of his expression. "Wait, no!" I shockingly replied. "So, you are telling me that Doctor 'Ivan Alkaev' was Alpha Z15?"

Jake nodded. "Yep," he answered. "Igor was undoubtedly left to watch his medical partner and one true friend suffer a fate worse than death. Watching his friend become a tormented monster would have been unlike anything he had ever witnessed."

"What happened next?" I egged.

"I don't know," Jake answered. "But I wouldn't be telling you this, unless I was ninety-nine percent sure that I'm correct."

I observed how intricate and detailed his paper was. "Okay, do you have anything else?" I asked.

Jake walked into his room and returned with an old dusty journal. On the front cover it said "Ivan Alkaev." "I translated this over the past week," he said. He opened the journal and began reading from it.

"Igor had a very hard life. When he was nine years old, his parents were killed by American military during a reconnaissance mission. After this tragic event, Igor was sent to an isolated orphanage in the slums of Moscow. In the time he spent at this place, he was mistreated and bullied by his peers. Not only this, but the man who the orphanage was a twisted individual. Apparently, he got a thrill out of sexually abusing and torturing the children. When Igor cried and writhed in pain, the man would laugh and claim 'that Igor was only alive for his pleasure.'

The orphanage was worse than a jail. Food was difficult to come by and often the orphans would have to beg or steal to survive. Whether it be malnutrition or hypothermia, many deaths occurred at the orphanage. Thirty percent of all the children that stayed at the place, after two years, either died or went missing. Yet, no matter how depraved it was, not a single person ever did anything about it.

At the age of twelve, Igor grew fond of experimentation. Having survived for so long, he was now older than the other children. With his higher intelligence and age, Igor was able to persuade the younger children to conform to his experiments. Even from a young age, Igor was destined to become a doctor.

Inserting objects under his peers' skin, or testing medication on them, Igor managed to kill a few of his subjects. Apart from this, the sexual abuse the children received seemed to be a major part of his experimentation, threatening and forcing his peers to take his place. Igor observed and devised a plan of revenge.

When Igor reached the age of 14, he had begun to mature. The man who ran the orphanage discovered this and knew that it was time for Igor's expiry. However, fortunately Igor knew the same for the man.

One night while the children were asleep, Igor dosed the man's alcoholic beverage with a synthetic neuromuscular substance. The substance that Igor had created from various medications enhanced pain receptors and caused paralysis. Through experimentation, Igor ensured that for a man weighing a couple of hundred pounds, the drug would last for four hours.

Close to a week later, the man was found by police. From the description of the body, the man had received lacerations of the eyes, a razor wire inserted up the urethra, removal of fingernails, testicles and tongue, a severely ripped anal cavity, a punctured voice box and a sharp rod implanted into his vertebrae to accomplish complete paralysis. The doctors were shocked to see how the man was still alive.

Water and food had been inoculated through tubes protruding from the man's chest. Ten liters of specific type A blood had been injected through delicate syringes to ensure the man's blood level remained stable.

After the doctors carefully extracted each instrument, they attempted to interrogate the man. Unable to communicate or move, the man was unable to provide any information. Funnily enough, instead of killing the crippled pedophile and putting him out of his misery, he was sent to a hospital where he would live out the rest of his life in pain.

The doctors also interrogated the children. All the children apparently all feared and admired Igor. They were grateful for what he had done to the pedophile. And they did not speak a word.

From here, Igor went into the drug business. He moved out on the streets where he illegally produced and sold drugs. Known as the D-Low of Moscow, Igor stayed in this business for ten years. He earned a lot of money working his way to the top. However, it was only until having a breakthrough with a new depressant was he able to convert his illegal business into a legitimate legal company. He went from a drug lord into owning a drug empire.

End of Sins.

People don't know this much about my close friend Igor. To all of his peers, he is a sincerely nice guy. He told me to write about his sinful past when his cancer became debilitating.

Unluckily, just a few days ago I discovered that I have got cancer as well... I hope that if anyone reads this journal, they still respect and think kindly of Igor. He may have done some disgusting things in his life, but he strived to the top and turned out to be a very nice and caring human being. Please don't regard this journal as Igor's life. He has completed amazing things in this wonderful world. I hope that one day people can comprehend the greatness of Igor's accomplishments and his rewarding vision to change the world. Signed: Doctor Ivan Alkaev."

Jake sat the book on the table and inquisitively looked at me.

I rubbed my eyes. It was a lot to take in for a small read. "Well..." I muttered. "What does this story have to do with anything?"

Jake squinted at me as if I was stupid. "Can't you see?" Jake said. "The death of Igor's parents, the fucked-up childhood, the vision to change the world. All of these things lead to one outcome. They lead to an angry and violent individual. And if a person like this gets power... they are one step away from becoming a terrorist... All they need is something to push them over the edge..."

I slammed my hand against the table. "A terrorist!" I laughed. "Didn't you hear what Ivan said? He said Igor was a good person!"

"Ivan is dead!" Jake shouted. "And it was America's fault!" Jake stood up and began pacing back and forth. "Think about it, Tyler!" he screamed. "Igor became a sick, sadistic human when his parents died! Think about what he did when his only true friend Ivan died!"

I shook my head. "Igor was dying," I muttered. "He wouldn't have been able to do anything…"

"Oh really!" Jake replied. "So, tell me… A man who now had full control over a multi-national, billion-dollar drug empire, as well as possessing the most unstable deadly drug in the world, had zero potential for terrorism…"

I stared at Jake in astonishment. "No, you can't mean it," I answered.

"Yep!" Jake shouted. "It was American military that killed Igor's parents…! It was American doctors that supplied the Psyriviox Z15 that killed Ivan…! It was America that consequently destroyed Russia!"

I couldn't believe what I was hearing and that it was actually making sense.

Jake tossed the paper at my face. "How do you think Psyriviox spread so easily throughout America?!" he screamed. "Igor distributed Psyriviox through Paramaxima! Igor was the person who gave the orders for bio-warfare!"

I was unable to say anything. I was stunned by the entire concept of bio-warfare. Eventually, I was only wondering one thing. "Where did you get this information?" I asked.

Jake grabbed the journal and piece of paper and threw them back in his room. He then got a glass of water and sat back down. "Do you wonder why that monkey didn't die the other day?" he questioned. "Do you wonder why Eli's parents actually visited Golden Willow Resort?"

"Yeah," I answered, intriguingly. "I was going to ask you if you knew anything about that?"

Jake sculled the cup of water and slammed it on the table. "I know pretty much everything about it," he replied, wiping the residue off his lips. "I found a research laboratory near the entrance of the resort. The monkeys were the Psyriviox Z15 test subjects that Nick told us about."

"Oh…" I murmured. "And I'm guessing that's where you found Ivan Alkaev's journal."

"Correct," Jake nodded. "I found a lot of stuff. In fact, there have only been two things that I've failed to find. One, actual Psyriviox itself. And two, any confirmation of Igor's death…"

I rubbed my chin. "Fair enough," I replied. "I have just got one last question. Why would Nick lie to us about all this?"

Jake tightened his mouth. "This is why I wanted to tell you alone," he whispered. "Igor needed assistance to distribute the Psyriviox through Paramaxima. He needed people that had close contact with American personnel. He needed the Richtons."

I knew exactly where Jake was leading with this conversation. I put my hand up to halt him. "Nope, this is going too far," I replied. "I know you dislike Nick… but this is over the top… Jake, you have got a grudge that you have to let go…"

Jake ignored me. "With the death of their beloved Uncle Ivan, Nick's parents would have been more than happy to follow through with Igor's wishes."

"Stop now," I replied. "You will start something within the group that I know will end badly."

Jake shrugged at me. "We've established from how Nick speaks that he hates Americans. From my tracking over the last few months, he keeps returning to the hospital. I have even overheard him communicating with someone else."

My eyes widened in shock. I finally understood why Jake was not upset about his missing parents. Jake had set all his attention on Nick. "So that is what you have been doing over the past few months!" I screamed. "Sneaking around and spying on Nick!"

Jake overlooked my astonishment. "Nick has been lying to us for a reason..." he seamlessly replied. "I fear that he is using us somehow..."

I could feel my face growing hot. All I wanted was for Jake to stop speaking.

"Nick drugged us last night..." he whispered. "Who's to say he won't do it again..."

I shot up out of my seat. "Shut the fuck up!" I shrieked. "I never want to hear about this stupid conspiracy ever again!" I covered my ears and walked away.

Chapter 21:
Downpour

lthough I walked away from Jake, his conspiracy theory lingered in my mind. It was fortunate though that it did not disrupt my daily life.

Over the following three weeks, zombie numbers noticeably increased around the house. The trench became crowded with zombies. Often it required clearing three times a day, as if left unchecked, the zombies would climb up one another and escape from the trench. Ultimately, the electric fence became the only obstacle keeping the zombies out.

It was a stinking hot day and I was clearing the trench. The humidity was the equivalent of that of a tropical jungle. My sweat was unable to evaporate, and I felt like I was covered in hot oil. I poured gasoline over the zombies and tossed a match into the trench. They alit like tinder, crumbling into ashes and bones in mere seconds. With the trench cleared for the second time of the day, I walked inside, grabbed a cool glass of water and sat down in the living room.

Jake walked into the living room and sat down beside me. "Urgh..." he moaned. "It's humid days like these that create thunderstorms."

I closed my eyes and fantasized about how good rain would feel. "There is not a single cloud in the sky," I sighed. "But by god, I hope you are right."

Jake got up and turned the ceiling fan to max speed, closed the curtains and laid down on a bean bag in front of me. "Did you clear the trench?" he asked.

I rested my head against the pillow. "Yep," I replied. "I will do it again in three hours. Just make sure you wake me up." I closed my eyes and went to sleep.

I was awoken by a sound louder than a gun shot. I opened my eyes and wildly looked around. The ceiling fan was no longer spinning a loud pattering on the roof could be heard. In curiosity, I stood up and pulled back the curtain. Outside, a humungous, dark cloud covered the sky. Rain was falling by bucket loads to the ground and howling winds were violently swaying the electric fence back and forth. Jake had predicted a thunderstorm; however, he had not predicted a hurricane.

A crack of lightning split through the sky, allowing me to take in the full extent of the situation outside. Through the pouring rain, Jake, Eli, Rufus and Nick were rushing around the house forcing huge wooden poles against the fence to stop it from falling. Rows of dead faces, as far as the eye could see, were standing behind the fence. Arms outstretched and clawing mid-air, the zombies were trying to get into our Haven. The lightning disappeared, and I was left alone amidst the darkness of the room. A rolling boom echoed through the air, quaking the house. I realized that thunder was the sound that had awoken me.

I raced to the front door and flicked on the porch light. The light beamed over the zombies. Their pale white eyes stared back at me. They began to relentlessly shake the fence. The light was making them agitated.

Eli burst through the front door. "Turn it off!" he shouted.

I immediately flicked the light off. "Sorry!" I replied. "I'll come help you in a second. I just need to get clothed."

Eli pulled me outside. "Not enough time!" he stressed.

I tried to break free, but his grip was too strong. He dragged me over to a stack of wooden poles. It was difficult to understand him through the pattering of heavy rain. He had to yell at the top of his voice just for me to hear. "Place the poles at any weak points in the fence!" he shrieked.

Being unclothed and drenched in water, unlike the temperature throughout the day, instead of stinking hot, I was now freezing cold.

I picked up a wooden pole and jogged around the fence. I was circling around the back of the house when I noticed a failing in the fence. A large group of zombies were weighing down a section, almost to the point of collapse. I slammed the pole into the muddy ground and positioned it to a forty-five-degree angle against the fence. The pole wobbled back and forth under the weight of the zombies. It was holding up the fence, but I could see that without another, it wasn't going to hold for long...

I sprinted back into the front yard to grab another pole. When I got there, I was alarmed to see that there were no poles left. Everyone came sprinting into the front yard with distressed expressions. "We need more!" Eli shrieked. "The fence won't hold!"

Cracks of lightning lit up the sky. The rain and the howling winds grew more intense. "We have got to go inside!" Jake shouted. "Get geared up and find any object that you can use to secure the fence!"

We dashed inside and equipped our armor. With my body sopping wet and clothed in leather, I felt very uncomfortable.

I dragged the living room couch out into the backyard and placed it vertically against the weak spot on the fence. The others tossed random bits of furniture around the fence in hopes that it would hold. The living room table was a piece that was used. I was disappointed to see the table outside in the rain as it was a one-of-a-kind piece of furniture that had occupied my house before I was born. It was my mother's prized possession. I sighed and ran back in the house.

When I got inside, apart from the fridge and a few heavy cabinets, the house had been stripped bare. I looked around in disbelief for I'd never seen a faster renovation in my life.

Rufus dashed past me, accidentally clipping my ankle with a long metal pole which he was dragging behind him.

I grabbed my ankle in pain. "For fuck's sake!" I shouted. "Watch where you're going!"

Rufus ignored me and ran outside. He dragged the pole up to the front gate and shoved it into the ground. Standing tall, the pole was close to fifteen-foot high. I had no idea where Rufus retrieved the pole, nor why he'd stationed it upright. Perpendicular, it added no strength to the fence whatsoever. I was about to walk outside and abuse him when suddenly Jake ran inside. "They have broken through!" he shouted. "The far-right side, I... I couldn't hold them..."

The pain in my ankle was excruciating and it made me furious. I picked up a light machine gun and loaded it with a box of ammunition. "These zombies better be excited!" I screamed. "Because they are going to get a once-in-a-life-time thrill!" I clocked the gun and hobbled outside.

Eli, Nick and Rufus came running past me, sopping wet with zombies tailing behind them. I gripped the gun tightly and opened fire. The heavy bullets exploded out of the barrel. The gun bounced up and down in my arms. It was difficult to aim, but it didn't matter. The bullets tore apart the zombies like no other weapon I had ever used. They shredded through the dead flesh like a hot knife through butter. It was immensely satisfying to watch.

I kept firing and moving forward. I aimed at the fallen piece of fence and blasted at the zombies trying to get through. I had it completely secured. Everything was going fine... until I ran out of bullets...

I pressed the trigger; the gun clicked.

"Shit!" I screamed. I tossed the gun on the ground and started hobbling away. The zombies charged over the fallen fence after me. At the speed that I was moving, they were catching me. I could hear their groans growing louder. The front door was only a few meters away, but it wasn't close enough...

Just when I thought I was done for, a tremendous frenzy of gunfire rained down from the roof. The ear-splitting noise sounded like a hundred fingernails scraping against a chalk board. I looked up to see Nick relentlessly firing the min-igun. Eli was standing beside Nick, feeding a long belt of bullets into the behemoth-sized weapon. The zombies that were following me were instantly ripped in half by a torrent of high-caliber bullets.

I staggered inside and sat down on the ground. The pain in my ankle was still noticeable, but it had subsided. Jake and Rufus each grabbed an assault rifle and walked outside. I took a few deep breaths and crawled over to the weapon stockpile. I searched for another light machine gun. I had only just begun my search when both Jake and Rufus ran back inside. They slammed the front door behind them.

Both of them were petrified and covered in mud. They looked as if they had gazed at Medusa's eyes.

"What are you doing?!" I shouted.

Completely ignoring me, Jake proceeded to shut all the windows around the house while Rufus stuffed his pockets with ammunition.

"What's going on?!" I shouted.

"There is more than one breakthrough," Rufus replied. "The house is completely surrounded by zombies."

A drumming noise resonated through the house's exterior walls. Zombies were trying to bash their way inside.

"Fuck me," I said. "What do we do if they break in?"

Rufus shrugged. "Let's just hope they don't..." he replied.

I frantically picked up a submachine gun and filled my pockets with ammunition. Jake strolled out of my room and sat down next to the weapon stockpile. He raised his hand, signaling me to stop. "Tyler, don't worry about the ammunition," he said. "If the zombies get inside, we are not winning..."

I stopped what I was doing. "What about Eli and Nick? They still have a vast amount of ammunition for that minigun... Maybe they could kill them all..."

"Unlikely," Jake replied. "The minigun cannot be angled to reach the zombies close to the house."

Rufus continued stuffing his pockets with ammunition. "Still, it is better to be prepared," he said.

Just as he said it, a zombie's arm busted through the wall. Its long rotten fingers swiped mid-air. The skin on its wrist fell to the ground as it wildly reached out for us. I aimed my gun at where I assumed its head to be through the other side of the wall and fired a single shot. The clawing hand went limp. "They are not getting in," I muttered.

Hundreds of zombie hands suddenly busted through the windows, covering the floor with translucent shards of glass. I got up and stretched my neck. "Arrhhhhh!" I screamed, furiously. I stumbled over to a window and mercilessly fired at the zombies. The bullets penetrated through their skulls as if they were no tougher than cardboard. They collapsed one after another, ceaselessly replacing each other in what felt like an infinite loop.

I stopped and reloaded. The sound of the minigun could no longer be heard. I looked around to see Jake and Rufus firing at zombies through different windows. Blood was splattered on their faces and a rain of empty shells covered the floor. I turned back and stared out my window. The zombies were roaring loudly. *If I was going to die,* I thought to myself. *This is how I'd want to go.* I aimed my gun at the zombies and continued firing.

The standoff lasted for another ten minutes. Blocking three windows was hard enough, let alone all of them. The house started to fail under the inexorable force of the zombies. The dead were prevailing and I came to the fated conclusion that this was how we were going to die. A zombie broke through the wall. We stumbled towards each other, a resentful tear dripping down my face. In my mind, the zombie inside my house represented our defeat…

It opened its mouth and lunged at me. I took a step forward and smashed an empty stick of ammunition into its eye socket. It faltered backwards. I clenched my fist and forcefully punched the ammunition stick into its skull. Blood gushed out of the eye socket and the zombie fell backwards onto the ground. There it lay motionless in a pool of its own blood.

With running eyes, I looked up to see countless more zombies rushing towards us. Their faces were cold and apathetic. As they overpowered Jake, holding him against the ground, his terrified shrieks did not scare me, for my thoughts at that fatal moment were of the zombies. Neither fully alive nor dead, they were an abomination to death. Innocence and empathy meant nothing to them. There were no sensors in their brain to warn them of right and wrong. All they could do was follow their instincts and subconsciously respond to differing stimuli. They were mindless beings… and yet they were winning. I closed my eyes, outstretched my arms and accepted the bitter end… *This is it*, I told myself.

The zombies hurled me onto my back. A surge rippled over me and everything went silent. A bright white light was all that I could see. *Was dying this easy?* I thought to myself. *Could it be this peaceful?*

I was hoping to awaken to the warmth of my mother. I was hoping she'd be hugging me tightly in her arms. However, some wishes are not meant to come true.

I opened my eyes to see Jake lying on top of me. He had a joyous expression stretched across his face. His mouth was moving, but I couldn't understand what he was saying. The ringing in my ears was too loud. I remained on the ground, disappointed.

Eventually, I was lifted to my feet by Eli. He propped my head up so that I was looking out the window. Outside, every zombie was dead. Some of the grass was charred black and smoke was drifting upwards from the tall pole that Rufus had placed beside the fence. I knew that gasoline was not the cause of scorch marks as flames could not exist in this downpour. I didn't want to believe it, but I had to. A bolt of lightning had struck the pole.

I gazed at the hundreds of smoking zombie carcasses scattered across the front lawn. "How is it even possible?" I muttered.

The ringing stopped and my hearing returned. Jake tapped me on the back. "Yo, Tyler," he said. "It's over."

I did not reply. I wiped water off my head and dazedly turned around. To my surprise, the house was in a better condition than what I had expected. Doors were unhinged and glass was everywhere. However, the roof was intact and only one wall was in ruin. A flicker of hope sparked inside of me. I knew that the house could be restored.

One last zombie was still squirming around on the ground. Eli bent down and shoved a machete deep into its face. "The storm is over!" he cheered.

Technically speaking, the hurricane lasted for another eight hours. However, as we were no longer in any imminent danger, all of us happily rejoiced.

The hurricane kept us in a lively mood. We sat in my bedroom and discussed the events that led to this catastrophe of a night.

I was still confused to why I was never awoken by anyone before the storm. "Why didn't you guys wake me up?" I questioned.

Jake raised his arm. "That was my bad," he replied. "I accidentally fell asleep. I only woke up a couple of minutes before you."

"Hmm..." I said, inquisitively. "Then why didn't anyone else wake me up?"

"Are you kidding?" Eli replied. "Rufus, Nick and I were at the pool all day. We only got home when the storm began. With the amount of zombies you and Jake left in the trench, we were lucky enough just to get through the gate..."

I tapped my fingers on the ground. I was trying to understand the occurrences that led to this near death of a night.

I looked at Eli. "Exactly how bad was it when you got here?" I questioned.

"Well, considering you and Jake came to help us only five minutes after we got inside. It was pretty bad!" Eli answered. "Plus, little dick over here..." he said pointing at Nick, "...stated that there was no time to go inside and that 'we' needed to reinforce the fence."

Jake shook his head in dismay. "You are a fucking idiot, Nick," he scolded.

Nick abruptly stood up and punched Jake in the face. Jake's nose cracked sideways. Gloopy dark red blood poured out of each nostril. It oozed downwards, drenching his chin and neck.

"What the hell?!" I shrieked.

Nick gripped Jake's throat and raised him into the air. "It was this little rat who fell asleep!" he shouted. "He was the one who forgot to wake Tyler up! It's his fault that all of us nearly died!"

Jake spat on Nick's face. A thick glob of bloody mucus dribbled down Nick's forehead. Nick gritted his teeth, his eyes burning with hatred. Rufus and Eli both jumped on Nick and pinned him against the ground. Nick thrashed and struggled. He was furious and he wanted to tear Jake apart.

With Nick unable to move, Jake ran up and kicked him in the ribs. It had to be one of the biggest dog shots I had ever seen. I rushed over and tackled Jake onto his back. As I tried to pin him against the ground he spat on my face. It made me furious. I repeatedly punched him in the nose. Blood splattered everywhere. Eventually, I was tackled off and punched in the testicles. It felt like I had been hit with a sledgehammer.

I writhed around in pain. With watery eyes, I watched Eli march around and punch everyone else in the testicles. Rufus, who hadn't even done anything wrong still copped a solid one. By the end, all of us except Eli were rolling around on the ground, squealing in agony.

"You stupid dickheads," Eli muttered. "You are all packed with so much energy that you decide to take it out on each other."

I gripped my tender nuts, knowing that he was correct.

Eli pointed at Jake. Blood was gushing out of his nose. "Tyler, that is mainly your mess," he said. "As I know Nick won't fix it, now you have to."

I rolled over to Jake. I stared at his nose, both surprised and disappointed. Jake's nose didn't look any different from when Nick broke it. My punches literally did nothing. I lowered my head and whispered in Jake's ear. "If you fucking spit on me again, I'll cut off your nose."

I pinched Jake's nose and snapped it back into place. Jake shrieked in pain. I wiped the spit off my cheek and flicked it onto his face.

Satisfied with my act of vengeance, I stood up and stretched. My testicles ached, but it was now bearable. I hobbled over to Eli and sat down beside him. "I guess we need more ammunition for the minigun," I laughed.

Eli looked at me confused. "More ammunition?" he replied. "We still have well over five thousand bullets."

"Wait... what?" I questioned. "Why did you guys stop firing?"

Nick sat up. "The gun jammed..." he replied.

Jake tilted his head forward and pinched the top of his nose to clog the bleeding. "And what about the electric fence?" he muttered. "Did that jam as well?"

Eli rolled his eyes. "Oh... shut up, Jake," he groaned. "Lately, you have been extremely annoying."

Jake took a deep breath. His adrenaline had subsided, and he clearly did not want to get punched again. "I'm sorry, Nick," he mumbled.

Nick smirked. It was obvious that he enjoyed Jake's forgiveness.

Rufus softly caressed his testicles. "So, what do we do now?" he asked. "The house is a wreck."

Apart from myself, everybody looked dumbfounded. I could tell by their expressions that they were contemplating whether we should repair or abandon our Haven. For me, there was only one option. I wanted to remain here. It was my home... I felt content knowing that my mother lay close... I couldn't just let all that I love rot away to nothing... I needed something to live for. I needed my house to remain a Haven...

I stood up. "Guys..." I said. "This place... It is 'our' Haven..."

Everyone looked at me both confused and inspired.

I began to pace back and forth across the room. I pointed at Eli. "Before tonight... how many zombies had broken into this house?"

"None..." Eli replied.

I nodded and turned to Rufus. "You call this house a wreck..." I proclaimed. "It's the only thing that has kept us together..." I gestured my hand around the room. "Look at us," I said. "We are together... Still in the same house... It is not a wreck... and neither are we..."

Rufus lowered his head in shame.

I pointed at Nick. "You would be dead if it were not for this house," I declared.

Nick smirked at me as if I were telling a joke.

"You think I'm lying?" I said. "The only reason we were able to contact you was because we were installing solar panels on the roof. If we hadn't decided to construct this Haven, we would have never received your messages and you would have rotted away in the hospital."

Nick looked at Eli to check if I was telling the truth. Eli smiled. "It's true," he said.

I walked into the center of the room. "Why spend so much time on something great, then abandon it after its first defect? Why toss away a diamond only because it has a scratch? Why not just smooth it until it's flawless...?"

Everyone looked at each other determinedly. They understood my analogy.

I knew that my speech had swayed them to retain the house. I pointed at Jake who was still pinching his nose. "How long will this Haven take to repair?" I questioned.

Jake muttered something under his breath.

"What was that?"

"Close to a week," he replied.

I nodded, pleased with the approximation of time.

Nick rested on his back. "Get some sleep, little sheep," he groaned. "Tomorrow we have work to do..."

We agreed with Nick and slept in the bathroom together on the hard tile floor.

We awoke the following morning to a disgustingly stupendous sight. The sun light revealed the aftermath of the downpour. It was not a pretty sight. A carpet of corpses was layered in a hundred-foot radius around the house. The trenches were brimming with soft, blue decomposing bodies and dark red water. The zombies had demolished the electric fence to the ground. From what I saw, not one section was standing upright. Inside the house, most of the walls had been refurbished with skin, brain and blood. The sour smell of chunky vomit, combined with the eye-watering aroma of festering and rotten meat, singed the nostrils.

All of us smiled and shrugged. We knew that we'd survived through impossible odds.

If we were to remain living in this Haven, it would need some cleaning and repairing. Each of us established a specific job and straightaway went to work. I fetched a bulldozer and cleared the corpses. Eli drained the trench and removed the flesh. Nick replaced the fence with an upgraded Volte 4000 and unclogged the minigun. Jake sanitized the house and filled the walls with concrete, to ensure that no more zombies could ever break in. Rufus may have done very little, but he still did something useful. He repaired a few parts of the roof with a few sheets of stainless steel.

Altogether, I was very pleased with our exertion of work. After five days of hard labor, we not only restored our Haven, but we also improved it into a more secure shelter. We ensured that if an incident like the hurricane were to ever happen again, that we'd overcome it.

The only thing left to do was to renovate the house with new furniture. Lying in the mud, my adored dining room table was rotten and cracked. I tried to repair it, but it was of no use. The table could not be fixed. However, it could be transformed.

While everyone else was shopping for new furniture, I stayed at home and worked on the table. Using the non-damaged sections, I constructed a small foot stool. It was no work of art, nor was it very useful. It only served one purpose. It was a happy reminder of the table's treasured qualities.

We had finished our renovations for the day and were relaxing on the veranda when a low noise appeared. A distant clapping of hands. I shielded my eyes from the sun and stared out into the afternoon sky. On the horizon, a shaky black dot could be seen moving towards us. It was not a bird...

CHAPTER 22:
Visitors

I squinted my eyes, trying to get a closer look.

"Is that what I think it is?" I confounded.

Eli stared out into the horizon. "Wait... it can't be..." he mumbled.

The clapping sound grew louder. The shaky black dot moved closer and an outline became visible.

"It is!" I shouted. "It's a helicopter!"

Everyone leapt to their feet and wildly ran off in different directions. "Try to get their attention!" Jake screamed.

Rufus started performing star jumps on the lawn. Eli rushed past Rufus and fired a flare gun into the air. The flare sailed upwards, creating a fluorescent red stream through the sky.

I glanced at the helicopter to see that it hadn't moved any closer. As I was about to ask Eli to shoot another, Nick walked out the front door carrying a bulky rocket in his arms. It was streaked black and orange and judging by Nick's wobbly feet, it was also very heavy.

Eli opened his mouth, astonished. "Where did you get it!?" he excitedly questioned.

Nick laughed and positioned it upright in the center of the front lawn. He then drew a lighter from his pocket.

I realized what it was... I had no idea where Nick had gotten it from as it was the only firework that was illegal in all but one state of America. "No way!" I shouted. "How did you get your hands on the 'Dragon's Sneeze Firework'?!"

Nick ignored me and lit the long fuse. All of us retreated back to the veranda and waited for the colossal eruption.

"How big is it meant to be?" Jake questioned.

"Shhh...!" Eli hushed. "Just watch it."

The spark scorched up the fuse and disappeared inside the firework. I cupped my hands over my ears expecting a loud explosion. What happened next was unexpected...

It was delayed, but two fiery spinning wheels ascended out the top of the firework. I stared at the spinners in bewilderment. "Huh... Is that it?" I questioned.

Eli rubbed his chin. "I thought there was more..." he mumbled.

Just as he said it, the fiery spinning wheels gained speed. The increase in speed caused the wheels to spit fire all over the place. Even from where we were standing, we had to shield our faces from the heat.

All of us stared through the gaps between our fingers. "What's it doing?" I questioned.

"It's tickling the dragon's nose," Nick smirked.

"What!" I screamed.

Suddenly, a massive firework shot upwards. It soared high into the air and exploded with a loud "boom!"

A silver mushroom cloud filled our vision. It glittered like a vibrant nebula. A cluster of smaller fireworks shot out from the cloud and exploded. Crackles of yellow and red danced through the sky. The combination of the three colors was mesmerizing. If dragons were real, I thought to myself. I would have wanted its sneeze to look exactly like this...

For some reason, the intense colors did not dissipate. They rained downwards and covered our Haven in shimmering ashes. The ashes caused a few spot fires on the grass, but nothing major.

It had to be the most amazing firework I had ever seen. I had no idea why it was banned in every state of America. Apart from producing a few burnt patches and attracting zombies, it seemed harmless.

With the firework display over, I climbed up the ladder and stood on the roof. As I looked outwards, I could see that the helicopter was pitching forwards, heading straight towards us at a high speed. "Guys!'" I shrieked. "It noticed the firework!"

By the time I'd alerted the others, the helicopter had moved so fast that it was circling the house. Its rotating propeller created an uproar that made it impossible to hear anything else. My hair rippled back and forth in the gale-force winds that it was producing.

It circled for a minute before stopping and hovering over the trench. Up close, I could see that it was a camo-colored, heavily armored and weaponized military helicopter. Its black windscreen made it impossible to see inside the cockpit, thus I could not discern the pilot's intentions. I waved my arm in the air as a friendly gesture. Instead of acknowledging my actions, it started circling the house again.

At this point, I started to grow concerned for it had not yet indicated that it was friendly. On its third lap around the house Nick shot up the ladder onto the roof. "What are you doing?" I screamed.

Nick couldn't hear me over the cleaving sound of the helicopter's gyrating propeller. He frantically pointed at the helicopter with an extremely worried expression. "What are you trying to say?" I screamed.

The helicopter turned so that all of its weapons were facing Nick. Nick stopped and stared at it, a sinister look in his eyes. The helicopter hovered perfectly still. It was a showdown. I stood in front of Nick and waved my arms in the air to try and break the tense moment. Unfortunately, Nick used my intervention to act out his goal for being on the roof. He mounted the minigun and aimed it at the helicopter. "No!" I shrieked. I dove at him in an attempt to knock him off the minigun.

As my shoulder struck his side, he placed his hand under my legs and used my own momentum to heave me over the top of himself, sending me flying off the roof. I thumped my back hard against the ground. The wind got knocked out of my chest and I struggled to breathe.

I was lying on my back, trying to revitalize my lungs, when all of a sudden the front veranda exploded into smithereens. A thick, cloud of inferno swooped over me. I shielded my face. After a brief moment of intense heat, I removed my hands and inspected my body. My hair was singed, but my skin was unburnt.

The sound of the mini-gun cranked up. A flurry of bullets pelted into the helicopter. The bullets ricocheted off the armor plating creating a fountain of sparks. The helicopter aimed all four of its turrets at the house and unremittingly fired. I ducked my head and crawled around the side of the house.

I sat against the wall and took a few deep breaths. The helicopter fired a missile. It flew straight past my head and exploded in the backyard. Roses flew everywhere.

I got up and stumbled into the backyard. The rose garden was destroyed. A huge hole in the ground was all that was left. I seethed in anger.

In the distance another explosion could be heard. I stumbled back to the front yard to see the helicopter smoking from its tail and spiraling towards the ground. It crashed into a nearby street and an enormous ball of fire ascended into the sky.

Nick stopped firing the minigun and climbed off the roof. Eli came rushing out the front door holding an RPG over his shoulder. "Fucking destroy it!" he screamed.

He noticed that the helicopter was destroyed and he immediately placed the RPG on the ground. The noise had settled and all was serene. In the middle of the front yard, Rufus lay lifeless...

"No... no... no!" I wailed.

Eli dropped his RPG and bowed his head in honor. "We have lost a great guy and true friend today..." he sobbed. "Rufus will always be remembered..."

Rufus leapt to his feet. "Gotcha!" he laughed.

Eli looked confused and angry. "Rufus," he said. "You realize that when you 'actually' die, it will now be seen as a joke..."

Rufus shrugged. "Eh..." he replied. "If I'm not alive to witness my own joke, then why does it matter?"

Eli scratched his chin in thought. It was a good point and Eli didn't know how to respond. To avoid an embarrassing eerie silence, Eli changed the subject. "Let's go check out the helicopter," he said. "You know... see who was shooting at us...?"

Seeing as though we were going to do it regardless, we accepted Eli's request. All of us jumped in a separate car and drove towards the rising smoke. When we reached the helicopter it was situated in the middle of the road, engulfed in flames.

We waited for the fire to burn out and cautiously approached the wreckage. The helicopter's framework and cabin were the only sections not consumed by the fire. From the outside of the wreckage, a burnt, flaky corpse could be seen smoldering in the pilot seat. Infrared goggles were melted over its eyes. Judging from the corpse alone, it was a male, only a little older than ourselves.

I grimly bowed my head at the corpse and stepped into the cockpit. Even though we'd seen who the pilot was, I still wanted to inspect the cabin. The helicopter's cindering remains melted the soles of my shoes. I quickly walked inside the cabin, leaving a trail of bubbling rubber footprints behind.

Inside the cabin, hot embers painted the ground a glittery red. A cloud of black smog filled the room. The confined smoke polluted the air. I held my breath and stepped out of the cabin.

As I stood inside the cockpit, I noticed that Eli and Jake had their eyes fixated on something behind me. They were looking back inside the cabin.

I waved my hand in front of their eyes. "Nothing to see in there..." I laughed. "I just checked."

Without speaking, Eli grabbed me and turned me so that I was facing the cabin. "What is it?" I questioned. I squinted my eyes trying to spot something I'd missed.

The smoke ascended to the ceiling. It wavered back and forth and for a brief moment, exposed something dreadful. It may have only been a glimpse, but it was unforgettable...

The vivid image was similar to a family portrait. Two parents, a mother and father were seated together side by side gently holding hands. Clutched on to the father's leg was a small girl. And curled up snug and tight in the mother's arms, was an innocent, little baby.

Sadly, even though the family showed heart-warming affection, their stiff, charcoal black corpses and terrified gaping mouths, captured the true panic and horror of the moment before their inescapable deaths.

I glumly stepped out of the helicopter wreckage and sat down on the road. I thought about the death of the family and if it was my doing. *I sought the helicopter's attention... Does that mean I am partly responsible for the cause of the family's demise?* I asked myself.

It was a difficult concept to understand. *It was one thing to be a ruthless zombie slayer, but it was another thing to be a murderer... Especially of innocent people.* Eventually, my train of thought was disrupted by a series of loud shouts and shrieks. I shook my head and turned around to see Jake and Nick arguing with each other. Eli and Rufus were standing a few feet away, watching the dispute unfold.

I got up and walked over to Eli. "What are they arguing about this time?" I questioned.

Eli shrugged. "I think Jake is blaming Nick for the helicopter engaging on us," he said.

I nodded and listened to the argument. Jake pointed at Nick. "You stupid fuck!" he yelled. "Your firework blew up our veranda! How did you expect the helicopter to respond!? The pilot would have perceived it as an RPG!"

I had assumed that the explosion that blew up the veranda was one of the helicopter's missiles. *Wow... I thought. No wonder the Dragon Breath firework is illegal in all but one state of America.*

Nick ground his teeth in anger. "I saved your life" he berated. "The helicopter had already decided to engage on us before the firework exploded. Jake, you are as stupid as the family that died in the helicopter.

Jake clapped his hands. "Oh... bravo, Nick," he mocked. "Go ahead and ridicule the innocent family you just killed."

Nick angrily raised his arm. "I think your nose looks better squished against your head," he growled.

I could see where this argument was leading. *It was leading to Jake's nose getting more busted than what it already was.* I stepped in between them. "Whoa! Whoa! Whoa!" I shrieked. "This is no one's fault. Let's just talk about it at home."

Nick glared at Jake and slowly lowered his fist. "Keep that pesky, little twat away from me," he snarled. "A person with his spiteful attitude, does not belong in a world like this." Nick shoved me backwards and walked to his vehicle. Eli dashed after Nick, trying to calm him down. Rufus, who couldn't care less about any of it, shrugged and hopped in his car. "I'll see you guys back at home!" he cheered.

I waved off Rufus and he drove away. Eli and Nick spoke for a minute before they too left. Once they were out of sight, I turned to Jake and grimly shook my head. "Come on man..." I said. "Just let it go... If it weren't for Nick, we'd all be dead..."

Jake uncaringly brushed the wrinkles out of his shirt. "If it weren't for Nick," he muttered. "That family would still be alive."

"You are overthinking, Jake," I said. "Just let it go..."

Jake sarcastically smiled. "You think Nick was helping us?" he replied. "Nick intended on destroying the helicopter. He just had to be clever enough to make it look accidental."

"What?" I questioned.

"Nick knew the firework's power and capability," Jake replied. "He precisely exploded it in front of the helicopter as he knew that it would cause the helicopter to engage. Nick wasn't helping us. He was helping himself..."

I grinned, sardonically. "Honestly..." I laughed. "How could destroying a helicopter help Nick?"

Jake rubbed his chin. "He is hiding something," he replied.

"Like what?" I questioned.

"A secret that he is willing to kill and die for."

"What do you suspect it is?"

Jake stared at me. "To be perfectly truthful," he answered. "I suspect that Nick is still testing Psyriviox."

"Wait what!?" I replied. "Why would you suspect that!?"

"I think it's the reason why I haven't been able to recover any Psyriviox yet..." Jake professed. "Nick knows more about the drug than me and he knows where to find it..."

"Trust me," I replied. "If Nick got his hands on it, even with the scientific mind that he has got, he would not touch it... Psyriviox is just too dangerous for an amateur to play with. Plus, what would he be trying to do with it? Find a cure...?"

Jake sat on the ground and crossed his legs. "As you may or may not already know, Tyler. Nick has a very disturbed view of death. He does not care about others dying, yet he himself fears it. It is a distinct psychopathic interpretation..."

I thought about Nick. I remembered when Nick helped me dispose of Mr and Mrs Cooper's corpses. I remember Nick telling me that death was "worse than the bitter end to the degradation of life." And that he himself was "death's cheat." I sat down on the ground and clasped my hands over my head. It was difficult to believe but *Jake's understanding of Nick... was correct...*

"Nick's psychopathic nature means that he will do anything to create a cure for himself," Jake said. "He doesn't want any interferences with his work and it's the reason why he destroyed the helicopter today..."

"But even if he was trying to find a cure," I replied. "He doesn't have the skills required. He would never progress in finding a cure."

Jake shook his head. "That is what I tried to tell you before," he said. "When I explained to you about Igor and the suspicion towards bio-warfare. I was trying to tell you about this part in particular…"

"What part?" I questioned.

"I suspect Nick isn't working alone…" Jake solemnly answered.

"What do you mean?" I asked. "Who would be working with Nick? Eli and Rufus definitely wouldn't be."

"Yep… they definitely aren't," Jake replied. "It is someone who has been working with Nick before we even met him. A person who Nick never talks about."

"Who?" I replied.

"Igor…" Jake muttered.

I took a moment of silence. This conspiracy just kept becoming scarier. After a couple of seconds of looking at the burnt helicopter, I continued speaking to Jake. "But Igor would have died from his cancer," I replied. "Why would you think Nick is working with him?"

Jake shrugged. "I have previously explained to you that I have found no actual evidence of Igor dying. Plus, Nick has kept information hidden from us and he keeps sneaking out."

"That doesn't mean that Igor is alive, though. You need more evidence…"

Jake pulled a mobile out of his pocket. "Is this enough evidence?" He switched on the mobile and held it to my ear.

I listened. A deep, croaky utterance became clear. What it was saying was incomprehensible as the language was Russian. The voice was what I imagined the grim reaper to sound like. After it stopped, I warily handed the mobile back to Jake. "What was that?" I questioned.

"That mobile is Nick's," Jake replied. "And that voice you just listened to... It was Igor's. Look..." He held the phone up to show the name of the recording. In big capital letters read: IGOR.

"Okay," I said. "What does the recording have to do with anything, anyway?"

"The recording you just heard..." Jake replied. "Was captured on the same day that we rescued Nick..."

"Wait!" I said, baffled. "How do you know that?"

"I cross-referenced the date with Eli's phone," Jake replied. "The day that Nick contacted Eli on the roof was the same day that this message from Igor was recorded..."

I couldn't believe it. "Bullshit," I said. "Show me."

Jake held the mobile to my face. "Remember the date of the recording. And when we get home, I'll prove to you it was captured on the same day that we rescued Nick."

My heart started to race. Jake's sheer confidence was troubling me. "I doubt it will be the same..." I unconfidently replied. "But if it is, I guess... I will begin to consider your accusations..."

"Good, good," Jake smiled. "I'll meet you back home, then."

I mockingly sneered and turned away. I walked back to my car, hoping to god that he wasn't correct...

CHAPTER 23:
Investigation

Despite the car trip home being short, the journey itself was slow. Even though that Jake had told me a life-threatening and justified conspiracy about a fellow member of our group, I was still respectfully thinking about the cold, black, corpses of the loving family. My body was twitching and shivering. My mind couldn't withstand being responsible for the death of a family, as well as having to fear Nick. The stress from both of the situations was tearing my mind apart.

When I got home, Jake walked me to his room, and ensuring that we were alone, he quietly showed me the evidence. The first piece of evidence was Eli's mobile. Jake used it to show me the date of the conversation between Eli and "Little Dick Nick" on the night that we rescued Nick from Southport Hospital. Unfortunately for me, Jake's confidence was not a bluff. The date of the Russian recording was identical to the date that we rescued Nick.

Filled with concern, I wiped sweat off my forehead. "But how do you know the Russian recording was sent by Igor?" I asked.

Jake handed me a strange electronic device that I'd never seen before. It was equipped with a touch screen interface, a microphone and speaker. "This is a top of the line, military language translator," Jake replied. "Just use the touch screen to set the language from Russian to English and let the recording play into the microphone."

To prove that the device had not been tampered with, Jake made sure that I test the recording myself. When I finished assembling the device to the correct figurations, I played the recording into the microphone.

The voice that reverberated out of the speaker was deep and electronic. It spoke in listless English: *"Everyone is dead..."* it uttered. *"It is up to you, Nicholai, to complete the task... Find me more Psyriviox... Allow me to experiment... Be your father's son... and just like myself, be death's cheat..."*

I paused for a moment. There was one particular section in the recording which stuck out to me. Over the time that we'd lived together, I'd never told Jake about Nick's peculiar concept of Death's Cheat. The fact that the concept appeared in the recording proved that it was not fraudulent.

Jake studied my face. "I hope you understand what the message conveys," Jake said.

"What?" I replied.

Jake pressed Play on the translator. It began to repeat the same message. *"Everyone is dead...It is up to you, Nicholai, to complete the task..."* Jake stopped the recording.

"In these short sentences," Jake said. "Igor is asking Nick to follow his orders." Jake pressed the Play button on the translator and continued the message.

"Find me more Psyriviox... Allow me to experiment... Be your father's son, Nicholai..." Jake abruptly paused the recording again.

"Here, Igor requests Nick to collect Psyriviox so that Igor can continue to experiment... Furthermore, Igor also states that Nick's father obeyed his orders and that Nick should do the same." Jake looked at me to see whether or not I understood his explanation. I sternly nodded to show that I did. Jake pressed Play on the translator and finished off the message.

"*...and just like myself, be death's cheat...*"

Jake rubbed his nose. "Igor is a smart person," he said. "In those last few words, not only does he say that he 'himself' has cheated death. But he uses it to bargain with Nick."

"Bargain with Nick?" I questioned. "What do you mean?"

"It's simple," Jake replied. "Igor was a terminally ill stage four cancer patient. The only possible way he could have survived up to the date that he sent the recording is via the one-drop-a-week injection of the extremely unstable Psyriviox Z15."

My eyes lit up. I finally understood what Igor meant by the term Death's Cheat. "Oh..." I moaned. "He literally defied death."

"Yes," Jake said. "With Nick collecting Psyriviox and suitable test subjects 'like ourselves'." Jake pointed at himself and I. "Igor can survive and experiment."

"Wait..." I replied. "How do you know that Nick is actually collecting Psyriviox?"

Jake looked irritated by my question. "You don't remember much, Tyler," he said. "I did tell you before that even with my rigorous searching, I am yet to find any Psyriviox..."

"Oh, yeah," I mumbled. "I forgot..."

"But that isn't the main indication," Jake said. "I am sure that Nick is collecting Psyriviox due to one reason alone..."

"Which one?" I asked.

"The bargain," Jake replied. "If you think about it. Igor offered Nick the only thing that Nick would ever want... A way to cheat death."

"Are you linking this back in with Nick being a psychopath?" I questioned.

"Correct," Jake replied. "Nick knows that if Psyriviox were to be altered to have no negative side-effects and also to be administered correctly. It could potentially be a drug that could make him immortal..."

"Eh..." I replied. "Not immortal. Fire would still do the trick."

Jake rolled his eyes. "You know what I mean," he muttered.

"Yeah... don't worry," I replied. "I understand."

"Anyhow..." Jake continued speaking. "Immortality is the pinnacle of ambitions. A psychopath like Nick would do anything and everything to obtain such a thing..."

I stretched my neck. "Is there anything we can do about it?" I questioned. "Like couldn't we tell the others?"

"No," Jake replied. "Not yet, anyway. If we did right now, 'Eli being very close friends with Nick' and 'Rufus being an idiot', both would think it was a big joke. They would laugh at us and inform Nick what I said to them, consequently making Nick cover up his tracks to an extent that his doings would become untraceable. That or he would speed up the experimentation, thus putting us in greater danger of being drugged."

"Fair enough..." I replied.

"Only once I have a hundred percent solid proof that Nick is working with Igor will I explain to Eli and Rufus the situation," Jake said. "Then together, we can sort it out…"

I sadly moaned. It was bad enough that Jake's conspiracy was genuine. It was worse that I had to keep it a secret. "Why are you telling 'me' this…?" I asked.

Jake picked up the language translator and placed it back in the cupboard. "I am worried for your well-being…" he replied.

"My well-being?" I muttered. "You told me that Nick is dangerous… It has only made me more stressed…"

"I know," Jake replied. "But the fact that 'you now know' means that you are in less danger… Not only that, you think you are stressed…? Think of how I have been with all this knowledge to myself… Up until now… my anxiety has been unbearable…"

"Oh… I understand…" I groaned. "You needed to share your burden to make yourself feel better…"

Jake shook his head. "No," he replied. "It was the perfect time to share it. I saw how torn up you were over the death of that family. Don't deny it. You were blaming yourself…"

"What?" I questioned. "No, I wasn't…"

Jake smirked. "Tyler, I can read you like a book…" He laughed.

Jake was uncomfortably correct and I wasn't happy that he could so easily perceive my feelings and thoughts. "Whatever…" I murmured.

"Just think about it," he said. "Now that you share this burden, you can understand that the family's death had nothing to do with you. From the moment that the helicopter was spotted. Whether you like it or not, Nick would have got rid of it one way or another."

I wasn't sure if Jake was lying to me or not. "Are you certain?" I stammered.

Jake solemnly nodded. "The family's passing was not your fault," he replied.

I sat against the wall and thought about the charcoal corpses of the adoring family. The unforgettable image burned in my head like a searing brand.

I closed my eyes and iterated what Jake had explained to me. *Nick's been lying to us,* I told myself. *Nick only cares for himself. Nick followed Igor's plans and sought to have no interference. It was Nick who intentionally destroyed the helicopter. The family's demise was Nick's fault...* A sudden rush of happiness flowed through my body. The guilt that I'd been feeling disappeared. I leant backwards and rested my head against the wall. With what Jake had explained to me, he was right. *I was not responsible for the family's death.* Jake shared with me his burden to not only ease his own conscience, but to rid me of my own burden.

Jake noticed my calmness. "Do you feel better?" he asked.

"A little..." I replied. "Just one thing..."

"What's that?"

"What are we supposed to do now?" I asked.

"Do as you normally do," Jake replied. "Nick probably knows that I am onto him. He's been doing weird things lately. His strange, misleading trails are becoming more and more common. I don't know why, but I bet it has something to do with all of us..." Jake ponderingly stared into the distance.

I clicked my fingers beside his ear. "Jake!" I shouted.

Jake snapped out of his pondering and sternly looked at me. "There is something we can do tomorrow while the others are out," he said.

"What's that?" I asked.

"You can fetch a zombie out of the trench so I can experiment on it."

I found it odd that Jake wanted to experiment. I mean, here he was just condemning Nick for experimenting, and now he wanted to do it to himself? "Why the experimentation?" I confoundedly replied. "What are you searching for?"

"I have got a suspicion, which can further prove Nick's been lying," Jake answered. "Come on, Tyler. From here onwards, it's me and you together!"

Jake seemed a bit too happy about something. "Okay..." I replied, trying to not raise any suspicion. "We will do it tomorrow, " I stood up and casually walked out of the room.

After the conversation, for the rest of the night, having to function normally in Nick's presence was a tiresome act. If I couldn't avoid him, I had to endure him. When we conversed, he would pat my head as if I was a small child and speak slowly to mock my intelligence. I couldn't believe how I found him bearable before.

Every time I walked past him, he would smile and wave. It was infuriating, as unlike what Nick assumed... I wasn't some oblivious stupid child. I knew that he was a psychopath and that everything he did was purely artificial.

Slowly but surely, the arduous night came to an end. The following morning, when Nick, Eli and Rufus went to search for food, I uncomfortably followed through with Jake's plan. The plan to experiment.

Preparing the experiment was relatively straightforward. The crowded trenches gave us many options for a test subject. All we had to do was choose one. Jake paced back and forth around the trenches until he found a particularly gruesome zombie. Small bulges of squirming worms could be seen writhing and pulsating underneath its skin. They crawled upwards and spilled out through tiny pocket holes of dead flesh. Jake pointed at the zombie. "Tie up that one!" he shouted.

With a K9 dog catcher pole, I noosed a cable around the zombie's neck and pulled it tight. I dragged it to the side of the trench and shoved a kinky gag ball into its mouth. I then heaved it out of the trench and tied its arms and legs together with a thick rope. Once it was totally secured, Jake threw it in a wheelbarrow and carried it around into the backyard. He tied it to a surgical bed and sat on a chair beside it.

Jake waved me to come over. "Grab that tray," he ordered.

There was a tray next to the bed. I walked over and looked at it. Inside were medical utensils, including a microscope, tongs, syringe, scalpel and a strange brown box. I picked up the tray and brought it over to Jake. "What now?" I asked.

Jake did not reply. He grabbed the scalpel from the tray and delicately sliced into the zombie's forearm. Maggots and worms tumbled out of the open wound and rolled onto the ground. "Ewww," I muttered.

Jake continued to slice a small chunk of flesh out of the zombie and used the tongs to place it on the glass specimen stage under the microscope. After five minutes of adjusting the microscope, Jake motioned me to look through the eyepiece.

With the zombie still struggling on the surgical bed, I bent down and looked through the microscope's eyepiece. "Do you see it?" Jake asked.

At first, all I could see was a blur. But as I increased the focus, what I was looking at became apparent. The microscope was showing quivering discolored cells of the zombie's flesh. I continued to stare at the cells until I noticed something odd. A single cell faded from red to black and as quickly as it changed color, another red cell beside it pushed it away and took its place.

I pulled my head away from the eyepiece and looked at Jake. "What is up with that color change?" I questioned.

Jake clasped his hands in his lap. "Tyler, have you ever wondered why zombies can get eaten alive by insects, yet still have flesh?" he asked.

"Not really..." I replied. "But go on..."

"What you just saw was a cell dying..." Jake said. "I don't know why, but Psyriviox clearly does something weird to cells. From the little evaluation of this zombie flesh, it seems that Psyriviox causes a cell to instantly replace a dead one."

I tapped my chin. "But don't cells have a limited number of times that they can regenerate?" I asked.

"Yep, that is why this is so peculiar..." Jake replied. "Psyriviox somehow gives an unlimited amount of regeneration. Remarkably it is also stable enough to not make the cells exponentially increase. It seems that it only works to replace dead cells. If it did in fact exponentially increase the cells, by now... the entire world would be three hundred feet deep in rotting zombie flesh."

"Urgh..." I muttered. "That would be disgusting..."

Jake scratched his head. "The zombies can keep living," he said. "Their flesh may decay and get consumed, but it's the Psyriviox that keeps it regenerating. It explains why the zombies are still alive today. With the dead cells constantly being replaced, maggots have a never-ending supply of food..."

It was actually quite simple to understand. I nodded. "Makes sense," I replied.

Jake looked at me and smiled. "There is just one other thing I need to check," he said. "All of us assume that the contagion is spread through saliva." He pointed at the zombie. "Can you reach into its mouth and extract some, please?"

I screwed up my face and took a step away from the surgical bed. "What?" I said. "I'm not untying that gag ball and I'm definitely not sticking my hand anywhere near its mouth..."

Jake rolled his eyes. "The other day you looked willing to die..." he muttered.

I knew that he was talking about my suicidal embrace during the downpour. I awkwardly looked away and stared at the sky. It was embarrassing to be seen as suicidal.

Jake walked over to the zombie and shoved a syringe through its cheek. He pulled on the plunger and filled up the barrel with an oozing transparent liquid. He then squirted it on the specimen stage and looked through the microscope's eyepiece.

After a minute of staring at the saliva, Jake lifted his head up. His expression seemed to be happy and bewildered at the same time.

"Did you find anything?" I asked.

Jake motioned me towards the microscope. I bent down and looked through the microscope's eyepiece. I stared at the saliva for a long time. Unlike what I'd expected, nothing happened. I couldn't find any abnormalities. The saliva seemed perfectly normal...

I lifted my head up. Jake crossed his arms and smirked at me. "Did 'you' find anything wrong with the saliva?" he cheerfully asked.

"No..." I replied. "I could have another look if you want, though..."

"No...no..." Jake ecstatically replied.

"I have got subjects that will test it." He reached into the strange brown box on the tray and pulled out a huge, gray rat.

I pointed at it. "Where did you get that?!" I questioned.

Jake rolled his eyes. "It's a dumbass rat," he replied. "They are everywhere..."

"What are you going to do with it?" I questioned.

"I'll show you." He picked up the syringe and jabbed it into the rat. It squirmed around in his hand, squealing and trying to bite him. Jake emptied every bit of the zombie saliva into the rat and sat it back in the box.

We watched the rat, closely. We knew that the contagion reacted instantly with living creatures. However, the rat did not change. It continued to run circles around the box, frantically squealing. We watched for a long time, eventually coming to the conclusion that it was not a zombie.

Jake grabbed it back out of the box. "There was a reason why the zombie saliva under the microscope looked to have no abnormalities," he said. "It's because it doesn't. The saliva has nothing to do with the contagion."

"But it has to?" I replied. "How else can it be transmitted?"

Jake smiled and untied the gag ball that was fastened inside the zombie's mouth. With its mouth free, it immediately lashed out at him, savagely trying to bite him with its huge, brown teeth.

Jake quickly pushed the scared rat into its mouth. A tooth from the zombie punctured directly through the rat's back, spluttering blood on Jake. The rat squealed loudly, crying in pain.

"Quick! Pass me the tongs!" Jake shouted.

I picked up the tongs and tossed them to him. Jake shoved them in the zombie's mouth and pulled out the rat. Clasped by the tongs, the rat was no longer squealing, but instead groaning and chattering its mouth.

Its eyes were albino red and its thick gray fur was falling off. Its guts were dangling out of its blood-covered body. "Now that's what I call a zombie rat!" Jake laughed.

I stared at the rat. Even though it was vermin, I still felt sorry for it. It was mean to use such a helpless creature in such a torturous experiment. "But what does this mean…" I mumbled. "Didn't we just prove that the zombie saliva doesn't contain the contagion?"

Jake pulled a tooth out of the rat's back and held it to my face. "Yes, the saliva doesn't contain the contagion," he replied. "The zombie teeth carry it."

I pushed the zombie tooth away. "Does its source of transmission matter?" I asked. "You killed an innocent animal…"

Jake tossed the rat on the ground and stomped on it, splattering it and covering my foot in entrails.

I knew that he purposely did it to annoy me. I angrily stared at him. "Does it mean anything?!" I screamed.

"Of course, it does," he replied. "I recall Nick saying that the 'zombie's saliva carried the contagion'." Jake pointed at the squished rat on the ground. "This right here proves that he was lying."

"Is that it?" I replied. "Is that why we did this shit experiment?" Jake smiled and reached into the box. He pulled out another rat. "Of course, not," he joyfully replied.

He grasped the helpless rat and twisted its head, snapping its neck like a twig. With its soft, lifeless body dangling in his hand, he then spat on it and threw it at the electric fence. It connected with the fence, convulsing then catching alight.

I shook my head in dismay. "Dude… that's harsh," I said.

"You see that?" Jake replied. "It was to teach you a lesson. What I did to those rodents, Igor and Nick could quite easily do to any of us."

"What?! This was a lesson for me!?" I shouted. It irritated me that Jake was experimenting on me. I picked up the scalpel and stabbed it into the zombie's head. It stopped snapping its mouth and rested still.

Jake happily nodded. "Well, I was never expecting to learn anything...?" He uncaringly replied. "It's good that we did, though."

I tossed the blood-soaked scalpel as far as I could. It disappeared over the electric fence. "Whatever..." I replied.

Jake patted me on the back. "Think ahead, Tyler," he said. "And remember, next time you see someone perform a dreadful experiment like what I just did, please be man enough to intervene. Or at least afterwards, give them their just deserts."

I turned around and slapped Jake on his bruised nose. Blood poured out of his nostrils. He grinned and licked up the blood that passed over his lips. "We may be rats!" he cheered. "But unlike these dead rodents today, we are not going to die by the hands of a doctor. We will bite the flesh off their fingers and shit on their life's work!"

I smiled and slapped him on the nose once more.

His eyes started to tear up. He held his head forward and pinched his nostrils. "Okay, that's enough," he muttered.

Chapter 24:
Trails

The experimentation on the rats was as gruesome as it was cruel. It was sick and twisted by Jake to torture and kill harmless animals. However, he did it for a reason. He wanted the possible dangers of Nick's plan to be memorable.

Oddly enough, his plan worked. I was no longer angry with Nick, I was scared. The haunting prospect of a painful, drug-induced death lingered in my mind. My caution and attentiveness around Nick increased immensely as I did not want to end up like the rats.

The only way I could stop worrying was to deal with the problem. After a couple of restless days, I decided that I should help gather evidence against Nick.

On a few previous occasions, Jake had mentioned that he'd been following Nick. When I told Jake my decision, he was overjoyed and he straightaway showed me how he'd been tracking Nick.

A tracking device similar to a GPS would be the first item of thought when locating a person. And it would have been perfect, if it weren't for the Trojan Tracker mounted inside Nick's ute. The device acted as a radar, displaying all functioning satellite devices in a four-hundred-foot radius.

Nick primarily used it to find operating mobile phones while driving through the city. However, it also prevented Jake from placing a tracking device in Nick's pickup as it would instantly be discovered. Consequently, Jake had to utilize a different method.

Jake explained that every morning, he'd attached a bottle of zombie blood to Nick's pickup and allowed it to seep onto the road. As zombie blood could not congeal or harden, its viscous, liquid state allowed it to be an extremely good tracking substance. Depending on the flow rate, the blood could seep out all day, without the need of being replaced.

The trails were so incredibly thin that the only way to properly see them was with an ultraviolet light. By the time I understood how it worked, Jake had already attached one to the front of my Chrysler. The first time I switched it on, I was totally amazed. Under the bright purple light, a morass of tiny silver trails could be seen shining down the road. They looked like a network of tiny wires running down an oversized circuit board.

Over the following month, Jake and I shared the trails. Every day at sunset, we would take turns in tracking Nick. We always made sure that we did it with no one else around as we didn't want the others to find out what we were doing. It seemed wrong to invade Nick's privacy, but we had to do it for our own well-being. And if we did it for long enough, we were certain that we'd find evidence to justify our cause.

Unfortunately, Nick travelled a lot. The tracking was not hard at first, but over time it became very tiresome. The trail's brightness determined how new it was. Often, we'd get lost thinking that we were following a new trail, when in actual fact, we had followed it before. The tracking consumed many hours of our day. We'd lose sleep, become lethargic and forget whose turn it was to track. I couldn't tell if Jake was lying to me or not, or just really good at proving himself correct, but almost every time, I ended up being the person in the wrong.

Following the trails felt like a full-time job and by the end of the month we were both exhausted. On the bright side, though, Jake's nose had healed perfectly. It was impossible to notice that it had ever been broken.

Jake walked up to me and slammed his hand down on the table. "I found the fucking evidence," he muttered.

I noticed that he was wearing yellow elastic gloves. He lifted his hand up from the table to reveal a small white tablet. It looked to be a paracetamol. I stared at it in confusion. "What's up with the tablet?" I asked.

Jake pressed down on the tablet and split it in two. A tiny droplet of a metallic turquoise liquid was in the center. I pointed at it.

"Is it supposed to have that inside?" I questioned.

Jake grimly shook his head. "That, my friend... is Psyriviox..." he replied.

"Bullshit..." I said in disbelief. "Show me."

In the top corner of the room, a small gecko scuttled across the wall. Jake ran and leapt on it. With it squirming around in his hand, he then placed half of the tablet into its mouth.

"What now?" I asked.

Jake looked at me and began to squeeze the gecko. He squeezed harder and harder. The gecko writhed back and forth in pain. Eventually, Jake squeezed it so hard, that the gecko's organs came violently tearing out its arse. It sprayed Jake's clothes in a thick coat of juice. The gecko looked like a drained orange.

"That's awful!" I shouted. "Jake, do you want to get a bleeding nose again?"

Jake held the gecko close to my face. "Look!" he screamed.

I watched, as the gecko's organs retracted back through its anus. Each individual strand of its innards looked like it had a mind of its own. The intestines slithered from side to side, flowing into the lizard like small, red snakes. They crammed inside the gecko's body and plumped it out to its normal size.

I stared at the gecko in awe. "It's an alpha gecko!" I screamed.

"Exactly!" Jake shouted. He walked over to a metal jewelry case and placed the lizard inside. He pulled the latch down and sat it in his room.

"Are you keeping it?" I questioned.

Jake smiled. "It's great evidence," he replied.

"As soon as the others come home, I will explain to them what Nick tried to do to me."

"What did he do?" I asked.

Jake pointed at the left-over half of the paracetamol tablet. "He offered me that tablet for a headache..." he replied.

I opened my mouth in shock. It was ridiculous, but Jake had actually caught Nick trying to experiment on him.

"Nick tried to poison you!?" I excitedly questioned.

Jake nodded. "Not only that, but he tried to poison me with what I already knew was poisoned."

"How did you know it was poisoned?" I asked.

"Because..." Jake replied. "The paracetamol that Nick offered me was created by the same company that I am sure engaged in biowarfare with America. He offered me a Paramaxima paracetamol!"

I fell back off my chair. I couldn't believe what I was hearing. What Jake was telling me not only proved that Nick was experimenting on us, but it also evidenced that the Russian company Paramaxima had originally used Psyriviox to attack and destroy America. Everything that Jake had suspected was suddenly coming together. His suspicions were correct. "You have got to be kidding me!" I screamed in amazement.

"Yep!" Jake replied. "Nick is officially screwed! When he gets back, I will show everyone what he is.... A murderous psychopath!"

I pushed the chair away and stood up. "Too right!" I happily agreed. "We have got him now!"

Jake high-fived me. "Tyler, just one last thing."

"Yeah, what is it?" I asked.

"Can you go out and track yesterday's trail?" he answered. "It's your turn to do it."

I was glad that we could finally convict Nick for his actions. The amount of effort we put into trying to find evidence against him was phenomenal. It was unrewarding as well, for not once did we find anything peculiar while tracking him.

Since it was the last time I'd ever have to track down Nick, I was more than pleased. "I'll be back soon!" I cheered.

Jake waved me off. I walked to my Chrysler with a skip in each step and flicked the ultraviolet light on. As anticipated, the bright purple light revealed a new, silver line. It stretched down the road and out of sight. I started up the Chrysler and followed it.

From my previous experiences, tracking Nick's car was often difficult. Nick may have been a fast driver, but he was also chaotic. Whether it be drifting around corners or swerving from side to side, the trails that he left behind would typically look like a maze. It was strange to see that the one I was now following had unparalleled straightness. Stretching through the morass of all the other silver trails, this one in particular, stood out like a rose among thorns.

I followed it as if my life depended on it. I traced it through the inner city and out into the northern suburbs. I gazed around at the forlorn streets. Huge monstrous houses sur-rounded me like skyscrapers. Their four-story shadows blocked out the setting sun. Not once had I tracked Nick into this area.

I was in the wealthy district of the city. I pushed my foot down on the pedal and accelerated down the street. I had a strong intuition of where the trail was heading.

I followed my hunch and hurried towards the location. As I was turning into the final street, I examined the road to see if I was still following the trail. As expected, halfway down the street, the trail could be seen turning into a mansion's driveway.

I drove down the street and stopped in the driveway. I got out of the car and stared at the depressive mansion that the trail unfortunately befell upon. The Coopers' tainted household was now nothing but a tragic reminder of hardship and despair...

Gazing at the crumbling, untidy house, I felt sorry for Eli. Throughout the entire time that we'd lived together, I'd never told him that his parents were dead. Instead, I let him believe that they were alive. I let him live in a lie of false hope. I gave him a "cup half-full" outlook. A cup which I know could never be filled...

I glumly saluted the house and walked inside. As I strolled through the front door, I straightaway recognized that someone had recently been here. All the drawers and cupboard doors in the living room were open. Books and paper covered the floor in a cluttered mess. It looked as if someone had been rummaging through the house for something...

I walked into the kitchen where I found a muddy boot print on the ground. Judging from the size of this one, it was definitely Nick's.

I walked upstairs and examined Eli's room. All of his trophies had been smashed on the ground. I remembered that Eli had to pick up a few essentials from his house a long time ago. He may not have brought back his trophies, but there was no way he would have found them redundant enough to break.

As I was about to walk back downstairs, I remembered something else. It was the night before Eli went to retrieve his possessions. I cleaned his house and disposed of his loved ones' corpses. I remembered that while disposing of his dead dog, Bruce, I saw someone staring at me through a window. They were in the second story. I recall Nick saying that he followed me alone and that no one else was in the house with us...

I don't know how or why, but something clicked in my head. A sudden realization. I now understood what was going on. *I now understood what was going on. Igor was the dark figure that I'd seen in the house. I couldn't believe that I hadn't figured it out earlier. After Rufus destroyed the hospital, Igor would have needed a place to experiment. The Coopers worked with Psyriviox.*

Igor would have known that their house had information and equipment related to the drug and would have moved in so that he could perform the experiments he desired. This whole time Jake and I thought Igor was living in the city center. It was ridiculous to think that he was living right under our noses in a close friend's house...

I ran to the room that I recalled the figure being inside. As I walked through the door, something instantly caught my attention. A cheerful portrait of Eli's and Nick's family. I remembered straightening the portrait when I was cleaning his house.

I walked up and examined it. Instead of seeing cheerful faces, everyone except Nick had their faces scratched out. I stared closer. Something silver glimmered behind the scratched-out faces.

I ripped the portrait off the wall. To my shock, behind where the portrait hung was a small steel safe. Noticing that it wasn't closed properly, I slid my fingers into the open gap and pulled back the safe door.

I took a step back in horror. Inside the safe, a broken test tube was leaking a metallic turquoise liquid. It was undoubtedly Psyriviox. However, that wasn't the most frightening part... Located at the far end of the safe was a message written in blood. In thick red, capital letters it read: "DEATH'S CHEAT."

I slammed the safe shut and ran out of the house. I jumped in my car and hurried home. I had to tell Jake what I'd found.

When I arrived home, another vehicle was already parked in the driveway. It was Nick's car... I ran inside the house. "Jake!" I screamed. "Are you okay!?"

Jake didn't reply. By the sounds of the commotion, Jake was already accusing Nick. The sound was coming from within Jake's room.

I crept up to the door and eavesdropped in on the argument. Nick sounded furious. He was shouting at the top of his lungs. In fact, it was difficult to hear what any of them were saying under the belligerent, incoherent roar of Nick's voice. I tried to open the door, but it wouldn't budge. The door was locked...

The shouting became increasingly louder and violent. They sounded like they were about to kill one another. With the argument intensifying, I had to get inside quickly. I relentlessly kicked the door in an attempt to break it down. With no effect, I pulled my pistol out of my pocket and aimed it at the door. I was about to shoot the lock off when suddenly... everything went quiet...

The trancelike silence stopped me in my tracks. I shakily held my gun and waited for something to happen...

The sound of vehicles could be heard turning into the driveway. Eli and Rufus had finally returned home. I took a deep breath of relief. I was happy that they were here.

I needed them with me. "Eli! Rufus!" I shouted. "Get here, quick!"

Suddenly, the door to Jake's room swung open and Nick came tumbling out. "Close the door!" he screamed.

I peeked past Nick to see Jake sprinting towards the door. He was moving at a phenomenal speed. His eyes were bloodshot red and he was gritting his teeth. Froth foamed out of his mouth like a rabid dog. He looked to be in a frenzy...

Chapter 25:
Loose Ends

Nick grabbed the door and slammed it shut. He sat down on the ground, breathing heavily. Loud thuds and crashes sounded as Jake bashed against the other side of the door, trying to break it down.

My heart dropped. I knew what Nick had done... He accomplished what he was unable to with the tablet. He had drugged Jake with Psyriviox.

"What did you do to Jake?!" I screamed.

"I... I didn't... do anything..." Nick stammered.

"We were arguing and then... then he went psycho..."

I aimed my gun at Nick. "You drugged him!" I screamed in anger.

Nick held his hands in front of his face, trying to shield himself. "No... no..." he worriedly replied.

"I swear, I didn't do it..."

"You think you are clever!" I shouted.

"You didn't think that Jake and I would catch you!"

"I swear on my life!" Nick cried. "I didn't do it!"

Eli and Rufus burst through the front door. "What's going on?!" Eli shouted.

"Leave me to it!" I screamed.

I pushed my gun against Nick's forehead. "Did you even care when you killed that innocent family in the helicopter!?" I shouted. "Would you swear on their lives?!"

Nick began to cry. "It was not my fault!" he whimpered.

Eli ran over and saw my gun against Nick's head. "What are you doing?!" he screamed.

I ignored Eli and glared at Nick. "You knew that Jake had learned about your psychotic plans and you didn't want them exposed. So, to protect yourself, you drugged Jake with Psyriviox and expected the rest of us to believe that he'd accidentally done it to himself."

"No...!" Nick sobbed. "You don't understand!"

"I understand enough..." I muttered. "Jake told me you'd do something like this... And he told me to give you your just deserts..."

"Please, Tyler...!" Nick begged. "Let me explain...!"

"No amount of explaining can save you now..." I snarled. "You are no friend of mine... and you are certainly not death's cheat..." I pulled the trigger.... *Bang!*

No!" Eli screamed. He ran over and tackled me from behind.

The gun sailed out of my hand and slid along the floor. Eli and I crashed to the ground. With my head pressed sideways against the floor, I could see that Nick was collapsed on the ground. His eyes were aimed in different directions. Blood flowed out of the hole in his head and a yellow, gooey liquid drizzled out of his ears. I smiled with revenge. My shot was a success.

"NO...!" Eli screamed. He leapt off me and ran over to Nick. He shook him back and forth as if trying to wake him up. "Tyler! What have you done?!" he shrieked.

I pushed myself to a stand. "I saved your lives!" I shouted.

Eli stared at me with watery eyes. I opened my mouth and was about to explain how *I'd saved his life*, but no words came out... The grieving look on Eli's face brought me back to a stable mind of thought. It wasn't good. Without my rage, I realized that one of the few people I loved in this horrible world was actually gone... I realized that my close friend Jake had become what I hated most. He had become a grisly alpha zombie...

Eli burrowed his head into Nick's lifeless chest and agonizingly cried. With Eli having succumbed to grief, I turned away and looked at Rufus. He was standing just a few feet away from Eli, frozen in shock. His body perfectly still.

As this was happening, furious groans and crashes were heard from the other side of the door. Jake had not stopped his frenzy. His drug-fueled madness was inescapable and endless...

I stared at the door. The hardwood was beginning to crack and splinter. Psyriviox had made Jake powerful and unyielding. His newfound strength was far beyond that of a human's. Piece by piece, the door fell apart. It was until his gory hand came smashing through the door did we stop our grieving and decide to take action.

Eli closed Nick's eyes and kissed him on the cheek. He stood up and wiped the tears off his face. Rufus looked at Jake's clawing hand and jogged outside. He came back in holding two rusty chains, a mallet and a large bolt. "Nick drugged Jake with Psyriviox... Didn't he...?" Rufus mumbled.

I sadly nodded in reply. Eli glared at me. "Tyler, you are showing me proof after we bury them..." he muttered.

Rufus walked up to the door and wrapped a chain around Jake's clawing hand. "If Jake is an alpha zombie... Unfortunately, we must incinerate him before we can bury him..." he said.

Rufus made me remember that the only way to kill an alpha zombie was through incineration. "Noooo..." I sobbed. "There has to be another way..."

Rufus lowered his head. "I'm sorry..." he replied. "But it's the only way..."

My stomach filled with butterflies. I dropped to my knees and started heaving. "I can't do it..." I spluttered. "I just can't..."

Rufus hammered the chain into the floor. The thick bolt jolted back and forth under Jake's merciless strength. Eli and I watched in horror as Rufus then opened the door. We expected Jake to rip us limb from limb; however, we were badly mistaken. What Rufus had done with the chain was bizarrely clever. He had intentionally immobilized Jake to the door.

Unable to escape, Jake writhed with fervor. He gnashed his teeth and smashed his head against the door. Each hard blow lacerated his face, at some moments revealing his skull. However, his cell regeneration was so far beyond that of a human, his lacerations remained open for less than a second before they were completely healed.

Jake twisted his head, his eyes locked with mine. I tried to look away, but I couldn't. His snarling face captivated me. He looked as if his mind was trapped in his own body. His groans sounded like pleas for help. A plea to end his restive torment...

Rufus weaved the second chain through Jake's arms and legs. He then wrapped it around Jake's neck and pulled it tight. Jake fell to his knees, gagging in agony.

I looked away in disgust. "I can't watch this..." I murmured.

"I have to go."

Eli grasped my shirt. "You are not going anywhere!" he shouted.

I tried to pull away, but I couldn't. His grip was too strong. "Let go of me!" I shrieked.

Eli moved his hand up my shirt and clutched my throat. "You are helping me bury Nick, whether you like it or not!" he snarled.

"Stop this!" Rufus screamed. He rushed over and jerked Eli off me. "Tyler! You are going to bury Nick!" he shouted.

I angrily pushed Rufus away. "I will never bury that filth," I retorted.

"Fine!" Rufus said. "Then you can help me incinerate Jake."

My options were either to burn Jake or bury the person who killed him. I scrunched up my face in frustration. Both options were horrible.

Eventually, I settled on the one that I thought I could at least withstand. "Fine..." I muttered. "I'll bury Nick..."

Eli tossed Nick over his shoulders. "Tyler, you grab the shovel," he said. "It's the least you could do..."

I rolled my eyes and curiously looked at Rufus. "Where are you going to bury Jake?" I asked.

Rufus glowered at Jake writhing on the floor. "I am going to bury him in the peacefulness of his home..." he calmly replied.

I faintly smiled. It was nice of Rufus to be so thoughtful. "Okay…" I sighed.

Eli trudged outside. I followed him, picking up my gun and a shovel on the way out. I knew that even though it was a tragic time, it didn't make the outside world any less danger-ous. Zombies were never going to hesitate in killing us, and apart from Jake, I was never going to hesitate in killing them.

Eli placed Nick in the backseat of my Chrysler and we drove off. I didn't have any idea where we were going and I didn't care. Eli was the one driving and it was his choice of where to bury Nick. If it was up to me, I would have left him to rot in a dumpster.

After a quiet and short trip, Eli stopped the car. By now, it was nighttime and it was difficult to discern our location. Eli flicked the car's headlights to high beam. In the distance, a row of gravestones were illuminated.

Eli hopped out of the car, hoisted Nick into his arms and cradled him like a baby. "Nick was a brother to me," he said. "And he deserves to be buried with my family…"

"Where are we?" I questioned.

Eli longingly gazed at the gravestones. "This is my family's cemetery," he said. He pointed at a gravestone. "That one over there is my grandfather. You wouldn't believe it, but he has the same first name as you."

I walked over to the gravestone and looked at the name engraved on it. In moldy gray letters it read: "Tyler Cooper." Eli was not lying. "Why is your family's cemetery so far away from your house?" I asked.

"We weren't always rich, you know," Eli answered. "In fact, it was my grandfather who brought the Cooper name into being. And it was in his wishes that he asked to be buried at the small shack that he grew up in. His shack was right where we are standing..."

"That's nice," I said. "So, his shack was changed into a cemetery to commemorate his hardship."

Eli nodded. "I can't remember him much," he said." He died when I was young. But my parents told me he was the nicest, most honest and hardworking person to ever walk the earth... It's a shame... I always thought much of you, Tyler... I even thought that one day, you could become as great as my grandfather. But now... after what you have done... You are nothing but a shadow of the leader that you used to be..."

Surprisingly, what Eli said seriously hurt my feelings. I never knew how much respect he had for me and why he thought I was a leader. "I was never a leader,"

I said. "Jake was. He determined what we did."

"No one listened to Jake," Eli replied. "Everyone ignored him. His disorderly outbursts about Nick and his constant need to show that he was the smartest, made him a joke. You may not have known it, but it was you who determined what we did. Apart from Jake, the rest of us, including Nicholai, depended on your judgment."

"But how?" I questioned. "I rarely had control over anything. Rufus for one would never listen to me. And also, you inflicted fear to control us. Your anger determined what we did."

Eli shook his head. "I may have directed you," he said.

"But in the end, you were the one with the control. From the creation of the Haven all the way to you becoming a murderer. Rufus, I and even Nick believed that you were the most rational out of us. Together, without your consent, we assigned you as the leader."

It was odd that Eli was telling me all of this now. If he had told me earlier instead of keeping it a secret, these events could have played out a lot different. "I guess Nick chose the wrong leader," I muttered.

"Correct..." Eli replied. He bent down and lowered Nick into a coffin. He then pushed the coffin into a shallow grave.

I stared at the grave in confusion. "Why did you get me to bring a shovel if you already have a grave dug out?" I asked. "And more to the point. Why is it already dug out?"

"There are two coffins and two unearthed graves here," Eli replied. "I did it in case I discovered the worst happened to my parents..."

I knew that Eli still had no idea about his parents' death. "Oh..." I murmured. "But what about the shovel?"

"Isn't it clear?" he replied. "I got you to bring a shovel so that you could bury the person you killed."

I angrily turned away. I realized what Eli was doing. He wanted me to feel remorseful for what I'd done. It was an impossible task. Nick's murderous betrayal was unforgivable. No matter what, I was always going to hate Nick and no story could change that. I walked over to the car. "Yeah, no worries," I cheered. "I'll just get the shovel."

"Thanks..." Eli replied. "It means a lot."

I reached into the car and foraged around. I deliberately made it look like that I was searching for the shovel, when in actuality, I was searching for the car key. Never did I have any intention of burying Nick. Instead, I wanted to bury the ashes of my actual friend. I wanted to bury Jake. And to do that, I had to get to Jake's house before Rufus did.

At last, my hand felt the cold metal of the car key. I grabbed it and clutched it tight. I then looked through the front windshield to see what Eli was doing. To my horror, he was walking towards the car. "It shouldn't be that hard to find!" he laughed.

With Eli closing in on me, I had to be quick. I leapt into the driver's seat and punched the key into the ignition. I glanced up to see Eli sprinting towards the car. "What are you doing?!" he screamed in confusion.

My heart raced. I had to do it now. I slammed my foot down on the pedal and speedily reversed out of the cemetery.

As I reached the road, the sound of gunshots echoed through the air. Unable to catch me, Eli had begun to shoot the car. I was in the middle of the road about to speed away when—Bang!—a front headlight exploded.

"Get out of that car!" Eli shrieked. He stood in front of the vehicle, aiming his revolver at me...

I was unsure what was running through his head. Was he capable of shooting me? Or was it all just an act? I wanted to find out. I daringly revved the engine. "Get the fuck out of my way!" I shouted.

Eli glared at me. "GET OUT OF THE FUCKING CAR!" he shouted.

I observed his body language. He was profusely sweating and the revolver was shaking in his hands. I discerned that there was nothing behind his intimidation. "You are a fucking coward!" I screamed. I slammed my foot down on the pedal and accelerated towards him.

Bang!

Eli fired the revolver.

The bullet exploded the remaining headlight and I was left speeding into darkness. I closed my eyes and kept my foot down on the pedal. What happened next made me grateful. I did not hear the impact of Eli with the car. I may have been accelerating towards him, but I never intended to crash into him. My initial plan was to just swerve around him at the last second. But it was ruined when he made me visionless. Eli may have been playing an act of intimidation, but so was I. The only difference was, I was better.

While dangerously speeding down the street, I remembered that I still had the ultraviolet light. Hoping to god that Eli wasn't chasing me, I stopped the car and switched it on. The dim blue light lit up the road ahead. It wasn't much, but it was enough for me to drive safely.

When I sat back in the car, the sound of heavy footsteps could be heard. I quickly accelerated. Eli fired at the car. The bullet exploded the rear windscreen with a frightening bang! I ducked my head and swerved to the right. Another shot fired, narrowly missing the car.

I sped down the street. "Save your last shot for a zombie!" I screamed out the rear windscreen.

I couldn't tell if Eli had heard me or not, but I did not hear another shot. I turned into the next street and returned to an ordinary safe speed. Eli may have wanted to chase me. However, I knew that he wouldn't until after he'd buried Nick. With Eli having no assistance from me, I expected him to be a minimum of thirty minutes before he would arrive home. And with that knowledge, I was free from worry.

I drove back to our Haven and hopped out of the car. I ran inside and searched for Rufus. From the bedrooms to the backyard, I explored everywhere. Eventually I came to terms that they weren't in the house. And that only meant one thing. It meant that Rufus was about to bury Jake...

I snatched a map out of the cupboard and spread it across the table. It meant that Rufus had cremated Jake and was about to bury him... I ran my finger over the map to try and locate it. But no matter how hard I tried, I couldn't... Throughout my entire life, I'd only ever visited Jake's house once. It was a pity that Rufus had planned the burial at Jake's house as I'd unfortunately forgotten its location...

I sighed in disappointment and moped out the front. I was staring at the road, glumly waiting for Eli's return, when something caught my attention. It was which vehicle Rufus had taken. Out of all the vehicles, Nick's pickup was the only one that could not be accounted for.

A spark of hope flickered inside me. I sprinted to the Chrysler and excitedly examined the road. To my joy, under the ultraviolet light, a brand-new trail stretched down the street. Unlike the trail that I tracked to Eli's house, this one was a web of confusion. I confidently smiled as I knew that it was Rufus's. With the trail guiding me to his location, I hopped in the Chrysler and followed it with hope.

With complete determination to get to Jake's funeral, I raced through the city. From the downtown ghetto, all the way to the industrial estate, I followed the trail. Eventually, I finished up in a most unexpected place. The winding trail terminated in the midst of the city slums...

I got out of my car and stared at the old, run-down shack that was stationed in front of me. A trail to this repulsive location was certainly not needed... Rufus hadn't led me to Jake's house. The idiot had led me to his own house...

The entire neighborhood was quiet. All I could hear were faint gags and shrieks of pain from inside the house... The voice was familiar. It was Jake's...

I glumly sat on the grass, heartbroken by his shrieks of pain. My attempt to reach Rufus fast had somehow worked against me. Jake still had to be incinerated. It was terrible... I didn't come to listen to Jake be incinerated... I came to bury his ashes...

I was about to stand up and walk away when something caught my eye. Beside the front door of the house, a silver object glimmered in the dark.

Curious to what it could be, I walked over to it and picked it up. In my hands, the object felt like a distorted cylindrical shape. A grimy padlock could be felt bolted to the top. I recognized what it was. It was Rufus's canister.

I couldn't believe that after all this time, he had kept the small canister that I'd created for him. I placed it on the ground where my hand brushed past another object. It was a flashlight. I picked it up, switched it on and aimed it at the canister. What I saw next made me shudder with fear...

The canister was leaking a metallic, turquoise liquid. It was Psyriviox and it was dripping out of a small bullet-sized hole near the bottom.

I immediately took a step away. Psyriviox was the most dangerous and rarest drug on the planet and the amount that had leaked from Rufus's canister had formed a small puddle on the ground.

It was at least a hundred times more than what I'd witnessed in the safe at the Coopers' house. It was a frightening amount... and Rufus had it for a reason...

I shone my flashlight at the door. Rufus had not closed it properly and Jake's piercing shrieks could be heard resounding through a small gap in the door. It sounded like a bat screeching in a cave.

Using my free hand, I pulled my gun out from underneath my belt and aimed at the door. I had a creeping suspicion that Rufus didn't want me here and I wanted to know why. I placed my foot against the door and gently pushed it open. Rufus had some serious explaining to do...

CHAPTER 26:
End of the Line

The flashlight shone a thin passage of light into the house. At the end of the light, in the middle of the gloomy living room, Rufus was perfectly motionless. In his hand, a can of gasoline.

I stared at him with concern. "Ah... Rufus... What's going on...?" I asked.

Rufus remained slouched, with his head bowed. Outside the thin passage of light, in the surrounding blackness, loud shrieks could be heard. I shifted my light to the side. It fell upon a shuffling creature. It was Jake. He was standing less than a foot away from Rufus, tormentedly trying to reach him. His mouth was open wide and his arms were outstretched. A thick rusted chain was constricted around his neck. He lurched forward and clawed at Rufus, trying to bite him with all his might. It was sad to witness. Jake looked like a restrained rabid dog and Rufus his depressed owner...

I shifted my light back to Rufus and stumbled back in shock. He was no longer slouched. His head was upright, his bulbous eyes glowering at me. "What is with the Psyriviox in the canister?" I worriedly asked.

Rufus did not reply. He retained his illusory blank stare. My gun was still aimed at him. He looked completely oblivious to the question and the gun.

I waved my flashlight back and forth over his face in an attempt to get him out of his trancelike state. It had no effect. Not even a blink. "Rufus...?" I asked. "What are you doing...?"

Someone responded, but it was not Rufus... It was a groan that I was unfamiliar with. Deep and croaky, it sounded like an old man who had been a heavy smoker their entire life.

I shifted my flashlight to the other side of Rufus. The light fell upon another creature. It was short, stocky and covered in tattoos. Its bald head glimmered like a diamond in the flashlight. My eyes widened in shock. I couldn't believe what I was seeing. It was Rufus's adoptive father... He was gnashing his teeth and clawing at Rufus like a wild animal. And like Jake, a thick chain was constricted around his neck.

I was about to ask Rufus another question when a third creature caught my attention. Two skinny arms were flailing about in the dark behind Rufus. I stepped to the side and redirected my light at the flailing creature. My heart skipped a beat. It came as another shock. It was a female with pale skin and long black hair. She wore a tattered white dress, patched in blood. Her small livid eyes glared at Rufus with pure hatred. It was weird to see that she looked healthier now than she had ever done in the past. The creature was easily distinguishable. It was Rufus's adoptive mother...

I knew what I'd stumbled upon was not good. It was a scary situation. Rufus was surrounded by his adoptive parents and Jake. All of which I could distinguish were alphas...

I shone my flashlight back at Rufus. "For the last time!" I shouted. "What's going on?!"

Rufus snapped out of his trancelike state and stared into my eyes. "It's all my fault," he whispered.

I squinted, unsure of what he meant. "Your fault?" I questioned. "What is your fault...?" Rufus did not reply. He bowed his head and stared at the ground.

It frustrated me. I wanted answers. "What's your fault?!" I screamed.

A tear trickled down his cheek and silently fell to the floor. "Everything is my fault..." he whispered. "I am the cause of every dreadful thing that has ever happened to us..."

What he was saying was nonsense. I shook my head in disbelief. "Stop lying to me," I muttered.

Rufus ignored my disbelief. He was captivated in his own emotions. "I have been hiding too much for too long..." he muttered. "If there is a god... he truly wants me to expose my mistakes... I can no longer hide what cannot be hidden... And I cannot lie myself out of this situation... So I am left with no escape... I will, once and for all, explain to you the truth of why I am trapped *here* in this hellhole, on this fateful night..."

He seemed to be certain that he was the cause of everything bad that had ever happened to us. It was absurd, but it also intrigued me. I tilted my head to the side. "Go on then..." I said. "Explain yourself."

Rufus stared deep into my eyes. "I will start from the beginning," he muttered.

"It was at the beginning of summer, last year. I was sitting in the treehouse playing with matches. I was bored, and I was seeing how far I could flick them.

"I'm not sure how I managed it... but I started a fire in the treehouse.

"By the time I realized what I'd done, it was already too late. My clothes caught fire, melting on my skin like plastic. I dove out of the exit. I landed hard on the forest floor and rolled around in agony. I was not on fire, but I did not need to be. The heat remained. My clothes bubbled and seared to my flesh, slowly roasting me alive...

"As I was being roasted, the radio toppled out of the tree house and landed beside me. It was half melted and steaming black. With my last bit of strength, I gripped the radio's microphone and screamed in my location...

"The next thing I remember, I was lying in a hospital bed. Perfectly fine, not a burn or mark on me..."

"I guess that explains why the treehouse was charcoal black," I replied. I shone my flashlight up and down Rufus's body. Not a single burn could be seen on him. "But you are not scarred... it's not possible..."

"It is..." Rufus sighed. "I was meant to die that day, but some people saved me. They barely even knew who I was. It was the Coopers."

"What?" I questioned. "How did they save you...?"

Rufus bent down and picked up a sharp rock off the ground. He shoved it into his forearm and dragged it downwards. It sliced through his flesh, splitting his skin in two. He raised his arm into the light, so that I could get a better view. I watched in horror as his skin sealed back together like a zipper. Once it was completely healed, he dropped the rock on the ground and looked at me. "I'm surprised that you hadn't figured it out earlier," he said. "But then again, I was never the center of attention. Eli and Nick were...

"I mean... would you believe me if I told you that for as long as I've lived with you, I've never been sick or injured...?"

I tried to think back to the times that he'd been physically wounded. I couldn't recall any...

"See... you can't..." he said. "There has been plenty of unexplainable instances that you have completely overlooked...

"Could you logically explain how I could crash a truck into a shopping mall and climb out without even a scratch? Or how I could hold my breath in the ocean for longer than what a professional surfer could do... I mean, you didn't even take notice of Bella's complaints, when she fired a shotgun at my chest and I said that 'she missed.'

"Your thought of 'me' being a 'mindless idiot' is what has allowed these occurrences to go past unnoticed... I have always been, and still am the first alpha in America. And it was the Coopers that chose me on the day of the treehouse fire to be their test subject."

I fell into shock. I couldn't believe it... *Rufus had been an alpha this entire time...* It sounded ridiculous... yet, from what I'd just witnessed, it was true...

Rufus discerned my dazed expression and continued with his story. "Of course, with this new-found healing and strength came burdens," he said. "For starters, I had to check in with Mr and Mrs Cooper twice a day at their house. My privacy was no concern of theirs. They explicitly experimented on me. I could withstand the affliction of pain, but the embarrassment I felt, when they experimented on my genitals, was far worse... I did not complain, though. They were risking everything for me. They weren't allowed a human test subject and they ensured that it remained a secret. They even went to the extent of threatening to kill me if I did not abide by their rules. It was weird, they were so willing to aid me, but at the same time... so willing to end me..."

I raised my hand and signaled Rufus to stop speaking. I found a flaw in his story. "The Coopers may have been nice people," I said. "But they would never give you Psyriviox, knowing how dangerous it is. They would have known that the contagion inside you could very easily result in a pandemic. They were not dumb people..."

"I don't think I even carried the contagion..." Rufus mumbled. "I had no idea that I was taking a form of Psyriviox... And by the time I did, it was far too late..."

"What happened?" I questioned.

Rufus longingly gazed into the distance. He looked to be recalling past memories. "Even though they experimented on me, over the time that I spent with Mr and Mrs Cooper, I grew close to them. For once in my life, I felt like I had an actual family..." He closed his eyes and shook his head. "I don't know why I did it... But I did..."

"What did you do?" I puzzled.

"One afternoon... my adoptive mother was in a frenzy. For once in her life, she was drug free. Sober is what you call it. She'd used up all her prescription medication and she needed more. She was acting strange, whispering to herself and twitching like she'd had one too many coffees. In her soberness she became very depressed, so much so that it came to the point where she threatened to kill herself..."

"Wow, that's rough..." I muttered.

Rufus shrugged. "I didn't care. I wanted her to die and I happily ignored her. I was about to walk out the front door, when I was stopped by my adoptive father. He stood in front of me like a brick wall. His arms were crossed and his face was clenched with anger. It was apparent that he disliked my smugness.

"Yet, I don't know what came over me that moment... But his serious expression made me laugh. A laugh which I regret...

"For as long as I lived with him, I'd never mocked him. Hence, I didn't know how he'd react. Unfortunately, he reacted the same way as he would to a disrespectful adult. He wound back his arm and slammed his colossal fist into my face, shattering both my nose and cheek bone.

"The pain was excruciating... But it wasn't for long. In less than a second, my face had reformed back to its normal self. Not a scratch or deformation on it. I remember my adoptive father's expression change from a deep anger to complete astonishment. It was at this point that I realized that I'd made a serious mistake. I realized that I'd done the only thing that Mr and Mrs Cooper told me not to do. I'd revealed my secret..."

"That's brutal, man... But it does not explain the outbreak."

"No..." Rufus sighed. "But this will...

"As soon as it happened, my adoptive father became overjoyed. He cackled at me, calling me a 'freak' and said that he was going to 'expose my oddity to the world.' He had some weird perception that he was going to be making money from me, or something...

"I pleaded and pleaded... begging him with all my heart, not to expose my secret. In the end, the only way I could stop him was to arrange a deal with him.

"The deal settled at this: 'He would not speak a word if I supplied him and his suicidal wife with a never-ending supply of strong medication.' It was ridiculous, I know... but I had no other choice...

"I mean... where was I going to get a never-ending supply of medication? The hospital, the pharmacy...? I'd be lucky to retrieve medication 'once' from those places, let alone every day for the rest of my adoptive parents' lives...

"But then I remembered something... It was what the Coopers had explained to me, right after they saved me. 'If a person were to inject more than a drop a week of the drug that I'd been taking, they'd die.' I realized that my drug was a perfect way to escape from the ridiculous deal. All I had to do was give my adoptive parents a little more than a drop."

I could see where Rufus's story was leading. "No..." I murmured in disbelief. "You didn't..."

"Yes," he sadly replied. "I did...

"You wouldn't believe it, but for a drug that was so secretive, it was actually quite easy to steal. You see, Mr and Mrs Cooper functioned around a schedule. Whether it be waking up, going to sleep, shopping, working or experimenting. Every day, they would follow the same routine.

"I was familiar with their schedule, and after having spent so much time in the Cooper household, I was also familiar with their home security system.

"It was three o'clock in the morning after my adoptive father had punched me when I broke into their house. I knew that it was in the midst of Mr and Mrs Cooper's experimentation timeframe, and I knew that they would be working with my drug.

"I bypassed the security system and snuck upstairs. I had a hunch that the small office room next to Eli's bedroom contained my drug. Without alerting anyone, I crept into the office room and hid in a cupboard.

"As I stood in the cupboard, staring through a small gap in the door, Mr Cooper strolled into the room. He was wearing a white lab coat and thick spectacles. Thinking that he was the only one in the room, he casually walked over to a portrait and tilted it to the side. To my joy, hidden behind the portrait was a thick silver safe. Unlike the rest of the Coopers' assets, the safe did not look expensive. In fact, it only required a six-digit number to open.

"Mr Cooper speedily punched in a code and placed a test tube inside. As soon as he left the room, I climbed out of the cupboard, crept up to the safe and attempted to repeat the same code.

"As you already know, my memory is terrible, so I was quite surprised when the safe door clicked open. It seemed a little too good to be true. Inside the safe sat ten identical test tubes. All looked identical to the drug that I'd been taking. The only difference between them was a numerical value on the side. I was so ecstatic about breaking into the safe, that I did not assess which test tube was mine, and instead seized one at random.

"When I returned home, I handed the test tube to my adoptive parents and told them that it was 'a drug that gives the best high in the world.' They were desperate and weren't expecting anything from me... So there was little convincing for them to try it. And try it, they did...

"Instead of a tiny amount, they split the drug into two halves, filled up the barrels of two rusty syringes and injected it into their arms.

"Unfortunately, instead of dying, they became the creatures you see beside me... Alphas... They chased me outside. However, when they could not catch me, they began attacking other people. My old, harmless next-door neighbor was the first victim. I remember his shrill cries of pain as my adoptive parents chewed off his face. After they were done with him, he was no longer harmless. I watched as he rushed over to his distressed wife and gouged out her eyes on the front lawn... It was the most horrific thing I'd ever seen, and it was my fault. It was like what I'd been seeing on the Russian news. I knew then that what I'd given my adoptive parents was a form of Psyriviox that carried the contagion...

"I was utterly terrified... So I ran from it all. I sprinted to your house, Tyler. By the time I arrived at your front door, I'd distanced myself far from my adoptive parents, and I was ready to start the first day of school back from summer..."

I gritted my teeth and glared at Rufus. "You fucking idiot!" I screamed. "Now I understand why on the bus you were so goddamn worried about Psyriviox spreading throughout Florida! You'd just released the contagion within the city and you wanted some fucking comfort!"

Rufus lowered his head in shame. "I'm sorry..." he replied. "I didn't know it would lead to all of this... I swear on my life!

I was going to tell you earlier... But I couldn't. Not after what happened to your mom..."

"My mom..." I mumbled. Rufus had begun the outbreak and I'd forgotten that he was the subsequent cause of my mother's death. Even though I was angry and heartbroken, I built up the strength to ask him another question. "What else are you responsible for...?" I asked.

"I don't know... Lots of stuff," Rufus answered. "You guys are my best friends, and I knew that if you found out what I did, you'd desert me. I cannot live in a world by myself... I just can't... I'd rather die...

"I tried to conceal my secret, but it made matters worse. I will explain to you all that I am responsible for. But I must start from where I just finished..."

I wanted to ensure that what I'd done to Nick was justifiable. Rufus seemed to know a lot. He was the evidence that Jake and I never got. He was the truth. I nodded in approval.

"From the moment I saw your math teacher Mr Vander as a zombie, I knew that the outbreak was going to be far worse than predicted. Unlike what you'd told me, 'America failed at cleaning up my mess.'

"A couple of days after the start of the outbreak, when we were creating our equipment in the school's industrial rooms, I realized that I was going to require my weekly dosage of Psyriviox. The difficulty was that the Coopers administered it to me each week. And amid a Psyriviox outbreak, I did not know if they were going to help me, or even be alive to do so.

So I came up with a plan. I decided that I would go to their house and retrieve another test tube of Psyriviox that they stored in the safe. It was not a reliable plan, but it was my only option if I were to acquire my weekly dosage.

"When Eli and Jake were chased by a horde of zombies from the school creek to the treehouse, I convinced you that they had run off to Eli's house. While you were rushing around the Cooper household in search for Eli, I hurriedly stole a test tube from the safe and placed it inside the canister that you had created for me in the industrial rooms.

"I had planned to share with you my secret later that night, however, after finding out what had happened to your mother, I couldn't bring myself to do it...

"Tyler... you blamed the zombies for your mother's death. And I remember how hard you took it... You sadistically smashed a zombie to mincemeat with a vengeful grin stretched across your face...

"I may be an alpha, but I didn't want to be your most hated person on the planet. The ordeal scared me enough to keep my secret hidden...

"The following day, I found a syringe and injected myself with the drug. It was dangerous and stupid, I know... but surprisingly, it worked. The countless hours of watching the Coopers inoculate me, had paid off. I could freely drug myself without the need for any assistance. All I had to ensure was that my supply of Psyriviox did not run out. You'd think that it would be easy for me to keep my secret hidden. But from that moment onwards it became a struggle. The fear of its exposure pushed me to drastic measures. My secret became the same as my canister, just another heavy weight which I could no longer detach...

"I didn't want anyone else to join our group. I wanted to live stress free, away from it all, where my secret could easily remain hidden. I wanted our group to remain just the four of us.

"It was after our first shopping spree... You guys were drunk and stupid and playing with sex toys. You could hardly speak, let alone notice my soberness. That night, after you guys had passed out, I drove to the power station and destroyed the city's power supply. My logic being that without electricity, we'd have zero outside communication. I look back at it now and think of how dumb it actually was. I mean... there was no possible way that it was ever going to work...

"The following day, even with your dreadful hangovers, not only did you restore power with solar panels, but you also received a text message from the last person that I wanted to join our group... Nicholai...

"At the time, you and Jake had no idea who Nicholai was. But I did... The Coopers always talked about the Richtons. They had photos of Nicholai and his family around the house.

"After witnessing him in person tussle with Jake on the first day of school, I knew that he was living in the city. And judging by the name of Eli's contact, 'Little Dick Nick', I was certain that it was him who had sent the text message.

"Nicholai's family's connection with Psyriviox terrified me. He was the last person I wanted to see, because I knew that if anyone had knowledge of me being an alpha, it was him...

"Later that night, when we were rescuing Nicholai from Southport Hospital, I purposely split away from the group. I thought that if I got to him before you guys did, I'd be able to stop him from joining us...

"While I was running around the bottom floor, I stumbled into the hospital's backup generator. At the time, it felt like I'd hit the jackpot. I thought that with the hospital power working, I could use an elevator to reach Nick first.

"I'd switched on the backup generator and was sprinting to the nearest elevator when I ran into my adoptive parents. It was the first time I'd seen them since the beginning of the outbreak. In the light, they stood out clearly. Their flesh hadn't rotted away... They looked completely alive... It scared me... I realized that if you guys saw them 'as alpha zombies', you'd know that I had something to do with the outbreak. They had to be disposed of for my secret to remain hidden.

"I was wielding a flamethrower at the time, however... unfortunately, it was also my first time using it and when I tried to set them alight, I accidentally set the room on fire... It was weird... I don't know what it was... It must have been the methane in the air or something... because just like the treehouse, the fire spread fast...

"Thinking that my adoptive parents were going to perish in the fire, I leapt inside the elevator and ascended to the top floor. When the elevator door opened, and I saw Nick running alongside you guys, I knew that I'd lost the race...

"It was after we'd escaped from the hospital, when we were driving home that I saw my adoptive parents in the distance, unburnt, chasing after the truck... And it was at that moment that my mission to eradicate them before you guys found out about them, started…"

"Ah…" I acknowledged. "That explains why you were so angry when we were driving away from the hospital."

"Yes," Rufus said. "I was pissed that my adoptive parents did not burn in the fire…

"Anyhow… With Nick in the group, as expected, everything became more difficult. He knew a lot about Psyriviox. I was injecting the stuff, and yet he seemed to know more about it than myself. Not only that, but he was very nosy. Pretty much straight away he had a keen eye on me. He knew that I was hiding something.

"There was an instance that I thought he'd caught me. It was in the middle of the night at Eli's house. Actually, now that I think about it… you were there, too. You were the one who shone the flashlight on me… ha-ha… I have got no idea how you did not recognize me."

I knew which instance Rufus was talking about. I'd originally concluded that it was Nick's evil companion "Igor" that had caught me off guard while I was disposing of Mr and Mrs Cooper's corpses. Now that Rufus had disproved that, I was concerned about my evidence against Nick. "So you were the dark figure that I saw through the Coopers' second-story window… What were you doing up there…?" I asked.

"The last time that I was in Eli's house I was in a rush," Rufus replied. "I retrieved one test tube of Psyriviox but left the others in the safe. As you already know, Psyriviox is a very rare substance. Without it I turn into a monster. I had no idea how long one test tube would last and I didn't want to find out. I was upstairs retrieving the other test tubes for myself because I didn't want to risk losing them to Nick."

"How did you escape without Nick finding you?" I asked.

"For the escape... After you'd spotted me with the light, I placed the portrait back over the safe and jumped from the second-story window onto the front lawn. Nick was downstairs at the time. I didn't even have to creep past him. It was an easy escape..."

Rufus's story made sense. Him being an alpha, he could jump from high places and not get hurt. I let him continue with his explanation. "What happened next?" I asked. "How could you be the cause of everything bad?"

"Well..." Rufus said. "Over the following five months, while you guys were searching for survivors, I was searching for my adoptive parents. Finding them was the only thing that was on my mind. However, with Nick always on my tail, it was near impossible... I mean can you believe it...? Five whole months and I accomplished nothing...

"Anyway, the next incident occurred at Golden Willow Resort. By shooting me in the chest, Bella had witnessed my 'undying' ability firsthand. She knew that I'd been hit and she knew that I was abnormal... It's just luck that the tiny bits of shrapnel were so camouflaged within my clothing that none of you could see that I had actually been shot..."

I remembered what Jake had told me as part of the evidence against Nick that "no matter where he'd searched, he could not find Psyriviox." I needed to ensure who was responsible for stealing it out of a lab in Golden Willow Resort, Rufus or Nicholai. "Wait... did you find a lab at the resort?" I asked.

Rufus gave me an odd look. "Yes..." he replied. "But how do you know that there was a lab there?"

"Jake found the lab as well," I said. "He was in search of Psyriviox. But he was unable to find any... Rufus... Did you take it...?"

Rufus squinted at me. "There was none in there when I checked," he replied. "I hoped that there would be... you know... with alpha monkeys rampaging around the resort and all..."

I smiled with hope. If Rufus hadn't found any Psyriviox in the lab, it either meant that there was none in the lab at all, or that Nick had stolen it for Igor to use. "Good," I said. "Very good."

"Now can I continue?" Rufus asked.

"Yeah, go ahead," I replied.

"Over the days that Bella had stayed in our Haven, I kept a close eye on her. I didn't intend to, but over the little time that I spent with her, I grew close to her... I fell in love..."

"No wonder you were so upset when she stole your car and deserted you," I mocked.

Rufus gritted his teeth. "Tyler... do you think that it was possible for her to steal my car, by threatening me with a gun, knowing that I cannot die?!" he said. "She never fucking made it! She died just like every other person!"

I stared at him in shock. "Wait, what...? I replied. "How...? What happened...?"

"I was dumb..." Rufus replied. "I had helped her through a lot and I thought that she liked me back... It didn't feel like the kiss that we shared was for show... I thought that it actually meant something... Oh... how wrong I was... We were sitting in the car and she was about to leave. I tried to give her a final good-bye kiss... Instinctively, she slapped me across the face."

"What...? So you got angry and beat her to death?" I questioned.

"No..." Rufus replied. "Her hand hit my mouth. My tooth scratched her and she became a zombie..."

My heart sank. Rufus was not lying. It made perfect sense. Jake and I had already proven that the Psyriviox contagion was transmitted through teeth. It explained how he could have kissed Bella and exchanged saliva without her becoming a zombie. Also, Rufus's buck teeth were an unavoidable target if a person were to hit him in the face... I lowered my head in grief. "You killed her..." I muttered.

"It was a moment of weakness..." Rufus replied. "For once, I actually felt human... I forgot that I was injecting myself with the same tubes of Psyriviox that my adoptive parents had used. I forgot about my contagion... I killed the person I loved... I fucked up, Tyler..."

I counted with my fingers all the dreadful things that Rufus was responsible for. *The outbreak... my mother's death... Bella's death...* "What more can you be responsible for...?" I questioned.

Rufus wiped his eyes. "Everything..." he sobbed. "I was also the cause for the helicopter engaging on us..."

"How?" I asked.

"None of you would have known, but infrared light shows zombies as pure green..." he replied. "There is no blue, yellow or red... our bodies, 'my body'... remains a stable temperature. From the moment that I saw the infrared goggles over the pilot's eyes, I knew that I was the cause. He would have identified me as a zombie and opened fire to try and protect the rest of you. If he wasn't wearing the stupid fucking goggles he wouldn't have died and neither would have the family that he was transporting..."

"But I thought Nick was the cause of the helicopter crash..." I mumbled. "Jake... He... he told me that it was Nick's fault... He proved it..."

"Proved what?" Rufus replied.

My mind raced over the information that Jake had told me. "He proved that Nick was collecting Psyriviox for a man named Igor," I stammered. "He proved that they were trying to create Psyriviox into a substance that would make them immortal... They were going to experiment on all of us. Rufus... You saw what Nick did to Jake... He drugged him... It's the reason why I killed him..."

Rufus squinted at me, confounded. "I have no idea of what you are talking about..." he replied. "But one thing is for sure... Nick did not drug Jake..."

I tensely stared at Rufus. "Wait... No..." I murmured. "It was Nick... It had to be..." Rufus sadly shook his head. "It was not..." he replied.

A feeling of dread swept over me. Rufus's entire explanation had led to this point. I did not want to hear it, but I had to... My body shuddered. Within the coldness of the night, I started to sweat... The flashlight trembled in my hand. "WHAT DID YOU DO, RUFUS?!" I shrieked.

Rufus's watery eyes glistened in the flashlight. "I... I didn't mean to..." he sobbed. "Nick... he had witnessed me capture

my adoptive parents and figured out that I was an alpha...
I was terrified and I didn't know what else to do... I injected
Psyriviox into a paracetamol tablet and some beef jerky
for him to unwittingly consume... I assumed that you and
Jake would think that he simply experimented on himself.
I swear on my life; I didn't mean for Jake to eat the jerky...
I don't even know how he came by it!"

"But the trail to the Cooper house..." I muttered. "The
Psyriviox splashed in the safe..."

"I... I knew that you and Jake had something against Nick
and I knew that you guys were tracking his car..." Rufus
sobbed. "The trail leading to the Cooper household which
you followed today... It was me, Tyler, I set it up... It was a
backup plan to discredit Nick in case he survived and tried
to expose my secret... I swear to god, if I knew plan B was
going to work I would have never injected the Psyriviox into
the jerky or tablet..."

I gritted my teeth, taking it all in. "You were willing to
'murder' over a secret..." I muttered. "You killed Jake... and
you did not stop me from killing Nick..."

Rufus lowered his head and started to cry loudly. He
hastily emptied the gasoline onto the ground.

I stared at him with pure hatred. "YOU FUCKING
MONSTER! YOU LET ME KILL HIM!" I screamed. "WHY
DID YOU NOT STOP ME?"

Rufus did not reply.

Even though it could not harm him, I aimed my gun at him.
"WHAT ARE YOU DOING?" I shrieked. "ANSWER ME!"

Rufus pulled a lighter out of his pocket and raised his
head, his sad eyes locked with mine. I looked at his face.

Unlike what I had just accused him of being. Not a monster did I see, but a scared child. A child that had made many mistakes, but a child that I still cared about... A child that was one of my only friends left in existence... A child with an innocence which I could forgive... Even though that Rufus had done terrible things, I did not want to see him die. Because in the end, his doings were accidents, not acts of evil. I lowered my gun. "I... I forgive you, Rufus..." I stammered.

Rufus closed his eyes. "I'm sorry..." he sobbed. "Tyler, you have been a good friend... but death is unforgiving..." The lighter fell from Rufus's hand and sailed downwards towards the ground...

"No... No! NOOO!!!" I screamed. Jake and his adoptive parents enclosed around him as a flame erupted underneath. I attempted to dash forward but was instantly driven back by the immense amount of heat.

I was sprawled out on the lawn in front of the fire. Timber crackled in the surge of heat while pain, anger and shame could be heard within the searing agony of Rufus's high-pitched screams.

Overwhelmed by everything around me, I collapsed to my knees. The dewy grass chilled my legs while the rest of my body embraced the torturous temperature. The fire filled my vision, each flicker devouring my mind and twisting my once forgotten soul. Tears filled my eyes and my vision went blurry. I could feel Rufus's pain fissuring through my veins as his shrieks died within his incineration...

I clenched the roots of the grass with all my might. No matter how hard I tried, I could not clear the horrible thought that was rushing through my mind. *Was it irony that Rufus died by his own arson? Or was it our fault for providing the fuel?* Layers of my flesh peeled and abruptly blistered all over. But it had no effect. The physical pain was nothing in comparison to what I was feeling inside.

I pulled my gun up... and softly pressed it against my temple. I closed my eyes and accepted the end. *This is it...* I told myself. *This will rid me of this nightmare...* I gently pressed the trigger and awaited the bang. *Click.* The gun jammed.

I opened my eyes and angrily hurled Rufus's canister into the fire. A fluoro-turquoise trail dissipated out of the bullet hole. I furiously rushed up and repeatedly stomped on the Psyriviox in an attempt to destroy the drug that had destroyed me. My face grew red with frustration. *How could this drug, which I'm not even addicted to, overpower my will to live...?* I asked myself. I kept stomping faster and harder, screaming at it like a little kid.

Eventually, I was stopped by a familiar voice. "Tyler... What are you doing...?"

I turned to see Eli with a puzzled look. He was covered in dirt and carrying a shovel over his shoulder. "Are you okay?" he questioned. "Where is Rufus...?"

I lowered my head and began to sob. "Rufus..." I muttered. "He's dead..."

Eli wasn't sure if he'd heard me correctly. He moved closer. "Wait... What...?" He said, baffled.

A crackle of wood burst into flames, illuminating our faces. I raised my head and stared into Eli's flickering eyes.

Eli could see I was telling the truth. He took a step back and aimed his gun at me. "What did you do, Tyler?!" he screamed. "What the fuck did you do?!"

I sat motionless with tears rolling down my face. *I just wanted the suffering to end.* "I... I killed him..." I replied.

Eli seized up and staggered backwards. "No... No... No!" he muttered in disbelief. "You are lying!"

I lunged forward and took hold of his gun. Using all my strength, I aimed it at my head. "Kill me!" I shrieked. "Fucking kill me!"

Eli tried to pull the gun away. "Why are you doing this...?" he stammered.

I took a deep breath and pressed the gun hard against my forehead. "Your parents are dead!" I screamed. "I spat on their rotting corpses!"

Eli began to cry. "Stop it!" he moaned.

"I also killed that fucking mongrel dog of yours!"

"Shut up...!" Eli shrieked. "Shut up!"

"The little cunt wouldn't stop squealing as I caved in his head!"

"Shut the fuck up!" Eli screamed.

I gritted my teeth and slowly moved my hand up the shaft of the gun. "What are you going to do??" I asked. "Do as what you've always done and watch everyone around you die! You are pathetic! A waste of human life!"

"Please, stop," Eli cried. The gun trembled in his grip.

My finger wrapped around the trigger. "Your fucked-up parents would be happy that they're no longer with you..." Then suddenly... *Crack!* Everything went black.

Chapter 27:
Death's Cheat

All was quiet. My mind at ease, my body at rest... Enclosed in a tunnel of blackness, I seamlessly drifted towards a dull, white light in the distance. It was beautiful. I was at peace... I journeyed through the void. The closer I drifted towards the light, the brighter it became.

Brighter and brighter, until eventually... I saw something through it. A face. Eli's... He held a small flashlight close to my eyes. "Tyler... are you in there...?" he asked.

I blinked a few times, trying to comprehend what was going on. *Was the flashlight that Eli was holding: the light at the end of the tunnel?* I thought to myself.

He pulled the light away from my face. "Tyler... Is that you?" he asked.

Without the light in my eyes, even with my blurry vision, I could distinguish that a ceiling was above me. "What..." I mumbled. "What's going on...?" I attempted to move but couldn't. Something was holding me down.

"Don't struggle," Eli said. "You are tied up."

I twisted my head and looked around the dimly lit room. I realized that I was back in our Haven tied down to a table in Jake's old room. "Let me out," I said. "I want to get out." I struggled from side to side, trying to break free.

"Stop it!" Eli said. "I am not going to let you out until you explain everything! How did Rufus die and why did you murder Nick?!"

I struggled for a little while longer before eventually giving up. Eli had me firmly secured. I was not going anywhere. "Let me go..." I moaned.

Eli waved the flashlight back and forth over my eyes. "Sorry..." he said. "But you are giving me an explanation, or I am leaving you here..." He moved his face close to mine and stared at me so that I could see the seriousness of the situation. I was a good judge of Eli's expressions and by the look on his face, he was clearly not joking about leaving me here immobilized and helpless.

"Why don't you just kill me...?" I asked.

He slammed his fist down on the table. "GIVE ME AN EXPLANATION!" he shrieked.

"WHAT HAPPENED TO RUFUS AND WHY DID YOU KILL NICK?"

I thought of the flames that had enclosed around Rufus before his death. "Rufus..." I muttered. "He killed himself..."

"What..." Eli mumbled. "Why...?"

I took a deep breath, readying myself for the explanation of a lifetime. It did not feel like the right time to say it, but I had to. Eli deserved the truth. "Okay... here it goes," I said. "Do not interrupt me. There is a lot that seems impossible..."

Eli nodded in agreement.

"Rufus was an alpha..."

"WAIT, WHAT?" Eli shrieked.

I glared at him, signaling him to be quiet. Eli acknowledged my glare and zipped his mouth shut.

"Rufus was an alpha…" I repeated. "He was in a bad accident in the holidays. Your parents gave him Psyriviox to survive. It was all behind your back. Behind everyone's back. Very secretive. No one, not even yourself would have known…"

Eli looked like he was about to explode with questions, but he kept his mouth sealed.

"Rufus was also the cause of the outbreak. He gave some Psyriviox to his adoptive parents and the contagion spread from there. Rufus tried to hide the fact that he was an alpha and that he was the cause of the outbreak. He kept it hidden because he did not want us to hate him. He did not want to lose us…

"When Nick joined the group, Rufus found it difficult to keep his secret hidden. Nick kept a close eye on him and after many months, he eventually figured out Rufus's secret…"

In an attempt to stop Nick from revealing the secret, Rufus tried to poison him with Psyriviox… His plan failed, though… and Jake was the one who got poisoned.

"I thought that Nick had poisoned Jake. And it was the reason why I killed Nick… Are you satisfied now…?"

Eli looked flabbergasted. I couldn't blame him, either. It was a lot to take in. He sat down on a seat and blankly stared at the ground. After ten minutes, he hopped up out of his seat and walked back over to me.

"Why would you think that Nick poisoned Jake…?" he asked.

I stared into Eli's eyes. "Jake told me things about Nick… He showed me evidence… You were right, though…

I should not have killed Nick... but believe me... Nick wasn't a good guy..."

"Why?" Eli replied. "Why was he bad? What did Jake tell you?"

As bad as it was, in my current state of mind I needed to believe that Nick was corrupt in order to remain somewhat sane. "Jake explained what Nick had been doing behind our backs," I said. "Nick was working with an evil man named Igor. Jake explained to me that the two of them were planning to experiment on us just to satisfy their own desires for immortality. I know that it makes no sense, but trust me... it will. I will show you the evidence."

"Igor..." Eli muttered. "You mean Nick's father?"

"What? Of course, not," I answered. "Igor... A man who worked with Ivan Alkaev, they were best friends. He got full control over their company Paramaxima after Ivan died."

"Yeah..." Eli answered. "That's Igor Richton..."

"Igor's last name is Richton?" I laughed in disbelief. "No... If it was, Jake would have told me."

Eli looked at me with concern. "Nick's father's name is Igor..." he bluntly answered. "You do realize that..."

I smiled at him. "Of course, it is!" I sarcastically replied. "And my name is Tyler Richton!"

"I think Jake was using you..." Eli muttered.

"No... I was the only person that Jake trusted. Hey!" I shouted, trying to change the subject. "Did you also know that Ivan Alkaev was actually the Alpha Z15 that started the outbreak in Russia?!"

"You are avoiding the truth..." Eli mumbled. "You think Nick was a 'corrupt human being' for working with his loving father...? What is wrong with you...?"

"I'm not avoiding anything," I answered.

"It's just that what you are telling me is untrue."

"But... it is true..." Eli said. "Jake used you... You are just too blind to see that..."

Eli's accusations had built up to a point which I could no longer withstand. "So what!" I shouted in retaliation. "Igor may have been Nick's father! What does that have to do with anything?! It doesn't change the fact that they were both psychopaths!"

"What did Jake do to you...?" he mumbled.

I was becoming more furious with each word that passed through Eli's lips. I struggled from side to side, trying to break free. "He didn't do anything!" I shrieked. "Just shut up! SHUT THE FUCK UP!!!"

"Jake brainwashed you, Tyler..."

I stopped struggling and gritted my teeth in rage. "Say one more word..." I snarled.

"You are fucked in the..." Before Eli could finish his sentence, I exerted all my force upwards. The table snapped at the legs and fell smashing against the floor. The ropes loosened and my arms came free. I launched at Eli and gripped his throat, lifting him high above my head. "I TOLD YOU TO SHUT THE FUCK UP!" I screamed.

Eli tried to break free, but he couldn't. My hand tightened around his throat. He gagged for air and wildly thrashed his legs about.

It took me a moment to realize that what I was doing was not physically possible... Eli was far stronger than me... Yet somehow... I was overpowering him... I immediately let go of him. He fell to his knees, rubbing his throat.

I stared at my hands and started backing away. "What... What did you do to me...?" I stammered.

Eli looked at me with teary eyes. "There was no other way..." he croaked. "Your burns... they were too severe..."

I knew what he had done. I just did not want to believe it. I staggered backwards, trying to pretend that it was a joke. "You're lying!" I laughed.

"Watch out..." Eli croaked.

Just as he said it, I tripped on a loose rope and slipped backwards. While plummeting to the ground, I instinctively shot out my hands behind me to stop the fall. Unfortunately, instead of stopping the fall, one of my hand's landed on a sharp object. The pain was sharp and excruciating.

"ARRGHH!" I shrieked.

I turned and stared at my hand. It was worse than what I'd thought. A thick splinter had pierced through my hand and was protruding out the top of my wrist. Dark, viscous blood oozed from it and stuck to the table like glue. In a panic, I yanked my hand upwards.

As the splinter left my hand, the pain immediately disappeared... I brought my hand close to my face to try to examine the gruesome cavity in which the splinter had created. As feared though, on inspection, there was no cavity. Not even a scratch... My hand was perfectly fine...

It confirmed what Eli had done to me. *He had injected me with Psyriviox.* "How could you do this to me...?" I whispered. "You... you turned me into the thing that I hate..."

"I'm sorry..." Eli muttered.

Even though I was mentally distraught and unstable, physically, I felt extremely lively. My body was exploding with energy. An energy which I knew only Psyriviox could provide. *I had to do something.*

I was about to get up and leave, when suddenly an old, brown book fell from a shelf and landed beside Eli. From where I was sitting, I was still able to discern from its cover that it was a diary. "Did Jake use a diary?" I eagerly questioned.

Eli picked up the diary. "Tyler... This is not Jake's diary..." he replied. "It's Nick's."

"Throw it to me. Let me see," I asked.

Eli hurled the book into my lap. I grabbed it and opened it to the first page. The first thing I noticed was that it was written in Russian. I flipped through the pages to ensure that the rest of the book was written in the same language. With each flick, it felt as if the diary was going to crumble in my hands. It was the most degraded book I'd ever felt. It was like it had been flushed down the toilet. The fact that it was so damaged, only made me want to read it more. But I couldn't, not until I had translated it into English.

I closed the book and carefully sat it down beside me. "It's written in Russian," I muttered "I will have to translate it..."

I looked at Eli to see that he was staring at me, holding a small blue book. It looked to be another diary. "Wait, whose diary is that?" I asked.

Eli waved the book in the air. "You wanted Nick's diary translated... Well, here it is..." he said.

"Who translated it...?" I inquired.

"I did..." Eli replied. "I found Nick's diary on the night that you were burnt in the fire..."

If what Eli was saying was true, it meant that he'd translated Nick's diary from Russian to English in just under twelve hours. "How could you translate it in one night...? I mumbled.

"Because it hasn't been a night..." Eli replied. "It's been three days..."

"Three days?!" I shrieked. "Was I in a coma?!"

Eli looked down in shame. "Yes..." he replied. "I couldn't maintain your condition... Today... before I injected you, you were on your last breaths of air..."

I rubbed my eyes, astonished at the fact that I'd been unconscious for three whole days. "Can you show me the translation of Nick's diary?" I asked.

Eli grimly nodded and tossed me the book. "To show the context of when each diary entry was written, I added a corresponding key event to the top of each page," he replied. "It should make sense for you to read..."

I stared at the book in wonder. Unlike Nick's brown, decrepit diary, this book was untarnished. Its velvet blue cover shone like silver in my hands. I flicked to the first page. At the top right-hand corner read "Entry 1." I then flicked through the book to see that there were eighteen sequentially set out, short diary entries all together.

I fascinatedly gazed at the diary. I had to confirm if my actions against Nick were justifiable and if Jake's conspiracy was true.

Entry 1 (A month before the beginning of the Russian Pandemic)

This is the worst day of my life... My father has just been diagnosed with stage 4 lung cancer and I'm not sure how much time he has left... It mustn't be long, though, considering that he has already signed documentation giving me his fifty percent share of Paramaxima...

It infuriates me that he doesn't care about dying... I mean... why doesn't he just off himself right now...? I wish I had a different father, one who cared about their own well-being...

Entry 2 (7 days after the initial finding of Psyriviox Z14)

This new drug is the best thing to ever happen! My father has only had one injection and he looks like a completely different person! I can't believe it! He still has a chance to live! Goodbye cancer!

Entry 3 (28 days after the initial finding of Psyriviox Z14)

Something is wrong. I know it... Father has not been home in a couple of weeks. Mother is also very quiet. She is hiding something. I hope that nothing is wrong with Father. I hope that he is okay...

Entry 4 (The beginning of the Russian Pandemic)

An outbreak has started. I think it has something to do with the drug which my father was using. I still haven't seen or heard from him... I am being forced to depart to America by myself... Also... my mother died today... She always told me to "be strong." I am not, though... A noose and chair are tempting... as right now, I feel like death...

Entry 5 (4 days after departing to America)

I started cutting myself. Not deep enough to kill myself. Just enough to relieve some tension. Like a pleasant tingling sensation that keeps my mind free from worry. I know it's bad, but it seems healthy right now.

I was correct about the drug being the cause of the outbreak. America has the Russian outbreak televised. The drug is called Psyriviox. I am now certain that it was the drug which my father was using...

Entry 6 (5 days after departing to America)

It's weird living in a foreign country by myself. I still know very little about whatever happened to my father. I am going to ask my American friends, the Coopers. They definitely know what happened.

Entry 7 (8 days after departing to America)

The Coopers claimed that they knew nothing. They seemed creepily cheerful to converse with. It is unlike them... I fear the worst for my father... But if he is dead... Why has everyone been keeping it a secret...?

Entry 8 (Beginning of the American Pandemic)

The Psyriviox Outbreak has spread to America. The hospital is in chaos...

Entry 9 (2 days after the beginning of the American Pandemic)

All the doctors in the hospital have become walking corpses. I am left alone in a surgical room. There is little food and I am slowly being surrounded in darkness...

Entry 10 (3 days trapped in the hospital)

I found out what happened to my father. It is far worse than what I could have ever imagined. I now understand why everyone was trying to hide it from me... He's categorized by the name of Alpha Z15. He is the creature that caused the horrific outbreak in Russia. From the looks of the "Moscow Massacre" recording, he is something from hell. In the recording, he chewed off his hand and somehow used it to plunge a syringe of Psyriviox into my Uncle Ivan. In a rage, Ivan then slaughtered his fellow doctors and changed them into something similar to zombies... The final part of the recording is of my mother... she sacrificed herself to stop Ivan... her brother... I don't know how to feel about the recording, for never does it show my father perish. I fear that if he is still alive, he may also have something to do with the outbreak in America...

Entry 11 (5 days trapped in the hospital)

The unbelievable occurred... I found Father... He is secured in the hospital. I also spoke to him... It was only for a couple of minutes, but it was enough to make me happy. He told me very important information. He knows how to reverse the effects of the drug. He says that "if he is able to stay sane for a few hours while being provided adequate equipment, he will be able to create a cure."

The only problem I have, is that I don't know where to find any more Psyriviox. It took two whole days to find a single drop in the hospital. And to be honest, where else could the drug be...?

Entry 12 (8 days trapped in the hospital)

I managed to find a little less than a drop of Psyriviox and inject Father with it. It was not a good idea... He was not himself... I tried recording him but had to stop after twenty seconds due to his sinking change in tone. I did not want to hear what he had to say while in a relapse, but I did regardless. He explained to me what it was like to be on the wrong end of Psyriviox. He said that "when he is not sane, he is trapped in his own body." "Paralyzed," he said, "a single minute feels like a year of suffering. And if he tries to resist, (which is impossible not to) he is engulfed in torturous physical and mental pain."

Luckily, I saved his initial inspirational words as a recording... Otherwise, right now... With him groaning and screeching, secured on a surgical bed. If I could... I would incinerate him and put him out of his misery...

Father may be the only person in the entire world capable of creating a cure. I strongly believe that if I give him the correct dosage of Psyriviox, he will have a sufficient amount of time to be able to accomplish it. He will suffer for an eternity... But if it means helping the greater good... So be it. I believe in the significance of what my mother told me. I believe that "this choice" is the implication of "being strong..."

Entry 13 (8 days trapped in the hospital)

I have contacted Eli. I am sure that he will come help me.

Entry 14 (1 day after the rescue)

Eli rescued me, but he brought friends. They are all fucking idiots. They burnt down the hospital... Luckily, Father did not perish. I found him under some rubble.

Because of the controversy in Russia, I cannot tell Eli or his friends about my father's condition, as they will assume that he started the pandemic in America which even I still don't know whether he did or not...

If they find out, I am sure that they will burn him... Thus, I need to keep it a secret, otherwise there will never be a cure...

My objective now is to collect Psyriviox to give to Father. He needs his sanity in order to reverse the contagion.

Entry 15 (2 days after the rescue)

One of Eli's friends is extremely odd. His name is Rufus. He acts dumber than what he is. I think he is hiding something sinister. I will keep an eye on him, just to be sure.

Entry 16 (3 days after the rescue)

I found Tyler snooping around the Cooper household last night. For some reason, I was half-expecting to see Rufus there... Tyler was not doing anything wrong, he was just cleaning up the corpses of Eli's parents. Eli has no idea about his own parents' demise... And right now, I think it's best if it stays that way. A sulking baby is the last thing that I need.

I searched around the house for Psyriviox but was unable to find any. I'm not surprised, though. The Coopers would have had to have been idiots to store it in their house.

However, there was something peculiar. I found a half-open, empty safe behind a family portrait upstairs. I'm not sure if it was ransacked or not. But either way, it most certainly would have had something valuable inside.

Entry 17 (2 months after the rescue)

I have accomplished nothing. Psyriviox seems impossible to find. I hope that Father will forgive me. The thought of his torture is grinding away at me...

I am correct about Rufus. He is definitely up to something. He knows that 'I know,' and he's avoiding me at all costs.

Jake is starting to annoy me. He thinks he's clever, but all he is, is a bothersome imbecile. If he keeps up his act, I will break his nose sometime in the future... undoubtedly...

Entry 18 (1 day after visiting Golden Willow Resort)

It's been months since my last diary entry. At long last, I have finally found what I was looking for. I found Psyriviox. It's an insufficient amount. But it's enough to give me hope.

I will find more! I will clean up the mess! I will save Father! I will save the world!

I turned the page, still half-expecting to find another diary entry. However, as already foreknown, the following page along with the rest of the book was blank.

As I closed the diary, a vile feeling rushed over me... A feeling of self-loathing. The truth had finally been revealed. Nick was not corrupt...

Filled with anger and frustration, I repeatedly bashed the diary against the ground. Pages tore off and flew every-where. They flurried downwards, landing to a still on the floor. "How could Jake do this to me?!" I screamed.

Eli looked at me with concern, but did not say anything. He knew that I'd discovered a terrible truth.

I continued to bash the diary until it was nothing more than an empty, blue, book cover. Only after every last page lay still on the floor, did I end my emotional outburst. I dropped the diary and looked at Eli. "Why did Jake do it?" I questioned, dismally.

Eli shrugged. "Jake never liked Nick..." he answered. "And whatever he told you, it was probably corrupted by his hate... It doesn't matter either way..."

I'd never actually thought about it. But it made sense. From day one, Jake had a grudge against Nick. He portrayed Nick as evil. However, I am certain that if he'd known the truth about Igor he wouldn't have told me the conspiracy that drove me to murder Nick. From the similar information between Nick's diary and the conspiracy, Jake undoubtedly had evidence against Nick, but not enough... And I can only assume that the pieces that Jake was missing, he filled with his own rancorous feelings...

Eli irately stared at my pondering face. "I don't know what lies Jake told you and honestly... I don't want to know," he said. "Jake's motive for creating the conspiracy and your motive for murdering Nick are as unjustifiable as each other."

Eli's accusations struck me hard. From his point of view, I was as corrupt as Jake. It was extremely offensive, but... I had to accept it... I was a murderer and without me, Nick would still be alive. My swift judgement and uncontrollable emotions are what ruined me. If I hadn't let Jake take advantage of my guilt, or if I listened to Nick's pleas, I would have never gotten stuck in this horrible mess. What I believed to be true was only true because I let it be... And no matter what I say or do, I could never justify my actions... In the end, I could only accept them... and try and live with what remained... I stood up and walked out of the room.

"Where are you going?" Eli asked.

"Out..." I answered.

Eli did not follow. He let me go. He knew that I needed time by myself... time to think. I walked outside and stood on the veranda. It was a beautiful day. Bright and sunny, there was not a cloud in the sky. Surrounding the house were zombies, all of which were stuck in the trench. As I gazed at their bemused faces, an odd thought came to mind. *I was more infected than them, but I was not one of them.* I walked off the veranda and sat on the grass. The zombies did not react to my movement. Now that I was an alpha, not a single one took notice. They accepted me as one of themselves...

I felt a little soothed while sitting on the grass as it was the first time since the beginning of the outbreak that I felt like I was not being watched. Alone and accepted, I laid back and embraced the warmth of the sun.

In this slight moment of relief, I came to a realization. I may be an alpha... But I was no longer a brainless zombie under Jake's command. Just like Nick, I'd endured through death and come out the other side alive. I was in truth what Nick thought I could never comprehend... I was death's cheat.'

Chapter 28:
Zaven

Over the following days I grew accustomed to my new condition. The fact that I could wind up in a terrifying sufferance from a faulty dosage scared me. However, being an alpha also had its perks.

Not only did Psyriviox sharpen my reflexes, but it also made me stronger. Measuring at six hundred pounds per square inch of force, my grip was as powerful as a lion's jaw. I could crush a zombie's skull just by squeezing it. It was lucky that I didn't crush Eli's throat when I'd choked him. The added physical strength also dramatically increased my agility. I was now able to run faster and jump higher than any regular human.

Asphyxiation is a very scary feeling and yet no matter how long I held my breath, I could never reach the painful sensation of my lungs about to explode. Rufus had kept this "unneeded breathing" ability very well hidden, for as long as we'd lived together, not once did I notice him not breathing.

The third perk was that I could not get mentally tired nor physically exhausted. It was as if my body was in a constant state of liveliness. Thankfully, though, I could still sleep.

"Not that I needed any, but it would have been dreadful if I could no longer dream…"

These abilities combined with the high health regeneration and being invisible to zombies, I was what some may have called "superhuman." But what I discerned was the opposite. I was "subhuman." After the tragedy, Eli treated me differently. The fact that I was an alpha was not the problem, nor was the fact that I had kept his parents' death a secret. Murdering Nick, one of his closest friends was unforgivable.

Grief was the main element that was holding our friendship together. Every day in each other's arms, we would mourn our deceased friends and family. Although it was depressing, it was also comforting. I found it strange that death had the ability to unite us.

Nick had mentioned in his diary that his father was on the verge of creating a cure. Thus, locating him became a top priority in our lives. I understood that a cure had the potential to save the world, however that was not the main reason why I became so motivated to achieve it.

Creating a cure was Nick's dream, and I felt as though if I were to accomplish it, it could provide me with some redemption.

From Eli's and my own research, we were certain that Igor was restrained in the city. It was a pity that Nick had never revealed the location, though, as the city was a very large place to cover…

When I wasn't searching for Igor or mourning the deceased, I was searching for information around the house that Jake and Nick had hidden from us. On the sixth day after the tragedy, I had gathered enough information, and although Eli did not want to hear it, I explained to him the conspiracy which Jake had created. With his help we pieced together everything that led to the disastrous night.

Probably the most unfathomable part we discerned from analyzing the information was that *from day one: everything that Nick had ever told us was the truth*. He may have had secrets, but his honesty was far beyond that of ours. It was upsetting that I only discovered this fact after his demise.

We also discerned that Jake's conspiracy contained a lot of truth. For instance, Igor and Ivan *were* the two leading facilitators of Paramaxima and they *were* experimenting with Psyriviox to find a cure for their terminal cancer. Igor was surviving on Psyriviox in America and the recording that Jake showed me was indeed legitimate. However, the most elaborate part of the conspiracy was how Jake depicted Igor as evil.

By finding a most brutal moment in Igor's past, Jake deduced Igor as a sadistic man who revered revenge. Paramaxima symbolized Igor's influence and power. And by assuming that "Ivan was Alpha Z15," he inferred Igor had a motive to attack America.

The recording that Jake found on Nick's mobile clearly provided evidence that Igor was living in America. However, Jake did not know that Igor was a deranged alpha zombie. Instead, he presumed him to be a sane alpha and thus a potential threat to us all.

Through Eli's and my research, apart from Nick's diary, never did we find Igor's surname cited on any paper. With a sinister past like Igor's, though, it made sense to hide in the shadows. Jake never told me that Igor was Nick's father because he himself did not know.

With all these pieces of information combined, without meaning to, Jake's resentful perception of Nick formed half the conspiracy. And sharing it with myself only made it all the worse...

Jake did not intend for everything to play out as it did. Fearing for everyone's safety, the tracking of Nick's vehicle was just a method to catch Nick out and prove the conspiracy to be true before any harm came to the rest of us... Now that I look back on it, though, it was never going to work... as Nick was 'what he'd once told me', he was untraceable...

It was a week after the tragedy had taken place and I was sitting on the couch waiting for my shot of Psyriviox. Eli stood beside me, flicking the syringe. "Are you ready?" he asked.

"It's now or never," I answered.

"Well... Not really..." Eli replied. "I did a bit of research and apparently you have a twenty-four-hour timeframe to have your seven-day interval dosage. So, in reality, at this point in time, you can have it in the next twelve hours."

If I was to continue to survive on Psyriviox, I needed to know as much as I could about it. What Eli had told me was actually very important, however, it was still a theory and I did not want to test it. "That's great to know," I replied. "But I'm not risking it. Drug me up now."

With that, Eli jammed the needle into my arm and pushed down the plunger. I felt a sudden rush of energy pulsate through my body as the Psyriviox entered my bloodstream. After the barrel was completely empty, Eli pulled the syringe out of my arm. "Another week, another injection," he said.

My entire body felt tingly. I stretched my neck. "Ahhhh..." I moaned. "That feels good."

Eli placed a cap over the syringe and sat it on the kitchen bench. "That's the feeling of a correct dosage," he laughed.

I smiled and stood up. "That reminds me..." I replied. "Where did you get the Psyriviox that you are using on me?"

"Oh that...?" Eli answered. "I scavenged it off Rufus's front lawn. There was also some in his canister that I managed to recover."

I realized that what Eli had recovered was the left-over Psyriviox that I'd stomped into Rufus's front lawn during my mental breakdown. Since I was now injecting one metric drop a week, I needed to know how many drops I had left. "How much did you recover?" I questioned.

Eli grimly smiled. "A little over five milliliters..." he answered.

I wasn't expecting much, but five milliliters was a minuscule amount. "How many drops is that...?" I asked.

"If you want to know how much time you've got before you run out of Psyriviox, it's two years..." Eli replied.

I was a little bit shocked by how bluntly he'd replied. "Ah..." I said. "I guess we have two years to find more..."

With my energy at a high, it was a perfect time to search for Igor. I walked outside. As I passed through the front gate my attention fell upon the sign that was welded to it. I gazed at it in disappointment. Most of the people that had resided in our house, 'an apparent haven,' had died. I was disappointed because our house was not what the sign had depicted. It was not a safe refuge for survivors. It was not a "haven" …

The sign needed to be changed to correspond to the place in which it was representing. Although it was welded to the gate, its secure position was no match for my strength. After a couple of solid whacks with a shovel, it broke off from the gate and fell to the ground. Lying in the dirt, blood smeared and lusterless, it looked like it had been through horrors. Its shabby appearance was not a bad feature, though. In fact, it was the only aspect that I admired.

My admiration created a problem, though. The problem was that: if I wanted to retain its tarnished features, I could not change its material. I musingly gazed at it, trying to devise a solution.

I don't know how long I pondered, but eventually a resolution came to mind. It was not difficult to complete, nor was it absurd enough to fail. It was perfect.

Using only my hands, I snapped off two diagonal pieces from the steel letter "H" and then proceeded to rotate it clockwise so that it looked like a capital letter "Z." After that, I sifted through some old, discarded wire for a strand which I could use to secure the sign back to the top of the gate. I searched through two knotted masses before finding a precious length. It was a short, blood-ridden strand with a notably burnt and mutilated rat seared to it, the sight of which filled me with disgust and despair. I twisted the wire around the sign as easy as a child would with string and secured it atop of the gate.

As I finished up, Eli came jogging outside carrying three objects. "Hold up!" he shrieked.

I leapt off the gate and looked at him confused. "What is it?" I asked.

Eli pushed one of the objects into my chest. It was Rufus's charcoal black canister. "I saw what you were doing," he replied. "Can you please place this on the sign? Here... use this footstool." He placed the footstool which I'd shaped from my mother's old wooden table at my feet. I reverently stepped up on it and positioned the canister so that it sat firmly above the sign.

In Eli's other hand were Nick's boots. "What about those boots?" I asked, pointing at them.

Eli hurled Nick's boots up on the sign. They got caught in the wire where they remained. I didn't quite understand the idea behind Eli's request, but I did not argue. "Is that it?" I questioned.

Eli did not reply, instead, he sprinted into the backyard. Before I could even ask where he was going, he returned with a flower. He held it out to me. "Place this on the sign as well," he said.

I extended my arm and carefully extracted the flower from his hand. Looking at it closely, it brought a tear to my eye. It was a large rose, identical to the one in which I had tossed on my mother's grave. I kissed it and gently pushed its stem inside the bullet hole of Rufus's canister. There it stayed fixed.

Without saying a word, I climbed off the gate and stood beside Eli. As we gazed at the sign, both of us smiled. A smile of hope...

My adjustment to the sign showed that our sanctuary could protect us from the undead but never from ourselves... Eli's addition displayed our agonized pain and reminded us of our mistakes.

Together, the sign was the perfect depiction of our struggle to create a zombie-free haven... Bound together by old gory wire, in large, faded letters read the word "ZAVEN."